The
Teacher

BOOKS BY DANIELLE STEWART

The Girl at the Party

The
Teacher

DANIELLE STEWART

bookouture

Published by Bookouture in 2023

An imprint of Storyfire Ltd.
Carmelite House
50 Victoria Embankment
London EC4Y 0DZ

www.bookouture.com

ISBN: 978-1-83790-316-0
eBook ISBN: 978-1-83790-315-3

PROLOGUE

ELIZABETH

"I believe that you are a danger to yourself and to others. You need to be evaluated immediately by your crisis assistance team and it is likely you will be involuntarily committed for an emergency psychiatric assessment and inpatient treatment."

These words. They change everything. Panic surges through me, a torrent of icy fear coursing through my veins. My heart hammers in my chest, a caged bird desperate to escape.

It's happening again.

The same suffocating feeling of being cornered, of having no control over the direction my life is taking. Everyone around me is going to decide what I need. What I'm capable of.

I try to steady my breathing, but the police officers closing in on me feel like vultures, their gazes unrelenting. I've been down this dark road before, confined to sterile rooms, stripped of my freedom, and labeled as something I'm not.

Crazy.

That's what they love to call women who dare to do what they think is right in the face of the world's assumptions. I want to scream. To tell these men that I am right. That I know perfectly well how to care for my students, my family, and myself. It is not crazy to want to save people. It is honorable to do everything you can for the people you love.

I feel a desperate urge to run, to escape this nightmare closing in around me. But I can't. Not with the police at my door, not with their authority, their power. They have me.

My mind races, searching for a way out, a lifeline in this sea of accusations. But for now, I am trapped, my world reduced to these haunting words and the chilling specter of returning to a place I never wanted to revisit.

I have to give in. I have to go. They'll call me crazy and, for now, I have no choice but to let them.

ONE

ELIZABETH

Now

It was random. It had to be. I work with teens every day. I know exactly how impulsive they can be. How they dare each other to do stupid things and feel compelled by peer pressure to follow through. My car was not the target. Or not specifically. Someone running their key in a squiggly line down my driver side, deeply damaging the paint, was not a message to me. I'm sure of it.

This had to be about how Mr. Tusken failed his entire sixth period because no one would fess up about the cheating scheme for his last exam. Or maybe it was meant for Mrs. Ellis, the art teacher, who made the cheerleaders miss practice to stay and clean up the mess they'd made in her classroom. I'm just accidental collateral damage.

I won't give the principal here the satisfaction of me reporting it. The school will go on some witch hunt. Punish the whole student body rather than trying to actually figure out who might have done it. And in the end, I know exactly what will be said. It will be twisted around on me. I am too close to my students. I make it too personal and therefore invite this kind of trouble onto myself.

So, I'll tell the principal nothing and when I get home, I'll explain to Rick that it happened randomly in the grocery store parking lot. Probably some nutjob who did it to a bunch of cars. My husband will believe me, because he'll want to.

Pushing the thought of the damage to my car out of my head, I think instead of this beautiful day. Of the excitement pulsing through my class. The spring sun beats down on us, as I lead my high school seniors outside, eager to take advantage of the lovely weather. It's almost curative to bring them into the fresh air. They have the energy of recently escaped prisoners and I beam with pride to be the one who broke them out.

This is the low-hanging fruit my peers miss. So many other teachers cling to the rigor of what has always been for the sake of ritual. They're certain that learning can only happen within the four walls of a classroom. But I know that to truly connect with my students, I have to think outside the box. And take them outside the classroom.

Today I've brought them to the field near the basketball courts, letting them feel the warm sun on their faces and the cool breeze in their hair. We discuss literature and life, weaving in modern-day connections that make the material relatable. Classic literature is not all that different than their current experiences.

I remind them that the themes we find in these novels and plays are exactly what they're living through now. Love and relationships. Social structures and class wars. Identity and self-discovery. Power and corruption.

"What happened to your car, Mrs. Meadows?" Bo asks in his husky, still sleepy-sounding voice as he flops down on the grass. "It looks like it got keyed."

"Who knows." I shrug, trying to look unbothered by the whole thing. It doesn't really matter anyway. We have insurance. We have money to fix it. Hell, we replace our cars every couple of years anyway. "Just some knucklehead. No big deal."

It had happened this morning after I'd parked in the school lot. Going back to grab my forgotten water bottle during morning break, it was there waiting for me. Somehow the kids in my class already know about it.

Bo grimaces. "People are so dumb. I saw it when I went to buy snacks at the concession stand by the gym between classes."

I wonder if Bo is the culprit. He's certainly dumb enough to think he's being clever right now. But he would never. Bo and I go way back. I taught him in eighth grade before I moved up to teaching the seniors three years ago. I got him through a very difficult time. Tutored him when he was at risk of getting kicked off the junior varsity football team. He comes to my defense whenever needed. Bo would never vandalize my car. Even on a dare.

"The bumper thing you'll want to cover up quick." Bo winces and looks away from me. "That's so messed up."

"The bumper?" I ask nervously, wondering if there was more damage I didn't notice in my haste to get back to class.

"You didn't see it? They carved the word 'bitch' into your back bumper." He's sheepish as he says the word. "I'm going to ask around and find out who it was. I'll get you a name. Seriously, it's screwed up."

I gulp down my nerves and push away the foul feeling spreading across my body. That sickening balm of shame and self-loathing that is smeared all over me when someone tries to label me with such harsh words. Not because their words wound me but because I believe they must be right about me. The idea that someone carved that into my car sends my mind spinning through the possibilities.

I glance up at the administration building and see Principal Awasa scowling down at us. His prying eyes remind me how this has to go down.

"I'm not going to report it and please don't try to figure out who it was. Some dumb prank is not worth all of you losing your next field trip or the dance getting canceled. You know that's what he'll do." I don't bother saying Awasa's name. They know who I mean.

I can feel his eyes still raking over the field where I'm holding class. The kids all sit comfortably on the grass, laughing and debating, but he sees only a lack of classroom management. Taking his judgmental glare personally would be foolish, since he spends most of his time looking for reasons to punish people. All evidence points to the fact that he can't stand kids and loathes education in general. Not the best career choice then.

At the end of class, I dismiss them with a smile, though I'm painfully distracted. Almost too distracted to remember the problem I'd been seeing and meant to follow up on. I've locked in on something that has my antennae up, and can't let my own parking lot drama get in the way of my job.

Daisy, a new student this year, has been struggling in the last couple of weeks. Sometimes things like this pass on their own but this seems to be getting progressively worse, not better. Bags under her eyes, her hair looking sparse in some spots as though she'd been nervously tugging at it, and an overall expression of sadness that seemed to follow her everywhere.

I pride myself on being able to spot these kinds of things. From disordered eating to the look someone has when they're being targeted online by a bully. A breakup. A failed test in another class. I'm in tune with my students and their lives.

"Is everything okay, Daisy?" I ask gently when the rest of the students file back into the building. Daisy is in the back, seeming to linger and I take advantage. I'm stacking books, pretending she doesn't have my full attention. Teenagers hate when you look at them full on. Spooking her would be a bad idea.

She looks away, her eyes filling with tears and I know

instantly this is a person teetering emotionally. I am painfully qualified to pull her back from the edge. I know the edge. I grew up on the edge.

"I don't know," she whispers, her voice barely audible. "I'm fine. I can help you carry these books in."

"Why don't you and I walk a bit. We can talk. I don't have a class next period and I can write you a pass to get you out of gym if you like. It's dodgeball today. It might be nice to skip that." I offer her a sympathetic smile. We leave the books in a pile on the picnic table and I wave at them as if they don't matter at all. She matters. That's what I want her to feel.

Daisy hesitates, and I can see the internal struggle written on her face. Sometimes speaking something out loud makes it too real. I've built a life out of keeping my pain to myself. Hiding my own past. I'd like to tell her it's an awful way to do things. That it creates a cavern in your soul that's nearly impossible to fill. But I don't need to. Finally, Daisy nods and agrees to join me under the old oak tree kids are constantly carving their names in.

This is not protocol. Students are supposed to be in their scheduled classes. If they have an issue, emotional or otherwise, they can make an appointment with the guidance counselor or go see the nurse. But Todd Digson, the current counselor, is about seven years past when he should have retired. His hygiene is the source of jokes among the kids. Case in point, he tries to hand the crying students his used handkerchief from his pocket. Something they find wholly cringeworthy.

The nurse, Laura Conkling, is nice, but overwhelmed by exam-induced stomach aches and gym class-dodging menstrual cramps. I can tell already this is not the type of problem either of them can solve.

I can't just send Daisy on her way, even if that's what the rule book says. People might give me grief about my tactics, but they know I'm out here doing the real work. The stuff that actually makes a difference.

"I messed up big time," Daisy sniffles, and I take in the pain she's clearly feeling. Her hair frames her face in soft, delicate platinum tendrils. The sun behind her giving her an otherworldly appearance with its bright hue. She seems suddenly younger and more fragile than a high school senior.

Even though she's clearly hurting right now, Daisy is a lucky girl. She's attractive and I know that has helped her transition into a new school without too much trouble. The popular girls accepted her quickly because she has delicate, princess-like features. Her nose is small and straight. Her lips are full and pouty, with a natural rose-pink tint. Her cheekbones are high and defined, giving her face a subtle sculpted look. Coming into a new school as a senior can't be easy, but she's managed well. Or she had until a few weeks ago.

"Is something going on with your friends?" I press, when Daisy doesn't offer any other information. "I know that it can be hard to be the new kid, but you've been doing great. We passed the halfway point for the year already. Almost the home stretch."

"It's not them." Daisy shakes her head. Despite her obvious distress, she is trying her best to hold it together. She's not sobbing or making a scene, but her body language suggests that she's barely hanging on. "It's me. It's something I did."

I lay my hand on her shoulder. "I promise there are very few things in life that can't be fixed with a good plan and someone to talk to." God, I wish someone had said this to me when I was her age. "What happened?"

"A party. I don't usually go, but I've been trying to fit in here. I said no to the last few and Stacy P. was starting to call me out on blowing them off. So I went."

"Okay, was this the one at Eli's house?" I'm in the know. I

get invited to half these parties, which I find laughable. I'd never go but they get a kick out of inviting me.

"No." She looks at me curiously, probably surprised I have my finger on the pulse of their social calendars. "It was... never mind. It was just a party that got out of hand. Like fifty kids showed up. It was a mess."

"Right." I nod, wanting to keep resting a comforting hand on her shoulder but thinking better of it when she hugs her arms around herself. "That can happen quick at a party. It can get out of hand."

"They had a bonkers bowl. That's when—"

"I'm familiar with those," I cut in with a little hum. It's a huge bowl of whatever alcohol the kids could get their hands on all mixed together with juice or soda. A disgusting concoction, but a popular one at these kinds of parties.

"I had a lot. Like too much." Daisy looks like she'd fall on her knees in shame if I wasn't standing here. I hate how tough kids are on themselves these days. I wish I could tell them more of my stories and the horrible things I got into. They'd feel instantly better about their own choices.

"It's easy to do with those bowls. There can be a ton of alcohol in there. Did you end up getting sick?" I don't let even a whiff of judgment cross my tongue. Nothing shuts a teenager down faster than judging them.

"I don't remember if I got sick." She looks at me desperately. "I don't really remember anything except for a few flashes and then waking up. It's the way I woke up. What was happening that..."

Daisy trails off unable to finish the sentence. But she doesn't need to. This is a tale as old as time. And it never gets easier to hear. She had too much to drink and some guy at the party, like a shark to fresh blood, was locked in on her. A bedroom off the hallway becomes a crime scene and even with a house full of people, no one intervenes.

"I'm so sorry that happened, Daisy." I don't make her explain any further. "There are things we can do. Things that can help you through this. Resources. Do you know who—"

"No!" She leans away from me. "I don't want anyone to know. I just want to forget about it. Trust me that's the best thing I can do right now. Otherwise it'll screw everything up. If you knew..."

It's a common response to something so terrible. Our brains want us to believe that with enough effort we can bury trauma deep and make it go away. I can't judge Daisy for trying. It's been my strategy for decades. But I know, logically, that's not the right way to deal with this. Not for Daisy. She shouldn't have to battle and hide crippling PTSD behind a mask of normalcy. That's only for people who didn't have support. People who were not believed. People like me. Daisy won't have to do this alone.

"We don't have to do anything right now if you don't want to." I keep my voice level and serious.

"We can keep this just between us?" Daisy asks, desperation filling her face. "I don't want anyone to know right now. It's hard enough being new here. The last thing I want everyone to think is..."

"Of course. I won't tell anyone. But you need to make sure that you're okay. If it feels like it's just too much to handle, I need you to reach out to me. Day or night. You're not alone in this anymore. We're in this together." I take my cell phone out and exchange numbers with Daisy. Again, it's a gray area but I categorize something like this as an emergency. Teachers are frontline workers, and sometimes we have to do what we know is right, even when it's not what they taught us to do.

"I can call you?" Daisy looks hesitant. Skeptical. I feel kindred understanding in this moment. People can be so disappointing, and she's not sure she can trust me.

"Or text. Whatever feels most comfortable to you. Just know that I'm here. No matter what."

"I didn't expect..." she trails off and then draws in a deep breath. "You don't really understand how bad this is. If you did, you'd never want me texting you. You'd call me a liar. Everyone here would think I'm lying."

"Because it's someone that—"

"I just want to forget it."

My gut wobbles and a wave of nausea consumes me. I can't place its origin. Is it the familiarity of being called a liar when I knew my own truth? Is it the weight of the burden all women carry? I dismiss my own unease and try to lighten hers.

"Don't worry about any of that right now. Just take it all one minute at a time and we'll get through it. I promise."

"I'm scared," she sniffles, looking up at the school as if it were a battlefield she'd have to storm soon.

"That's completely fine if you're afraid. Do you know why?"

"Why?"

"Because I'm not afraid at all. You can be afraid if you need to, because I know exactly what to do when you're ready. I can be brave enough for both of us."

Daisy is a long way from looking relieved but there is a small shift in the tightness of her shoulders. She believes me. Or wants to. That's progress.

I let her head into the building on her own with the late pass I've written. I padded it with an extra ten minutes so she could freshen up in the bathroom. I'll juggle the stacks of books back to my classroom myself. If I can get there without fainting.

My body jolts at the triggering of my own long-buried trauma. The cement I've poured over my own hurt begins to crack. I am back there. The school in front of me crumbles away and I am Daisy's age again. Fighting. Fighting for my life.

Fighting to get free. I am touched. I am held down. I am silenced.

A tapping on the glass above my head shakes me from the panic. Awasa stares down at me curiously and I remind myself there is no time for fight or flight right now. I'm not being chased. Held down. It's not me anymore. My life is safe. My life is perfect. And if I'm going to help Daisy, I can't be swept up in old pain.

TWO

ELIZABETH

By the time I'm nearly back to my classroom Awasa is there waiting for me. He's pacing and frowning like he's practiced this in the mirror. I've never met a man who so enjoys wielding his power to try to fix something that isn't broken. He doesn't offer to help me with the books so I put them down myself with an annoyed huff.

"What's going on?" he asks, deepening his voice as if that might intimidate me.

His vague question is intentional, a snare he wants me to step into, but I won't. "What do you mean?" I smile and shrug just to get under his skin.

"You took your class outside again today? The other classes can see them out there sitting in the grass and laughing." He folds his arms across his chest and doesn't realize how ridiculous he sounds.

There is a chance he doesn't know about my car being vandalized in the school parking lot. Maybe he hasn't heard what Daisy is saying happened to her. I don't know what has become common knowledge and possibly made its way to his office. What I do know is whatever situation he interjects himself into will be made infinitely worse.

He's normally slow to the hot gossip flying around the school because no one trusts him. Not students. Not staff. He's kept out of the loop often and I'm hoping that's the case with the car and with Daisy. If he's just here to bitch about my teaching practices, that's a battle I can win.

I sigh as though I'm exhausted by him already. "If all the other classes are jealous, their teachers should consider doing the same. I don't think nature and laughing are the antithesis of learning."

He doesn't like my answer and injects venom into his next question. "Why did you have that student out there after the bell rang? She should have been in her next class. You know our policies and you flout them every chance you get."

"Our students need more from us than just quizzes and test prep. You and I won't ever see eye to eye on that." I brush by him and busy myself in my classroom, but he's not ready to let this go and follows me in.

"We don't have to see eye to eye. You have to follow the rules. It's as simple as that. You can't continue to step outside your role. Your probation two years ago should have been enough of a warning to set you on the right path. You need to comply. I've been in education for decades. When I started all the ladies that worked for me understood—"

"They should obey you?" I cock up my brow and dare him to go on. "They did what they were told? I'm sure it's not to your liking, but the world is different these days. What students are facing is nothing we've dealt with before. Our tactics need to adjust. Sorry if I'm not being a proper lady about it." Awasa will never understand what it's like to be in Daisy's position. And though he believes it is, a rule book will not be enough to save her.

He rolls his eyes. "This is not some attack from the patriarchy. This is about not blurring the lines that separate us and our students. The world might be changing but some things are nonnegotiable. You need to dial back the antics and the unconventional outings. Teaching in your classroom is more appropriate."

The bell rings and students flood the hallway, some gathering outside my door getting ready to come in. Awasa knows he's on my turf now. The students will pour in with excitement and joy, glad to be in my class. It undercuts his argument of me being a terrible teacher, so without another word, he leaves.

It's not easy to stick my neck out again and again, but I'll never regret it when I can look back and see the lives I've saved. The girls like me. The girls like Daisy. Because the thing no one tells you when you sign up to be a teacher... these days... it really is life and death.

THREE

ELIZABETH

The sparkling white kitchen, adorned with a bowl of fresh fruit on the granite counter and expensive stained-glass drop lights, elicits a profound sense of gratitude within me. Our house is no mansion, but every inch of it makes me feel like I've won the lottery.

The hungry, lonely little girl I used to be would never believe that I'm standing here with an apron around my waist. An apron. It's laughable. The soothing sounds of classical music fill the air, harmonizing with the tantalizing aroma of the pot roast I've skillfully prepared. I am the fulfillment of dreams I could barely dare to dream. I have become the mother I saw on television. The tidy house full of character. The aesthetically pleasing decorations, changed out seasonally. I have turned a house into a home. My first real home.

The hungry child that once resided within me has found solace in the knowledge that my own child will never experience such uncertainty. Not on my watch.

My child.

A flash of Bryson's sweet face erupts in my mind and then disappears just as quickly. As much as this house is the fulfillment of my deepest desires, Bryson is the answer to all my prayers. He is my life well lived. Though I hardly see him these days.

I turn up the music to drown out the silence that's now invading my house like a destructive weed. It's crawled into every corner and taken over. Things are changing. I have to acknowledge that. Everything is different recently. It's slow. Manageable. Bryson, now fifteen years old, doesn't have those childish, frenzied needs that he did when he was younger. There are no fires to put out. He doesn't seek my attention at the same rate he used to, and while I miss it terribly, I know that he is growing into the man I've always prayed he would be. One of the good ones.

This new slow pace of life should be comforting. I always thought of it as the prize at the end of the parenting tunnel. But the one part I can't explain to anyone, or even to myself, is that I miss the adrenaline that comes with simply surviving. From my earliest memories right through all the years raising Bryson, it was perpetual motion. When you have to fight to live you feel indisputably alive. Now I'm just coasting and I might as well be asleep.

As Bryson transitions to a new phase of his life, it becomes more important than ever to feel like what I'm doing matters. Like all the pain I endured will be for a purpose.

To help someone. Someone like Daisy.

"Some jerk at the grocery store," I say the words in a low whisper, trying to practice which tone will be most convincing. "He didn't like how I parked, I guess." I shrug casually and try it again, this time with more anger in my voice. "Some jerk at the grocery store didn't like how I was parked. Can you believe how terrible people are?"

Rick will be much more comfortable with believing this was some stranger rather than the truth that it happened at school. Much like Awasa, he'd like to make the conversation deeper than it is. He'd speculate and want to turn it into something it's not. "Some jerk," I say it again to make sure my cheeks don't blush, giving me away.

I'm jolted out of my thoughts by the sound of my phone ringing. I'm disappointed when it's not Daisy calling. I need to hear from her. I need to know she's okay.

Instead, it's my sister, Jules, and we exchange the usual pleasantries before she notices what I'm trying to hide.

"You sound a little off," Jules asserts, and I can tell she's already picked up on my unease. I've got Daisy on my mind. The word "bitch" on my bumper. And Bryson, who is more like a ship passing in the night than my son right now. But none of that will make sense to Jules. We've never occupied the same spaces in this world. We're never in the same season of our lives. A nine-year age difference will do that to sisters.

I offer only a small glimpse because she won't stop asking until I do. "Everything's good, but sometimes I'm just not sure that I'm doing enough. Do you know what I mean? I like to stay busy, and things are changing so fast around here lately. Rick is working on that new case and it has him at the office constantly. Bryson is almost never home. But things are perfect. I can't complain." I wonder if she'll read between the lines. If she thinks I'm ungrateful for even mentioning it.

Jules laughs. "Girl, you're like the queen of perfect. You've worked hard to have a boring life. Enjoy it."

"I love my life." My voice is a bit too high to sound convincing but Jules gives me a pass. "Forget I said anything."

"Not a chance. Better just spill it now. You know you can't keep anything from me. It's my job, as your sister and an investigator, to find things out."

Before I can tell her what's on my mind, Bryson, with his shaggy hair and tattered sweatshirt drags himself into the kitchen. There are exams this week and he's holed up in his room buried under a pile of textbooks and study guides. I've been trying to give him his space in spite of the fact that I could be the perfect person to tutor him. I know better than to even offer.

Now on a short break, his ears are plugged with headphones and his eyes fixed on his phone. I remind myself this is all age-appropriate behavior. I can't take his pulling away from me personally. He works hard at school, is crushing it with soccer five days a week. His teenage brain is going haywire. His hormones are taking over. So staring at his phone and listening to music during his downtime is not an attack on me. Or that's what I keep telling myself.

My pot roast is resting on the stove and he looks at it funny. Even though I'm on the phone he groans out his question.

"Can we please order pizza? I'm starving and I really want pizza from Tony's. I need pizza to study." As annoying as his question is, I love the way he sidles up to me and leans his head on my shoulder. No matter how old he's gotten these special moments of sweet affection still happen.

"Dinner is ready in fifteen minutes. Say hi to Aunt Jules." I hold up the phone and he pulls away.

"Hey." He breathes the word out as though it's painful to have to communicate with anyone. I can still see my darling little boy in there. He's buried under the new muscle and stoic expression but he's there. "I really want pizza. Can we order?"

"It's pot roast. You love pot roast. I made the potatoes the way you like them." I poke his side where his chubby belly used to be but I hit only muscle. Soccer dominates his free time now and the team is obsessed with the weight room.

"It's fine." He shrugs and moves to the pantry. The type of pantry I used to dream about when I was a child. Full of snacks. Color-coordinated baskets. Labeled jars loaded with flour and pasta. All things he hardly seems to notice. That's a good thing. He shouldn't have to appreciate food. Food should just be there. And for him, it is.

"Are we out of chips? We have like nothing to eat here." His head snaps back and he looks up at the ceiling as though this hardship might crush him.

I count backwards from ten in my head. Another lesson I've learned is you don't have to show up to every argument someone invites you to. Bryson will eat pot roast in fifteen minutes and feel better once he does. I ask Jules to hang on for a second and she giggles, getting a kick out of this interaction.

"Hey." I call him back before he can slip away. "Do you know Daisy Marello? She's a senior."

"I guess." He answers with a shrug and plugs his ear back up with music. "She's new this year."

"Yeah. I was talking to her today. She's having a hard time. Do you know anything about that?" I don't elaborate. There is still a bit of innocence to Bryson I'm not ready to snuff out. These kids are two and three years older than him and dealing with much bigger issues.

He shrugs again and drags himself out of the kitchen and calls over his shoulder at me. "You always think everyone is having a hard time. School sucks. That's the hard time."

"These are the tough years, right?" Jules tries to sound upbeat. "I think it's so you don't miss them so much when they leave for college."

She doesn't realize that missing him when he leaves for college keeps me up most nights. Even though we still have years left, it's not enough. I've poured myself into this child and he will take all that with him when he leaves. The emptiness, the quiet, the time to think might kill me. These tough, grumpy days do not dominate our relationship. Things are still good between us. Our love still ever present and our jokes we share still funny. I am one of the lucky mothers. Even when the teenage angst hit, Bryson and I found a way to still maintain all the parts of our relationship that work.

I laugh out the thought that I know Jules will appreciate.

"It's just so ironic. Can you imagine anyone making us pot roast and us not wanting it?"

"I can't imagine anyone ordering us pizza either." She giggles and we're clearly both transported back for a moment. I'm jealous of how young she was when it was really bad. How much she doesn't remember. Trauma is the death of youth. I was transformed into this miniature adult the first time I had to protect my infant sister from the world. It's a metamorphosis that cannot be reversed.

Resting against the counter, I look over at the pantry door Bryson left open and smile. We have everything we need and more. "It's hard not to tell him about how we grew up and try to give him some perspective. If he only knew."

Jules hums out her suggestion. "Maybe you should. Rick and Bryson both ask every now and then but you always dance around things. I just follow your lead."

"I don't keep anything relevant from them," I shoot back defensively, even though she didn't mean it as an attack. "I'm not that person anymore, so there is no need to introduce them to someone who doesn't exist."

"Well, Bryson is a lucky boy to have a mom as patient as you. It's a charmed life he has and he doesn't even realize it." Jules is always on my side. I love that about her.

I try to find some perspective as I think of Daisy. "These kids do have different challenges than we did with all the technology and stuff out there. That's probably why I sound off. I'm actually in the middle of some tough stuff with a girl, Daisy, at school. I didn't want to give Bryson the details but I think something happened to her recently. An assault."

"Assault? Has she reported it?" The shift in my sister's tone is abrupt and unmistakable. But also predictable. I am filled with regret for bringing it up, but I want someone to talk to about this stuff. No one at work gets it. Rick is just a problem-solving man. I want Jules on my side.

"She's not ready to." I take the butter dish from the counter and put it on the table I've set. We always had the margarine you could get in a tub from the food bank if they had it. This is butter. The real stuff. I still don't take it for granted.

"It doesn't matter if she's ready." Jules is deadly serious now.

"I don't have all the details but it's clearly shaken her up. I gave her my number so I'm hoping she reaches out to me and we can talk more about it."

"But she told you she was assaulted?" Jules has always been black and white. She knows unequivocally what is right and what is wrong. It serves her well as an investigator but in the world of teens it's not quite so easy. It makes her rigid and inflexible and sometimes a situation calls for a more fluid approach.

"Not in so many words. Just that something happened at a party. She was extremely drunk and—"

"That's assault. She needs to call the police. I can get you in contact with an officer." I can hear her voice rising with the assertion. The most important thing I ever did for Jules was make sure she wasn't a victim in the way Daisy is. I fought to keep her out of situations I had unfortunately found myself in. I am glad she's made it through this world unscathed by such things, but it also means she lacks the perspective Daisy needs right now.

"She's not ready, Jules," I reiterate, this time more firmly. "She'll text me. I'll encourage her and support her."

"Do they want you doing that? Are there policies on students communicating with teachers after hours? I feel like you have a target on your back at that school after that thing with Bethany. You don't need any more trouble." There is genuine concern in my sister's voice. I know these questions come from a place of love.

"That was two years ago. It was different for Bethany and

that turned out perfectly fine. I did the right thing. This situation is just as precarious and I can't let Daisy deal with it on her own. I don't think her family situation is great. She never talks about home. I'm going to do what I need to."

She might think I cross the line sometimes, but there is no line between me and my students. There can't be.

Jules knows we won't find common ground here and she gives in. "Just let me know if I can help at all."

"I will." *I probably won't.*

"And tell Bryson to quit complaining and eat the pot roast."

"You'll need to tell him that. Everything I say lately just makes him roll his eyes even more."

"Then you must be doing something right."

We say our goodbyes, and I hang up the phone, feeling grateful for my sister's love, but also a little bit lonely in my own thoughts. It feels isolating to not be understood. To look at the people I love and know they've never known the hurt I have. It's not a club I want them to join, it's just one I wish I wasn't in. One Daisy is in now.

FOUR

ELIZABETH

I call out for Bryson and Rick to tell them dinner is ready and shove down the feeling of restlessness that's trying to take hold of me. This is my life. It's all I ever wanted. It's enough.

I am not a bad teacher like Awasa thinks. I am not a bitch like my bumper says. I am not that broken person who was lost in this world before Rick came along. I have to believe all of that.

My phone chirps with a text and Rick sidles up to kiss me on the cheek. I breathe in his familiar cologne and take note of the stubble on his cheek. He's almost out of razors so I add them to the mental shopping list I keep running in my mind. Work is dominating his life now and my gift to him is carrying the mental load of the little things. It's the least I can do.

"It smells delicious, babe," Rick says through a warm smile.

I want to look down at my phone to see if Daisy has reached out but instead smile back at him.

He's got his eyes on his watch as he breaks news that he thinks will bother me. "I've got two calls to get on in an hour. I'm really sorry. I'm glad to finally be able to have dinner together though. This case is going to be the death of me."

"I'm glad too. Don't worry about the calls. I know you're working really hard." Rick is just another space in my life where I am profoundly lucky. His kind features and toned body project a confident yet gentle demeanor. His eyes are warm and inviting, a deep blue and focused gaze that constantly shows thoughtfulness. Eyes that he handed down to our son.

Aging has only made him more handsome. Men are lucky like that sometimes. He's ten years older than me but now at this age we can't really even notice the difference. We joke that we've caught up with each other. I'm like an old lady most days. His late forties have brought only a touch of gray to his neatly styled hair. Anyone would find it easy to figure out why I fell for him; the more difficult question was what he saw in me. I was a troubled, misguided, lost soul and yet he never gave up on me.

I glance quickly down at my phone and see the text is from Jules. A link to military school as a joke to address Bryson's attitude. The disappointment that fills me is shocking. I wanted it to be Daisy. I wanted her to need me.

An urgency fills me and I fire off a text to Daisy even though I swore to myself I wouldn't. I'd let her come to me when she was ready. But I know I'll never be able to refocus on what's right in front of me until I hear from her.

Me: *LMK if u r good*

The three little dots pop up to indicate she's writing back and the adrenaline that pulses through my body seems disproportionate to the situation. A frantic lack of control that was ever present in my childhood.

Daisy: *Not sure*

I know all the shorthand for texts and I try to make sure I'm not using punctuation. That's a dead giveaway that I'm not cool enough to be trusted.

Me: *What can I do*

Daisy: *idk no matter what I do its shit*

Me: *it feels that way*

Daisy: *If you knew what happened.*

My gut tightens as I run through all the boys in her class. I'd like to believe none of my students would do such a thing but I'm not naive. That group has been together since elementary school and are incredibly close-knit. They are affluent and on track for perfectly cultivated lives. An accusation from Daisy, an outsider, would be met with fire. She also knows how close I am with my students and probably perceives some loyalty. But I want her to know there is nothing more important to me than her safety, and justice for whatever happened.

I believe victims. Rick, a seasoned criminal lawyer, occasionally pulls me into a debate about this, tossing around statistics and citing examples of false accusation, but I'm never swayed. People change on a cellular level when they are assaulted. There is no faking that kind of brokenness in my experience. And I saw it in Daisy.

"Everything all right?" Rick asks, furrowing his brows and eyeing me closely. "You have that look."

"Which look?" I tease, crossing my eyes and sticking out my tongue. "This one?"

Guilt swims like a goldfish in my gut, swirling around, looking for a way out. I know Rick has earned the truth over the years and yet giving it to him right now won't work. Like Jules, this is an aspect of my life he doesn't know and couldn't possibly understand.

"That look you get when you're trying to solve everyone's problems."

Rick and Bryson are both staring at me as I force my attention off my phone and back on them.

"All good," I call back in a sing-song voice as I untie my apron and join them at the table. "Just some school stuff."

"Thanks for dinner, Mom," Bryson offers, probably at Rick's insistence but I'll take it.

"We'll do pizza tomorrow," I assure him, proud of my compromise. "Oh, you'll never guess what happened today." I clap my hand to my forehead as though I'd just remembered. "Some jerk at the grocery store keyed my car. I came out and there it was. I guess he didn't like the way I was parked."

"Your car was keyed?" Rick puts his fork down and eyes me closely. "How bad is it?"

"It's not great." I shrug and fill my mouth with food. Bryson's eyes are on me as he furrows his brows in that same way Rick does. I don't like being looked at this way, but it happens a lot in the house these days. I am alien to them sometimes and I don't like it.

"It happened at the grocery store?" Bryson asks with a funny tone.

There is a very slim chance Bryson has heard that it happened at school. But my students don't run in the same circle as the sophomores. Our school is huge and if Bryson did hear, he'd have only heard some fifth-hand rumor I can refute, if it comes down to it.

"Yeah. I stopped on the way home for some fresh carrots. You caught the bus, so I figured I'd be able to run in really quick. Guess I parked like crap and it pissed someone off. I'll get it dropped off tomorrow and grab a rental from the body shop."

If Bryson knows more, he doesn't say. Instead he fills his

mouth with potatoes and pretends to be busy pulling at a loose string on the placemat.

Rick's phone rings and he groans as he silences it quickly. "Sorry. This case is never-ending. I'll call them back in a few minutes."

"Did you find the forensic specialist you were looking for?" I change the subject and lean in with intense interest, something Rick can't help but engage in. The conversation turns quickly to the big case he's working on and soon dinner is over.

We all ate quickly, running off to our own worlds. Bryson will study. Rick will make calls. I'll clean up. Or I should clean up. I should call Bill at the body shop to tell him I'll be dropping the car off in the morning. But the dishes wait untouched and I don't make the call. Instead, I start mentally drafting my next text to Daisy. Every word is critical to pull her from the abyss. I have to reach out to her. I have to pull her back.

FIVE

DAISY

She's probably eating dinner. Some delicious homemade dish with all the fixings. I bet her kitchen sparkles and her family jokes easily with each other. I'm an interruption to her nice night, so I toss my phone down and try to get her text message out of my head. I am nothing to her. A speck of dust floating by her very busy life.

The difference between our circumstances is glaring. Mrs. Meadows has it all. She's pretty, clearly has money and a family that loves her. Everyone likes her at school. Well, the only people who don't like her are the teachers no one else likes so they hardly count.

I on the other hand am not sitting down with my family for a nice home-cooked meal. My grandmother is snoring in her worn-out armchair, the sound of the Weather Channel blaring in the background. Why she's so fixated on the forecast I'll never understand, considering she doesn't leave the apartment. What would it matter if it was raining tomorrow or not?

These four walls are all she sees. They're covered in wood paneling and the carpet is a putrid shade of green. This apartment is my hell and yet it's still my best option for a place to call home.

I'd planned to boil some water to make pasta and use the last of the jar of sauce to pour over it. If I added a bit of water to the jar and shook it really well, it might be enough to cover the noodles. But I'm missing an important ingredient to this recipe.

"Grandma," I call, shaking her roughly. "When is the water going to come back on? And why wasn't the bill paid?"

My grandmother stirs, her bleary eyes focusing. I can't help but take it personally that her face sours when she realizes it's me.

"What do you want, girl? Can't you see I'm trying to get some sleep here?"

I grit my teeth, frustration building inside me. "The water bill, Grandma. When can we turn it back on?"

My grandmother lets out a heavy sigh, her nicotine-stained fingers reaching for a nearby ashtray. "I don't have the damn money for it, Daisy. You need to start contributing more. Get a job, or something."

It wasn't as simple as just getting a job. I did things for money. Babysitting. I tutored a few kids over the summer. But getting to and from work would be a challenge since we don't have a car. Getting my grandmother to take her meds and keep from imploding our lives is a full-time job too. Balancing school and this hellscape of home is too much to throw in anything else. This shit show of getting the water turned on is the perfect example of why I have to be here.

"You're supposed to have enough money with your disability check and the check you get for me every month. Where is that money going?"

"Don't stick your nose in my business. Get out of my face." She lights a cigarette and coughs out loudly on the first drag. She's fought and beaten cancer twice and I remember my mother saying it was because you can't kill evil. I wonder if she'll die soon. I wonder what that will mean for me.

I feel a wave of anger and helplessness wash over me as I walk to my room. It's hardly a bedroom. More like a closet with a bed squeezed into it. Everything is a mess. Everything is falling apart. I think of that bedroom. The one with the fish tank and the soft sheets. Just for a moment before it turns my stomach.

Now, without water, I worry about how I'll shower in the morning. Brush my teeth. Am I going to turn into the smelly kid? The one people tease for their greasy and unwashed hair? And what about my clothes? I'll have to go to the laundromat.

It's already starting to show. I know people must be wondering why I haven't bought the latest fashions. Why my 'favorite' designer sweater makes so many appearances even though it's warm out. My expensive clothes from my former life are showing wear. Under the bright light of high school life it will be impossible to hide this forever. And now I run the risk of being something worse than the new kid. The poor kid. The accuser. The ruiner of lives. The labels are heading my way faster than a freight train.

Everything is unraveling but I don't cry tonight. Sadness does not fuel change. Only anger does. That's what my mother used to say. I should probably discount her advice considering how her life turned out. Maybe she's not the best source of guidance. But I know that, so far, sadness has gotten me nowhere. Maybe she's right about at least that.

My emotional state is fragile, and everything I had planned for myself is falling apart. The envy crawls down my throat and burrows in my stomach. Sitting like a rock. Everyone at that school has it made. Their biggest drama is whether or not their parents ground them from their Mercedes for the day.

No one at school knows this kind of hurt. They don't know

this betrayal. What's been taken from me. I'm cursed and they can't even see it. But I consider for a moment, that maybe they need to see it soon.

SIX

ELIZABETH

I never leave a sink full of dishes but tonight I do. I tell Rick to take his calls and he kisses me as if I'm the best thing that ever happened to him.

It feels sneaky to be texting Daisy and not telling Rick what's going on, but he'd have a million questions I couldn't answer. As good of a man as Rick is, he's still a man, and biologically he'll feel compelled to give me solutions I'm not asking for. To try to solve this very complicated problem as if there is some obvious course of action. He can't begin to imagine what it feels like in the wake of an assault, and he won't know what to do or say. I'll spare him the feeling that he should.

Me: *U there?*

Daisy: *Ya*

Me: *Crazy busy*

Daisy: *K I guess*

Me: *it's ok if you're not. You don't have to act like everything is fine. Not with me.*

Daisy: *Things are messed up.*

Me: *Are you safe? Do you want to meet?*

Daisy: *Now?*

Me: *I was just going to grade papers. I take them to the coffee shop behind the old Sears. We could meet there if you want to talk.*

Daisy: *I guess*

Me: *Good. U need a ride? I can pick you up.*

She's one of the few seniors who takes the bus to school still. I've heard her talk about a car being fixed or upgraded or something but I don't know the details.

Daisy: *No. I can get there.*

Me: *See u in twenty?*

Daisy: *K*

My palms sweat as I craft my escape route. Leaning into the living room I don't catch Rick's eye.

"I've got to go grab some snacks for a party for Gennie tomorrow." That sounds exactly like something the math teacher would expect on her birthday. "I forgot I said I'd bring them in. We're surprising her for her birthday."

"Want me to go for you?" Rick asks, his eyes fixed on the

legal pad in his lap as the basketball game plays quietly on the television. "You've got to grade some papers, right?"

"I'm good," I say over my shoulder as I grab my keys. "I'll be back in a bit."

"Love ya."

"You too."

"Mom, wait," Bryson shouts as he comes breathlessly into the kitchen just before I can leave.

"You need something from the store?" I try to look curious and engaged but my mind is already in the car heading toward Daisy.

"Can we talk for a minute?" He's got his baseball hat turned backwards and his hands tucked into the pockets of his jeans. His face has changed so dramatically but I focus on the three freckles on his cheek. The constellation I used to trace out again and again as I rocked him to sleep. The bullseye where I would land all my kisses. They are still there. Even as everything else changes, they remain.

These requests to talk with me are getting less frequent these days. I used to be the one he confided everything in. From big gossip at school to little thoughts that just randomly crossed his mind. I used to be the full moon in his life and now I am just a sliver.

"Sure," I say, gulping back my nerves and trying not to do the math to see if I'll be late to meet Daisy. "I've always got time to talk."

"Want me to ride with you to the store? Is that easier?" His eyes darting away and his effort to make this more convenient for me is a dead giveaway. This has been on his mind for a while, whatever it is.

"No, it's fine. Let's just talk here. Is everything okay?" I count my blessings that while his problems feel enormous to him, compared to what some of my senior students are dealing with, it's still pretty manageable. He's not dating anyone yet. He can't drive. We still have some time.

"I just wanted to say sorry for how I've been acting lately. You do so much for me and I'm such a dick sometimes."

I fight the urge to react to his language. He's not ten years old anymore. It's good that he feels comfortable enough to speak freely in front of me. He's talking about himself, not calling anyone else a name. I let it slide. And you know what, he has been a dick lately.

"This is part of growing up," I assure him. "You are an amazing kid with a great heart. You and I are going to have some tough moments but you know, at the end of the day, Dad and I love you so much. Nothing will ever change that."

"I just feel like I keep screwing everything up and you hate me." He looks down at his sneakers, the ones that cost two hundred dollars and he almost immediately ruined by wearing on his bike even though I asked him not to. I think of the math test he just failed and has to retake. How we took away his phone last week because he kept turning off his location when we've told him not to. As these things were happening, they felt colossally important. Like he was falling down this slippery slope toward doom. Now with the perspective of what Daisy is going through, I see my little boy again and his manageable tribulations.

We can do this.

"You're not screwing everything up. You're figuring things out. If you're not making mistakes, you're not taking enough chances. We're not looking for perfect. You know that. I promise things will be okay."

A strange look crosses his face. It takes me a moment to sort it out. For the first time, he doesn't believe me. My comforting message doesn't seem to offer any comfort at all.

He shakes off whatever is running through his mind and tries a different approach. "Can we watch the new Marvel movie this weekend? It's going to rain Saturday so I won't have practice." There is more here. I can feel it. I make a mental note to use Saturday as a catalyst to dig deeper.

I tick off the list on my fingers. "Popcorn. Candy. Beanbag chairs in the living room. We'll do it just like we used to." I pull him in for a hug and kiss his cheek right on those freckles. "Bryson, you're not screwing everything up, and I really appreciate you talking to me about this so I have a chance to remind you how much I love you."

Bryson walks to the counter, grabs one of those imperfect apples out of the slightly lopsided bowl and takes a bite. "You sure you don't want me to go to the store with you?"

I only shake my head and wave him off, the lie about my destination getting sour in my mouth. I don't want to say it again. I draw in a deep breath as I step outside. As much as I hate keeping the truth from them, I feel a surge of something familiar. The adrenaline of being important. Needed.

I have never found more peace in my life than when I am fixing things for other people. Part of me knows I am sometimes building their houses as mine falls down around me. But I've lived this long in an internally crumbling life. I can keep going. I have to keep going.

Daisy will not suffer alone. She will not question if this is all her fault. If she should have made different choices or if life is worth living. Not on my watch.

SEVEN

DAISY

The bus takes longer than I thought and I'm late. Mrs. Meadows is already sitting at a corner table in the coffee shop with two drinks in front of her. I slink in feeling self-conscious but the sweet smells make my hungry stomach growl loud enough to distract me. I'm almost certain she heard it too.

"I got you a hot cocoa." Mrs. Meadows beams, gesturing at the rich-looking drink covered in whipped cream sitting on the table. "But if you'd rather have a coffee—"

"Cocoa is fine." I force a smile and slide into the chair, pulling the drink toward me. "Thank you for getting this. I didn't bring my wallet but I can pay you back tomorrow at school, Mrs. Meadows."

"I think while we're here you can just call me Elizabeth. And the drink is on me. I'm glad you decided to come and you're doing all right." I can see her pulsing with energy like she's ready to jump out of her skin. But she's always sort of amped up. Excited and ready to do something great.

I dip my finger in the whipped cream and then taste it. "Thanks for coming. You were probably doing other stuff."

"This is exactly where I need to be right now." She reaches

her hand across the table and covers mine for just a beat. "Are you hungry?"

"I'm okay." The lie is hard to choke out. Without water at the house I couldn't make dinner and I'm starving.

"What have you eaten today?" She's not letting this go.

I feel like this is a trick of some kind. Like she knows somehow that I'm starving. I don't answer. She tries again.

"I spotted you at lunch today and you didn't have anything but a few chips from Bo's bag. You barely ate. I know that when stress is high and things feel so serious and confusing the first thing we do is stop caring for ourselves. I'll feel a lot better if you get something to eat. They have waffles. Egg and cheese sandwiches. I think even some muffins. Please, try to eat something. For me."

"My wallet," I say, gesturing back toward where the bus dropped me off.

"It's my treat. Please."

I nod, and place my order, making sure I look both grateful and reluctant. It's a relief to know food will be coming. I thought for sure I'd have to go until the morning where I could get into the cafeteria early and grab some of the free fruit.

"Do you want to talk?" Mrs. Meadows asks, leaning back in her chair, trying to look casual. She's anything but. There is an urgency, a bubbling over in her. It makes me uneasy and I want to change the subject.

"What happened with your car today? People were all talking about it in study hall at the end of the day. Did someone really write 'bitch' with their keys on your bumper?"

Waving her hand, she dismisses the rumor. "Some prank or something. I am sure I wasn't the target. There are like three teachers that have the same SUV as me. I'm going to drop it off in the morning and get it fixed. No big deal."

"Yeah, no one would do that to you. You're so nice." I watch her light with pride.

"Thank you. I do try. You're very nice too. It's why it's been so easy for you to settle in at a new school that's loaded with cliques and really judgy friend groups. You've done well."

"I've always been good at fitting in. I think it's that thing you were talking about in the class the other day. Duality."

Nodding at me, I can see the wheels in Mrs. Meadows's mind turning. Trying to morph the conversation into something I can use in real life. Her specialty.

"You found that interesting?"

"It made me curious. Do you really think people can be filled with so many contradictions? That they can present two sides of themselves that are polar opposites?"

She leans in the way she does in class and beams with excitement to discuss a topic she finds fascinating. "In that text we read, that was what was happening. The author was trying to show how a person can be multifaceted and some-times to the point where they lose sight of their authentic self."

"But in real life, do you think that people can be like that?" I sip on the cooled-off cocoa and scrutinize her face. I need to know her answer. How many versions of ourselves can exist in one body?

"Yes. I do. I think it happens quite often." Mrs. Meadows taps her fingers nervously on the table as she sorts out what to say.

"Why? Isn't one version of yourself enough?"

Now it's her turn to hide behind her coffee cup for a few extra seconds, clearly trying to say the right thing. "Honestly, I think it comes from trauma. People have to split in two some-times to protect themselves. We have to be someone we're not and we hide the person we are. If we do it right, it gives that hidden-away part a chance to heal."

I notice the way she says "we". She's counting herself in this twisted coping strategy. "Faking it with all the people in your life seems cruel. It's like playing pretend and lying all at once. It's wrong."

"It's survival." Her eyes glaze over with a shadow of tears but she gathers herself quickly. "Some people won't ever understand it, which is why it's better to shield them from it. They want you to hide it away so they don't have to feel all that discomfort. But then you find people who understand it and can carry it with you."

The waitress disrupts the conversation by putting my food down in front of me. It's glorious. The stack of waffles and the pad of butter melting slowly on top. I quickly slather it with syrup and unroll my silverware from the napkin like I'm cracking a whip.

"Need anything else?" The waitress is halfway back to the counter before the words are out of her mouth, so I just whisper back that I'm all set. I don't have the patience to eat slowly or worry about any eyes on me. I'm starving. But halfway through my plate of waffles and side of bacon I realize how ravenous I look.

"Sorry," I say with my mouth half full. "I guess I lost track of when I ate last. The stress."

"For sure," she replies, but I can tell she's not convinced. "I'm just glad you're eating now. Do you want another waffle? Maybe one to go?"

"No." I clear my throat and look away. "That would be too much."

"I insist."

Her phone chimes and it has her expression shifting to something mysterious. Maybe worried. "I'm sorry I can't stay longer. I don't want to run out on you but—"

"It's okay. Really. I know you've probably got a lot going on. I don't even know why I came. I don't want to make this whole thing bigger than it is. The best thing I can do is just forget about it."

She walks to the counter, points over to me and then comes back and gathers up the rest of her stuff. "They'll bring you over a sandwich to go. Can we do this again tomorrow night? I'll have more time then. I really think we should talk about what happened, because the worst thing you can do is pretend it didn't. Trust me, it'll cause you more problems in the end."

"You say that like you know."

"I do." She smiles at me deliberately.

"Tomorrow?"

"Yes, are you parked out front?"

"I took the bus. I'll just catch it back."

"The bus?" She looks horrified. "It's late. Dark. Where is the bus stop?"

"Just a little ways down."

"How far?" She's holding tightly to her purse as her brows are weighed down with worry.

"Half a mile I guess."

"Half a mile?" Her voice is high and sharp. "No. You can't take the bus back home. I'll drive you. Come on."

"You can't. My house is not on your way. Really, the bus is no trouble." I feel my throat begin to close.

Her expression is soft again. "Grab your to-go food and meet me out front in a few. I just need to make a quick call and then we'll be off."

"Mrs. Meadows, I don't—"

"Call me Elizabeth. Come on. I won't take no for an answer. I'll meet you out front. The blue SUV with the word 'bitch' carved into the bumper. You can't miss it."

"I really think we should just drop this. It will end bad for everyone." My palms are slick with sweat and I try to figure out how to convince her there is a disaster on the horizon.

She looks down at me and thinks for a moment. "Bad is bad no matter who does it. It might seem complicated, and if you think that just because I know the person I won't be on your side, you're wrong. You'll be believed, and you'll be safe."

I blink slowly at her, wondering if she understands the magnitude of this. "And I think maybe that's why they vandalized your car. They know you'll help me. I don't want you to get any more involved in this. You know the person."

"And I know you. And I believe you." She pulls her keys from her bag and heads out the door as though all our problems will be solved with her strength and conviction. She has no idea how wrong she is.

Like everyone else, she's wrong about me too. And the second she pulls up to where I live, she'll know that for sure.

The apartment building Mrs. Meadows will see when she drops me off will give me away. The half-hanging shutters. Trash in the yard. The caution tape around the porch to keep people from walking on the parts that would have them falling through. She'll see it all. The colliding of the two parts I've been keeping separate. I should fight harder to turn down her offer for a ride. I should just get on the bus. But Elizabeth is going to make sure I get home. Because right now she still thinks she wants to help me. It's like milk growing sour in the fridge. Soon she'll realize she's not on my side at all. She can't be.

EIGHT

ELIZABETH

Rick did not appreciate my brief and dodgy call. I was gone too long to excuse it away as getting birthday snacks, and now with dropping Daisy off on the other side of town I've really been out for an unreasonable amount of time.

He's waiting at the door, holding open the screen so I can walk through. "Need me to carry anything in?"

"I didn't buy anything." I scoot by him awkwardly, keeping my eyes cast down. "I had to do something else."

Dropping my purse down on the counter I spin and feel instantly guilty for the look of hurt on his face.

"Elizabeth, I need to know what's going on." There is a posture he gets. A rigid back. His hands tense. I usually do everything I can to keep him from getting this worked up. His job is endlessly stressful and the last thing he needs is me making life more difficult. It's not easy loving someone like me. Everything I never learned as a child became his burden to carry. Poverty and a lack of support deprives you of more than just meals and clothes. There are a million aspects of life I was never exposed to, things that were never explained, that Rick has had to guide me through. I try to remember that fact on the days where I make his blood pressure rise with a circumstance he didn't see coming. He's already done so much for me and yet I do things like this.

"I had to meet with a student. I didn't tell you before I left because I didn't want to debate all the nuances of the situation. She's in a tough spot and I couldn't leave her on her own." My voice is more timid than I planned but I can already hear every counterpoint he plans to make. Rick is so damn good at this. He talks circles around me until I just give up. It makes me want to keep more things to myself but that never seems to work. The man is astute and he can sense the slightest change in me. I should be glad he pays that much attention. All the other women I know complain that their husbands are oblivious. Rick is the opposite.

"Okay." He stretches the word out as if he's processing and there's a jam in his brain. "Which student?"

"That's not important. But it's worse than I thought. She approached me after class and disclosed that she's struggling with something that happened. Now, after sitting with her, I think she might be having some trouble at home too. She was starving. Eating like she hadn't had a decent meal in ages. Then when I dropped her off at home, the place was... Rick, she's living in squalor. I had no idea. She acts as though she's just like all the other kids at school, but she's hiding her real circumstances." I intentionally leave out the details I have about the assault. He will take a hard legal line that Daisy is not ready to face.

Rick paces. He's sorting out solutions and I want to stop him. I don't need his problem-solving skills. I need the space to help Daisy the way I know is right.

Before I can tell him this, or try to, the ringing house phone has us both jumping.

"Who the hell is that?" Rick asks and I take a quick stride to beat him to it. It's not going to be Daisy. She doesn't have this number but I still feel compelled to find out before he does.

"Hello?" I press the phone to my ear and keep my back turned to Rick.

"How's your car?" the voice asks. It's rough and unfamiliar. Obviously, someone trying to mask their real voice.

"What?"

"Bitch."

The line goes dead suddenly and I feel a chill run up my back. All my rationalization and excuses for how this happened to my vehicle evaporate. There is no way to pretend that message was meant for anyone else.

"Who was it?" Rick is at my side and I can feel the color has drained from my face.

"Wrong number." I croak the words awkwardly and I can tell he's unconvinced.

"Who did they ask for?" His hand is on my arm and he turns me to face him. Rick can see through me. He always hones in on any kind of unease in me and won't stop until he gets to the bottom of it.

"I don't know. It was just some kid. Maybe a friend of Bryson's pulling a prank." I force a smile.

"You look like you've seen a ghost. What did they say? Was there a number on the caller ID?"

"No, it was blocked. It was seriously just some kid trying to change his voice and swearing like a tough guy. It's nothing."

"Let me see the phone." He extends his hand but I don't make a move to give it to him.

"Drop it. Really."

Rick pinches the bridge of his nose and groans. This is the look he gets when I exhaust him. "Do you think maybe it has something to do with you meeting this student tonight? Could it be her father? Or someone else in her life who doesn't like the idea of you butting in. This is exactly what I was talking about.

Do you think it's a coincidence that the night you meet her this happens?"

"It's not related." My gut sinks thinking about Daisy's warning. If the person that assaulted her believes I will help bring him to justice, then maybe he might try something like this. But worrying Rick isn't the right move yet. The second he hears about the assault, he'll steamroll my attempts at helping Daisy the way she actually needs to be helped. He'll call the police before she's ready to report. He'll dominate the entire process and treat these random threats as if they are more dire than they are.

"Please just give me some space on this thing with my student. I can handle it."

"You've said that before. I can't let you walk yourself down the same dangerous path. Please take my advice and just drop this. Point your student in the direction of resources and then let it go. It's the most prudent option, to protect your job and maybe yourself."

"Rick, I know the lens you look through as a lawyer is—"

"You need to back off of this." The disappointment on his face pains me. I prefer him being angry. Angry I can deal with. That's the language that was spoken fluently in my home growing up. But his disappointment is unsettling to me. "If you aren't going to report it then leave it alone. You cannot afford to get overinvested in a student's home drama. That's not your job."

"You don't understand." I plant my sweating palms on the cold granite counters. "You have no actual perspective on this issue or what I should do."

Like the gentle man that he is, Rick centers himself. Closes his eyes. Takes a beat. Softens his expression and lowers his voice. No one can cool down a rising temperature like Rick. I'm often in awe of how calm he can stay no matter how much I do that might rile him up.

"Elizabeth, I can see this is really hitting you in a personal way. I want to support you. But supporting you is protecting you from losing your job, or worse. That's what could happen if you don't separate yourself from this situation. These students have plenty of resources if they need them. You cannot save them all."

I can hear Awasa's voice ringing in my ears. They are very different men. My husband is noble. Kind. Forward-thinking. Believes in equality and fights for it. Awasa is a dinosaur and the undercurrent of most of his conversations come back to the fact that women should know their place. I know that is not how Rick feels but at the moment, the ideas swirl together.

"I appreciate that, Rick." In fact, I do not. "But I know what she needs right now. I went through this. I refuse to just let her try to navigate it all herself. She deserves—"

"Slow down, babe," Rick pleads as he takes my hands in his. He's transitioned out of frustration and is now fully in worry mode. "I've always tried to give you your space when it comes to your past. You've made it really clear that you don't want to revisit that time in your life. I respect that. But I'm getting the sense that you're connecting your own experiences with that of your student and—"

"Rick, the reason I don't talk about every little detail of my past is because that's not who I am anymore. It's irrelevant. I'm not projecting my own abuse and trauma onto my student."

He takes a step back. "I've never heard you call it that before. Abuse. You and Jules are always so pragmatic about your childhood. It's all jokes and changing the subject. But it's not something you can just stuff down and forget. This is serious stuff, and I think you've gone long enough without addressing it. You and Jules experienced—"

"I made sure Jules had the best childhood possible. I never let anything bad happen to her."

"By letting it happen to you?" Rick is probing in a way he

never has before. I used to think he was being kind by letting me keep my secrets, but over the years I realized it was easier for him not to know. He preferred not to see me in that light. It became an unspoken agreement between us. I think he knew as well as I did that if we opened that door, horrible things would climb out and they could ruin what we have now. But he sees how this new phase of our lives is changing me. The quiet is giving me too much time to think lately. Jules has her life sorted out. Bryson is so busy. He's not wrong that I'm struggling but that's not why I will help Daisy. I'll do that because it's the right thing to do.

He tries again. "There is something changing here at home. I can feel it. Something is shifting in you. I'm worried. Now I see you're falling into a bad pattern at work."

"Pattern?" My back stiffens. I know what he's getting at.

"Two years ago with Bethany. That turned into quite the fiasco. Probation. Something in your permanent record. They warned you that you'd crossed the line. I don't want you getting involved in something like that again. It wasn't just the impact it had on your job. It affected you deeply."

I don't allow him to rewrite history. "You agreed with me two years ago that Awasa and the school were just covering their asses. Lawyer shit. Bethany was suffering from extreme disordered eating. I was the only one to step in and do something to help her. And I was right. She needed inpatient treatment. The doctors said she was in serious danger."

Rick is again conflicted. It's written all over his face. His love for me is deep and his urge to protect me is primal. Sometimes he thinks he has to save me from myself. "I know that. But you were going to her volleyball games on the weekends and having her eat lunch in your classroom. Calling each other. You interjected yourself into her life. The optics of it were not great. It could have turned out much worse. You can't do that again."

"I cared more about Bethany being well, which she is right

now. She's in her sophomore year at university and thriving. I got a slap on the wrist that everyone agreed was just for the paperwork. You know her parents were very grateful for the support I gave her."

"They were. I know you feel compelled to take in strays and be the shoulder to cry on for your students. I see all the extra hours you spend tutoring the kids that fall behind and making sure everyone feels like they've got a place to fit in. It's admirable. But I'm concerned that you don't know where the line is. No one would blame you for that. You have some unhealed things that compel you to get involved."

Biting at my bottom lip I make sure not to say something I'll regret. He doesn't deserve that. He's earned my self-control in this moment.

My silence has him doubling down. "Don't you feel it? Bryson is getting older. He's pushing us away. You've poured yourself into that kid and into Jules for their whole lives. Now they are both needing less. I think it has you out searching for something to fill that need in you. But what you could be doing instead is dealing with your past. Finally facing it."

The house phone rings again and this time Rick beats me to it. "Hello?" he demands angrily. "Who is this? Hello?"

Clearly no one speaks this time. He waits a beat and then slams the phone down.

"Do you see what's happening? You have to go and get help for yourself."

"We're not getting into all of that." I hold up my hand to quiet him. "It's not about me, but I do have perspective and empathy that you couldn't bring to this situation. It has to be handled a certain way. I didn't go out looking for someone to help. The world is shit, Rick. People everywhere are in pain. It's our job to help who we can."

His eyes are wide with disbelief. More disappointment. "Are you even hearing me?"

"Just let me do this."

I understand his shock. Our arguments never go this far. By this point I normally come around to his perspective. "Do what exactly? Are you going to fistfight her father or move her in here or something? Are you going to wait until something more serious than phone calls start happening?" He slaps his hand to his forehead. "The car. The person who keyed your car. Is that connected? Listen, this ends now. We don't know what her situation is. You need to be practical, Elizabeth. You're a teacher, not a therapist or a social worker."

Intent matters. Or it should. Rick isn't trying to belittle my job or my education. He's being literal and direct. But it still hurts me. "I know you went to law school, Rick. You speak three languages. Your pedigree is very impressive. I barely made my way through college and just blather on to tuned-out high school students all day. You're right. I'm not qualified to help anyone."

He drops his head and pinches the bridge of his nose again. "You know that isn't what I meant. You busted your ass to get your degree. You had Bryson your sophomore year of college and still graduated with honors. I don't know anyone stronger than you. You carry all of this very well, Elizabeth, but that doesn't mean it's not heavy. It doesn't mean you shouldn't try to lighten your load eventually. Life for us has been a million miles an hour since we met. But now might be the right time to really give yourself what you deserve. Some professional help."

"Rick, you did that. You helped me with everything I ever needed. I was floundering when we met. I had nothing. Couldn't get myself together to get a decent job. You walked into that doctor's office with your niece that day and when she and Jules started talking, you took pity on us. Took us both to lunch. You saved me. Literally. You pulled me out of that shitty life and gave me this one." I gesture around our glistening kitchen.

"Not even close, Elizabeth. You worked for everything you had. I helped you with school and did what I could for you and Jules, but you were the one who did all the heavy lifting. Using my father's money to support your efforts hardly makes me a hero."

"You're my hero," I correct as I put my hands on his cheeks and focus his eyes on me. "And everyone in your life surely told you that being with me was crazy. You could do so much better. Someone from your own social circle. Someone with class and who knew about the world."

"You knew about the world." He drops his voice as though I'm being ridiculous.

"I knew about the streets. About how bad things could be. But not about the world you grew up in. You could have done so much better. Yet you bet on me."

"And it's paid off tenfold." He leans down and kisses me.

"I need to bet on her. I need to know that this life I'm living means something. That I can help someone who's hurting and pull them out of this shit. The way you did for me. I need that right now."

Rick is not convinced. In fact he looks downright agitated. "Elizabeth, that's different. We were adults."

"I was barely an adult." I laugh and roll my eyes. "You were robbing the cradle." It's a familiar joke between us, but this time he's not laughing.

"You were—" He shakes his head like I'm talking circles around the point. "I think we should at least call Dr. Crovitz."

"What?" I gasp and recoil. "The therapist I saw after I had Bryson? Are you kidding me?"

"You were struggling. Some very similar things to right now. Impulsive. Erratic. It was a slippery slope you were on. I don't think we should wait so long this time."

My urge to slap him is strong. A feeling I've never really had with him before. His suggestion is a betrayal. Worse than being cheated on. The fact that he wants me to get therapy for trying to help Daisy makes me want to lash out. "I had post-partum depression. Are you suggesting I have that again? Fifteen years later?" I laugh humorlessly.

"He helped you. Do you remember how bad it got? You trusted me then and I want you to trust me now. I'm seeing something that's making me worried for you. I don't want to wait so long this time."

I don't allow myself to flash back to that dark time. To the hopelessness and downright lack of reality that came along with those first few months of motherhood.

"Rick, you saved me when you started dating me and showing me what life could be like. You helped me through school. You married me when I got pregnant. And we've navigated this marriage beautifully. I don't know where I would be without you."

"You make it sound like a business acquisition." He wrinkles his face in disgust.

"I love you and I appreciate that you're feeling worried. But that's a you thing. Something you have to deal with. I am not spiraling or being impulsive. I'm helping someone who needs it. My head is clear. I know what I'm doing. You just have to trust me. Give me a few days to sort out what is best for her. That's all I need."

Running his hands through his hair in exasperation, I can see him clenching his jaw in that dangerous way. The way he gets before he breaks down. Rick is not a violent man. He's not cruel or vindictive. His pain doesn't splatter outward like paint thrown on a canvas. Instead it's like the cartoon character who swallows dynamite and implodes, smoke coming from his ears. It's a shutdown. A self-contained disaster. Something I hate for him. It crushes me to know I cause him that pain.

"I'm sorry this is stressing you out." I fold my arms around myself now that I know he won't be pulling me in for another embrace.

"Maybe I've been wrong all these years letting you disassociate from your past. Pretend it never happened. I thought I was doing you a favor, but now I can see it's just been there the whole time."

"I'm not that scared little girl anymore, Rick. You made sure of that. I'm not hiding from my past; I'm standing on the ashes of it. You've always had my back, please have it now."

My words twist him into a conflicted pretzel. He loves me. Deeply. But in his eyes there has always been an element of doubt that I can be who he wants me to be. He's so accustomed to winning these arguments. I acquiesce because who would I be without him? But lately I ask myself a more frightening question, who would I be on my own? Who would I be if I won more of these arguments?

"Okay." Rick nods and clears his throat. It's as if he can sense how dug in I am. How unmovable my position is. "A couple of days. But that's it."

He opens his arms to me and I fall into his embrace. The way he clings to me is alarming. He's trying to squeeze me together. To keep me here in this kitchen. Making the pot roast. Parenting our son. Rick doesn't want me to be more than that. And I don't blame him. This is the life we both said we wanted, and my foray into Daisy's problems puts it at risk. What I don't know is if it will pay off, or blow up in my face. Will Rick have a solid *I told you so* or will we be stronger because I've grown in my own resolve? Even taking that risk seems dangerous.

Before I can consider the question, the damn house phone rings again.

NINE

ELIZABETH

I pretend to be looking for a book in the library when I approach Bo's table. He's the star quarterback of the football team. Broad shoulders, slow on the uptake, and loud. He's always yelling something down the hallways. Chanting something that can be heard from across the campus. I'm hoping for now, in the library, he can be quiet while I talk with him. I thought of a few other students I could approach about this but Bo will be the easiest to persuade to tell me something.

"Studying hard?" I whisper and tap my polished nails to his table. Most of the kids are eating lunch outside today. If Bo is in here, it's because he's fighting for a passing grade on some upcoming test.

"I think I've read the same line a hundred times. I really don't care what the Egyptians were doing back then. We get it, pyramids. Do we need all this other stuff?" He bangs his meaty hand down on the book.

"It's a lot to juggle with your sports schedule. Hang in there."

"I'm going to fail." His head is in his hands.

"Try to stay positive, Bo. What are you using for study tools?"

He gestures at his open text book and I laugh.

"You've got to change the material into something you can really use. Multimodalities. That's the key. You like movies?"

"Sure." He shrugs and sighs.

Grabbing his blank notebook and pen I lean over him. I know his eyes are on me. He's a flirt. It's not appropriate and I'm always quick to send him on his way but at the moment he's right where I need him to be.

"I'll write down a few movies that would help you pick up this information. A couple of them are really action-packed. Watch those and make some flashcards based on the chapter summaries of the textbooks. That'll be enough to get you a passing grade."

"You're a lifesaver." Bo brightens up as I slide the paper back to him. "If you ever need a favor, I'm there." He licks his lips a little provocatively and looks away. He thinks he's a big man but really, he's still a boy. We both know this, which is why he can't hold my gaze for too long.

"I do have a question." I wrinkle up my forehead like I'm giving this a lot of thought. "Did you go to a party a few weeks ago? A pool party that got a little out of hand."

Bo's eyes light up at the question. He's excited to tell me about it. "Oh yeah, I was there. It was crazy. It was supposed to be all low-key, but you know how it goes." His reaction is telling. He has nothing to hide. I feel confident he isn't the one who took advantage of Daisy, and I feel relieved that he's not giving any indication that he was. Nothing to hide. Then suddenly he thinks better of his response. "Wait, are you pissed about it? I thought you'd be cool with it. You're like that."

"I'm not pissed. Why would I be?" I say, with a chuckle, playing it cool like usual. "High school kids are going to party. So it got a little crazy. Did anything happen?"

"Tons happened." He claps his hands together and laughs again as though we're both in on the joke. "Did someone break something of yours though? I thought I heard like a glass break or something, but people were trying to be crazy respectful because we all like you."

"Something of mine?" I ask, trying desperately to keep a poker face.

"Yeah, or your husband's, or whatever. When we heard the party was at your house, we thought that was pretty ballsy of your kid. A tenth grader throwing a rager and inviting the seniors. But then we figured if he's your kid he must be pretty chill."

"Right." I choke on the word and force composure. I could shut Bo down with a sudden shift in demeanor that makes him think he's screwed up. "I didn't know you knew Bryson?"

"I didn't really before the party. I guess he's trying to get in good with us. The kid has game. Bagging a senior, especially a cheerleader, is a big deal. You must be proud."

A cheerleader? My head spins. Of all the emotions welling up in me, pride is about as far from the top as possible. Confusion. Anger. The urge to scream. That's all ever present, but pride is not. "Bryson has always been ahead of his time," I stutter out through a smile. "Was Daisy there too?"

"Everyone was there. But yeah, she was a hot mess. I try to warn people not to hit the bonkers bowl too hard but that stuff goes down way too easy. Bryson said you wouldn't care if we hit up the liquor cabinet. Did she puke in your house? I was super worried she would yak up all the pizza Bryson ordered."

I brush over his question as the earth shifts seismically below my feet. "No puke." I roll my eyes as if this is all so laughable. A small nuisance and nothing more. "Did you take any pictures or videos or anything?"

This question finally sounds alarms in his head. It's almost shocking how much he's said without a filter, but that's why I chose Bo. I knew he'd be ready to talk, I just could have never imagined what he had to say. "It's not because anyone is in trouble. It's nothing like that."

"I don't usually take many but I have a few. Why do you want them? Are you trying to live vicariously through us? You should just come next time." He winks at me. "Half of us were hoping you'd show up."

"We were staying in the city for our anniversary." I think back to that night and how Rick had insisted Bryson could be trusted to stay home alone. I'd spent the last fifteen years being called an overprotective helicopter parent. That night, I caved to the pressure. Now I see just how big of a mistake that was.

"Can I see what you have for videos? It's no big deal but I'm trying to get ahead of something. A little chatter, and if I can get to the bottom of it before Awasa hears anything it'll be good."

"Ugh, he's such a buzzkill. Hopefully you can deal with him." He swipes the screen on his phone and then hands it over. "I don't have a ton of pictures but here, you can look at these."

"Thanks." My voice is a whisper now, not just because we're in the library but because this feels suddenly clandestine. Something I don't want anyone to overhear. I'm involved in a new way. My family is.

I watch the few short videos on his phone and feel my blood drain from my face. Kids are milling around my kitchen, one juggling the fruit from my counter, while another fills red solo cups to hand around.

"Don't judge though. We were all pretty drunk."

"Right," I say, trying to hide my disappointment. "I was in high school once, too. I get it."

How did I not notice the remnants of a party in my own house? Weren't there stray cups lying around? Some beer bottle tops that rolled under the couch? Pizza boxes? Bryson is a terrible liar. I've always counted on him selling out his own screw-ups with that twitch in his eye and the gulping thing he does. Is it even possible he was able to pull this off without us knowing?

"And you wouldn't bust any of us, right?" Bo laughs as he asks, so confident that I'd be cool with whatever. He can't tell that I'm raging on the inside. Furious that my son lied. That something catastrophic happened in my home.

"No trouble from me." I give him a reassuring smile, hand back his phone and pat his shoulder.

"Oh wait, here's one more video. I forgot about this one." He turns his phone back toward me but holds it in his hands.

I feel a pang of terror in my chest as a cloud of vape smoke parts to show more of my students invading my house. Laughing. Yelling. People wet from falling in the pool fully clothed. Beer pong on my kitchen table. A knocked-over vase in glass shards and people standing around to pose proudly with it.

"I knew something broke. I deleted this video because I felt so bad." Bo crinkles up his face sympathetically.

Ignoring his apology, I lean in when I see Bryson on the screen. He's in the background. His cup looks full. His eyes worried. I know that posture. Bryson is not relaxed and having a good time. I take a little comfort in his discomfort.

I scan the video for Daisy and a second later she comes into view. There is a wildness to her movement. Something between dancing and falling, but somehow she stays upright. A loud laugh erupts as she bangs into the couch and puts her arms up like a gymnast who's just landed a difficult dismount.

A moment later she's talking to Bryson, leaning against him, staring up at him. Now he's smiling. Left arm out, he steadies Daisy and I watch as her hand curls around his bicep. There is something. A spark. A connection. They move away, Daisy and Bryson in the far corner. They are too far off for the camera to pick up the nuance of their interaction. Just before this video ends, they walk away to the stairs. I can't tell who is leading who. I can't see who is saying what. They are simply both gone.

I don't ask permission, and quickly take his phone and send the video to my phone before I hand it back. I don't know what I'll use it for, but I know I need to watch it a thousand more times to make this feel real.

"Was it expensive?" Bo bites at his lip nervously.

"What?" The ringing in my ears grows louder.

"The vase. Was it expensive?"

"No," I assure him. "I didn't even notice it was gone." That part is true. The vase was a wedding gift from one of Rick's rich uncles and something that never really matched the look I was going for in the house. It was on display purely out of obligation. The fact that it no longer sat on the living room credenza didn't matter. It's everything else in the video that matters now.

He nods slowly, seeming to believe my act. I pat his shoulder again and take a few steps back, stumbling over a chair and nearly falling.

I call to him, too loud for the library. "Watch those movies. Make those flashcards. You'll do great on the test." I do everything I can to not run wildly down the hallway to find my son. To interrogate him. I want to wave this video in his face and demand answers.

"Thanks, Mrs. M., and see you in class." Bo is a sweet idiot who has no idea what he's just put in motion. I'd feel bad for manipulating him if I had room for any other feelings at all.

"Oh there you are," Mr. Awasa says as I nearly bump into him just outside the library. "I was calling your classroom. Can you come down to my office, please?"

"I, uh—" My mind snaps back into the real world. "Lunch is finishing up. I've got a class coming in soon."

"It's covered. Just come with me." He's curt but that's how he usually is with me so I try not to be too alarmed.

Following two steps behind, resentment grows in my chest like a parasite taking over. I look like a scolded puppy lingering behind its owner, hoping for forgiveness. The anger morphs quickly to concern as I realize this might be about Daisy. My normal readiness to argue with Awasa fades. I don't have a lot of moral high ground to stand on anymore. The assault took place at a party at my house. If she's disclosed what happened and mentioned that I knew there will be little for me to say. As a teacher I am a mandatory reporter. It's a legal matter, and all my confidence about my strategy evaporates.

"What's this about?" I croak out the words as we cross the threshold into the administrative office. "I've got a lot planned for my class."

In reality the only thing I'll be doing this afternoon is counting the seconds until I can get Bryson in front of me and start asking questions. The only silver lining about this whole thing is that I'll be able to hear from him who was at the party. Who might have been vile enough to hurt Daisy.

The words *speak of the devil* crawl into my mind. Bryson is there. Sitting alone on the bench outside the office that holds the 'bad kids'. The ones sent to Awasa because of something they've done wrong. My mind moves like skidding tires looking for traction. Is this about the party? Why is Bryson here?

TEN

ELIZABETH

"What's going on?" I ask, trying to keep my voice steady. "Are you okay, Bryson?"

Principal Awasa looks at me gravely and I'm sure it's only for effect. "I'm afraid there was an incident today. Bryson and some of his friends got into a physical altercation with some juniors."

My heart sinks even further. "What? Why?" I demand, my mind racing. I wonder just what he means by altercation. Bryson is not a physical kid. He's great at de-escalating things with his friends. I've spent a lot of time focusing on communication skills and how to handle tough situations. "If he was fighting it must have been for a good reason. Bryson, were you trying to stand up for someone?"

The pointed expression I get back from the principal is alarming. Though he looks a bit smug too. The majority of times I leave his office the winner. Not that there is really a scorecard, but we both know when I've backed him into a corner and he'll need to give up. This time it seems obvious I'll need to surrender.

"Witnesses say that Bryson started the fight and used some very hateful language in front of multiple teachers."

Is he smiling while he tells me this?

Before I can decide how much of an ass Awasa is being, the accusation sinks in. I feel like I've been punched in the gut. Bryson? My sweet, intelligent, thoughtful son? He knows the power of words. I sat him down in the kitchen when he was thirteen and we squeezed a whole tube of toothpaste out on a plate and I challenged him to put it all back in. The brilliant metaphor of words and how impossible it is to take them back. I can't believe he'd use any hateful language.

"That can't be right," I protest but only weakly, mostly because of the guilty expression on Bryson's face. I nearly start the argument about how Bryson would never... Then I remember, the moment you say your child would never, they go nevering like they never nevered before.

"I was a bit shocked myself." Awasa groans out the words and fixes his eyes on Bryson. "I know this is hard, Mrs. Meadows, but we have a zero tolerance policy for violence and hate speech. Bryson will be suspended for three days."

Bryson won't look my way. I don't blame him, the daggers coming from my eyes would be dangerous.

"What was the fight about?" For some reason this feels vitally important to hash out right now. If I leave here and only get Bryson's side of the story, I'll be left wondering. There is still a part of me holding out hope that this was Bryson doing the right thing, even though it looks like his methods were wrong. That I can connect with. That I can understand. Stick up for the kid being bullied. Shove your friends for putting their hands on someone without consent. When I ask again the answer is not what I want.

"Nothing," Bryson barks back, and the harshness in his voice catches me off guard. Awasa clears his throat as he offers the explanation he has.

"I think it has to do with the big breakup. That's what I surmised from speaking with a few students. Apparently, Bryson and Allison have broken up and it's caused a lot of trouble for different friend groups."

"Allison Gauvin?" Bo's comment about Bryson dating a senior finally sinks in. It was the least important part of the conversation at that point but now I can see just how connected it all is.

"Yes. Allison Gauvin." Awasa nods sympathetically. "When a relationship goes that long in high school it can make for some fireworks when it's over." Awasa tosses his hands up as if this is just how things are.

"A long relationship?" My mouth is agape as I snap my head back over toward Bryson.

Awasa chuckles. "In teen time, yes. Four months. It's a lot."

The list of things I did not know were happening in Bryson's life is growing by the second. I fill with fury. An old kind of rage I've tucked away. It's had no purpose in my life for the last fifteen years. I try to stuff it back down.

"Let's go, Bryson. I'll grab my bag from my room and we'll head home. You have my classes covered for the rest of the day?" I cock up a brow at Awasa who simply nods. I hate that he's loving this.

Bryson moves at a snail's pace as though dragging his feet will save him from the conversation we're about to have the second we get into the car.

When he slinks into the front seat of the rental car I'm shocked by his posture. The ire is radiating off his body like steam off hot pavement.

"This is such bullshit." He punches his fist into his open palm. The fact that he thinks he gets to be the angry one in this situation is laughable.

"Excuse me? After all that, you're going to get in my car and curse? You must be out of your mind. You're suspended for three days, but you're grounded for a hell of a lot longer."

"Whatever." He sinks low in the passenger seat as though he wants to disappear. Not happening. I'm locked in on him and whatever the hell he thinks he's doing. A party. A relationship with a senior. Is he having sex? Why didn't he tell us?

"Bryson! What is going on? This is not you. We talk about everything. Now I find out you've got a girlfriend. You're fist-fighting in the hallway. Using hate speech. And you lie about—"

"It wasn't hate speech. I called someone an asshole. Which they are. So it was more like a well-fitting nickname."

"Stop." My voice is sharp and my horn honks by accident as I slam my hand down onto my steering wheel.

Bryson jumps. This is not a side of me he's seen before. Good. We're even then, because he's acting like a stranger himself.

"Chill out." He says this quietly, like he's pleading with me instead of ordering me around. That's an improvement.

"Bryson, please just tell me what happened? You and I have always been able to talk."

"Right." There is sarcasm on his tongue.

"You disagree?" My brows are high. I'm challenging him to accuse me of being one of those moms who doesn't listen. One who freaks out at the littlest bit of trouble. I have a great poker face. Anytime Bryson has come to me with anything, I never overreact.

The time he was going to a sleepover at his friend Nathan's house and told me they were planning to check out his father's gun. I didn't freak out. I handled it. When he kept getting put on a school group chat with monstrously bad homophobia, I helped him figure out what to say and get himself off of there before they all ended up getting punished. We've always answered all of his questions. Guided him without judgment or making a bad situation worse. We are a trio. A team. It's us against the world. Or it used to be.

He doesn't double down on his accusation but still tries to make his point. "We talk. I'm not saying we don't. But you don't get what's going on in my life. You're always so caught up in your students. Like they are the only ones with problems. How many times do we sit around the table and talk about someone who's failing class because of their home life. Or they are overextended in sports and other activities and you're going to help them prioritize their free time. You save the girls with eating disorders and you mentor the boys with anger issues. You're always there, swooping in for everyone else."

Now I'm the one who wants to call bullshit. Bryson has given no indication that anything at all was going on in his life that needed to be fixed or supported. His grades are solid. His sports are well balanced in his schedule. He eats. He socializes. No signs of drug use or addiction. He'd have the absolute most boring after-school special made about him. Or at least I thought so.

"I didn't realize you were struggling." The words I carefully choose push their way past the ones I want to say. The ones I want to yell. Like a harried businessman trying to catch the train, shoving his way forward. But I don't let those words out. I speak sweetly and stay calm.

"Of course you didn't. How could you? You're pretty busy being a *try hard,* acting like you're a teenager who is desperate to fit in."

Hurt people hurt people. I force myself to stay calm and remember that. My son, who I love dearly, is in pain. I am his emotional punching bag at the moment and while I want to take a swing back at him, I know it wouldn't be productive.

Keeping my eyes fixed on the road as I drive, I make sure he knows I'm calm. "You've got my full attention now. I'm sorry it took something so disruptive and painful for us to get to this moment, but I'm glad we're here. What do you need?"

"Nothing. Seriously. I just want to be left alone." Folding his arms across his chest he digs in even deeper to his anger.

"You know I can't leave you alone completely. I'm your mother and like it or not we're in this together. I can give you some space, but I need to make sure you're safe and supported, even if you don't want it coming from me. We can call Aunt Jules or—"

"Please stop." The groan of annoyance makes me feel like a snake coiled up and ready to strike. This child has no idea what I'm holding back right now for the sake of our relationship. He also doesn't realize how close I am to releasing it on him.

I guess I should be grateful for the use of the word please. "Let's go home, take a deep breath, eat something and talk this out. I heard something today that was pretty worrisome and I had already planned to talk to you tonight before all this happened." I don't want to pile on, but the party is by far the most alarming part of all of this. What happened to Daisy in our home needs to be front and center. I need Bryson to tell me who was there. What he saw.

"What did you hear?" He's insulted by my accusation of more trouble coming his way. I want to knock that look off his face. I've never raised a hand to him but in the last forty-eight hours both my husband and son have said things that are making me want to choose violence.

It's completely unfair that in this situation he is the one with an attitude. But I have some things he doesn't. A fully developed frontal lobe and the ability to regulate my emotions.

"You threw a party. That night Dad and I stayed in the city for our anniversary after the orchestra. You had a pool party at our house and it got out of control. Drinking. Smoking."

This was a conversation for the house. A level-headed approach with both Rick and I having a united front. But

Bryson has pushed the patience out of me. I curse, then praise the red light for slowing us down. Maybe it's better I have him as a captive audience as long as he's in the car. Or at least I think I do.

"Are you spying on me? Asking your little friends, I mean students, to rat on me. You can't believe what they say about you. I have to hear all the shit they say about how you act. It's embarrassing. I just want this to—" He pulls open the door, snatches up his backpack and bolts from the car.

"Bry—" My words are eaten up by the honking of a horn. The impatient driver behind me wants me to go. The red sedan was familiar but I couldn't place it as they start honking incessantly at me.

This driver that doesn't care that my son, or whatever alien snatched his body, is running away. They honk again and I flash the middle finger and gnash my teeth in their direction. I can't catch up with Bryson, who's already weaved his way between houses and is out of sight. Instead, I pull up through the green light and drive toward our house.

The red car barrels by me, illegally crossing the yellow lines and cutting me off. He only nearly misses my front bumper and then slams on his brakes. I've got nowhere to go. I watch as the reverse lights flicker to life and the engine revs. He's threatening to smash into me. The buried part of myself who always chose fight over flight flips him off again and holds my other hand down on the horn for a long and loud blast. I don't recognize the man buried under a baseball hat. I can't see him clearly enough as he tries to intentionally avoid my stare.

This is the part of myself that had to be put away years ago. The seething anger that was once essential to survival and then had no place in my new life. I'm daring this fuming stranger to reverse his car into mine. Road rage is dangerous these days. An encounter like this can turn quickly into something deadly. I know that logically. But as I'm filled with rage because of my son I direct all of my fury at this bully in front of me.

Finally letting off my horn, I can see other drivers looking our way. My heart thuds against my ribs and I wait for something else to happen. Will he step out of the car and shoot me? Will he run his car into mine? Follow me home and come back later to seek vengeance on my whole family?

Sense is returning to my body and I understand the mistake I've made. I put my car in reverse and back away from him, holding my steering wheel tightly, looking away to show I'm done with this. It's over.

A moment later his reverse lights flicker back off and he pulls away. It's over for him too. Crisis averted.

My hands shake wildly as I pull out my phone and look at Bryson's GPS location. I could track him down. That's why I put this app on his phone, right? For moments just like this. But I know better. This incident with a stranger in another car makes it perfectly clear why I can't try to have a calculated and logical conversation with my son right now. There is too much anger. It's all too raw.

I can tell by the direction he's walking on the GPS that Bryson is heading to the mall. He'll be safe there and can slink around furiously, get a slice of pizza and cool off. If I show up there, it'll just make things worse.

We are his soft place to fall. Our love is wholly unconditional. I know he heard me all those times I said it. Now I just have to have faith, that when push comes to shove, my love is enough to bring him home. The home I never had. I learned the hard way, if you have a place to come home to, you don't have to run toward danger. Desperation drives you into the clutches of evil. I remember that choking grip all too well.

ELEVEN

ELIZABETH

Then

Playing with fire. That's what my mother always called this type of thing. Lingering in the corner booth of the dingy café this late at night is dangerous enough but I have a motive. I can pass for fourteen even though I'm only twelve. That can help.

As I keep my gaze fixed on the man a few tables away from me, I know exactly how close I am to the flames. He's older than me, by at least fifteen years, with a disheveled beard and tired eyes that hold a hint of curiosity. It's that curiosity I know I can use.

I've never fished, but I feel like bait. Waiting for something to happen. Having only one job. Be alluring enough to reel something in, even if it destroys you. It's the way his brows go up and he's switching his toothpick from one side of his lips to the other that lets me know I've got him.

Or he's got me.

Every flit of my tired eyes. Every time I tuck my hair coyly behind my ears, I loathe this degrading process. I hate that my blossoming body has become my best tool. My only tool really.

The hunger gnaws at my stomach, a constant reminder of how survival requires danger. This is nature in action. If I want to eat, I have to play this game.

Each time I consider getting up and going home, the image of my younger sister flickers in the corner of my mind like a candle fighting against a gust of wind. Jules depends on me, her small frame a constant reminder of my job. If I don't bring food home tonight no one else will. She can't afford to skip any more meals. But I am sometimes glad that she's so small for her age. The younger she looks for the longer she can the better. She won't have to deal with anyone like the man staring at me now. I wish her as many years as possible without this.

My well-practiced flirtatious smile curls at the corner of my lips as the stranger slides into the booth where my hot chocolate mug sits empty.

"Awful late for a young lady to be out alone." He runs his hand through his beard thoughtfully. This is how it always begins. A feigned concern. I've found the truly worried people never come over. They whisper to the waitress that they'll pay for whatever I want to eat. They quietly offer me a nod of their head and a look of sympathy. Sometimes the waitress will bring over enough money for a bus pass that someone left for me. The good people don't come over. They don't lean too close. They don't want anything from me. This man is not one of the good ones.

"I just wanted some cocoa." I sigh, looking down at my empty mug. "I couldn't sleep."

"Tough day at the office?" His joke is punctuated by a booming laugh that turns my insides into a nervous heap. I laugh too because his ego is the wall I have to climb over to get to where I want to be.

"Just couldn't sleep." The shrug I offer is all part of the game as I repeat the same complaint.

"Past your bedtime?" He cocks up an overgrown eyebrow,

checks his watch, and chuckles. "A little girl like you isn't safe out here on your own. Where are your parents?"

This is fact-finding, not simple curiosity or concern. Am I alone? That's what he wants to know.

"Do you drive a truck?" I already know the answer. I saw him pull his rig in a half hour ago. Tucking my hand under my chin I pretend to really take him in, as if he's endlessly fascinating. I look at him the way he wants to be seen.

"I do. You need a ride?" He's ready to jump up and toss me in the cab of his truck if I agree.

"No. Just wondering. I live close. I was going to get some food to bring home but I didn't have enough money."

I have spun the correct combination to this man's brain and unlock it with ease. I've given him exactly what he was hoping for. Leaning to the side he pulls his wallet from his back pocket, making sure I see all the cash he's got.

"My treat. You order whatever you want." He flags down the waitress, looking thrilled with his control in the world, as if he can do anything. Buy my food. Order the waitress around. Have whatever he wants.

"No, that's too much. I'm okay." I look down in that way that I know has me seeming younger than I am. "I don't have anything to give you."

"Sure you do." He reaches across the table and touches my arm, sending a chill up my back. "We'll just sit and talk while you eat. That's worth every penny for me. These long hauls are lonely as hell."

And the transaction begins. We do talk. Or he does. He brags. Lies. Laughs. Waits for me to laugh too. I watch him inflate as if this is the pinnacle of his manhood. I am the audience of his one-man production of masculine bravado and he's owed a standing ovation.

I lean forward, my fingers lightly brushing his arm as I listen intently to his words, my eyes filled with a feigned enchantment.

In this twisted game of survival, I am both predator and prey. I navigate the fine line between getting a meal and having to give more than I'm willing to sacrifice. It's a high-stakes gamble, a dangerous dance where one wrong move could tip the scales against me.

"My sister is probably hungry too," I say as I shovel more pancakes into my mouth.

"Bring her home some food," he suggests as though the idea was his own. I light up, indicating his brilliance and generosity is continuing to astound me. The act sours my stomach but I keep eating.

The familiar refrain in my head is echoing now. The realization that haunts the quiet moments in my mind. I am on my own if this goes wrong.

No one is coming. There is no one coming to save me.

The best-case scenario tonight in the diner is this man's ego is fed well enough to say goodnight when I pack up my food to leave. That his paying the bill and me keeping him company is an equal exchange. He's been heard, fawned over, given control and then peacefully he gives it back to me.

Because while my mother is right, this is playing with fire, sometimes a girl's got to stay warm by that flame. And some day it won't be like this. I'll have an exceptional life. Magazine-worthy. And when I do, I'll be the person I needed on a night like tonight.

TWELVE

ELIZABETH

Now

I'm regretting having to send this text but I'm not sure what else to do.

Me: *Fam drama. Meeting might be hard.*

Daisy: *K.*

My gut sinks. I'm trying my best not to internalize Bryson's accusations against my parenting failures. My attention to my students does not account for him lying and fighting. What I do to help Daisy does not take away from my support of Bryson. It's a ploy and I can't fall for it. And now my obligation to Daisy is greater than ever. It was in my home that she was victimized. My foolish decision to trust my son home alone overnight created the nightmare she's living in. I never should have listened to Rick. But that's what I always do. Cave.

It's important for me to be here for Bryson, but now, getting more information out of Daisy seems paramount. I need to know what she remembers. How this might impact our home. Our family. There is a new level of urgency.

I pull open the front door and listen for a long moment. He's not here. Glancing over my shoulder back toward the street I see a flash of red at the cross street and I wonder if it's the same car. I tried to ensure I wasn't followed, as foolish as that seemed at the time. But now I'm not sure what I just saw at the corner. I shake off the eerie feeling and remember the even scarier fact that my house is empty. My son is not here.

I can tell instantly. His shoes aren't by the door. His back-pack isn't half open and the contents spread across my counter. Today would be one of the first days I wouldn't bug him about that. It's clear he needs a little more time. I can give him that. I'll have to. He's turned his location off on his phone and I'm trying not to freak out about that. If I can't talk to him, I need to talk to Daisy.

Me: *I can maybe meet right after you get out of school. Same place?*

Daisy: *You left school already?*

Me: *Just some home drama. Had to go.*

Daisy: *It's fine. We don't have to.*

I'm scaring her off. This fragile trust we've built is going to snap like a twig if I don't do the right thing here, and it feels more important than ever.

Me: *Seriously. Let's meet. I'll be there at 3. Need a ride?*

Daisy: *I'm good. Bus from here is np.*

Me: *Talk to you soon.*

I can do this. I can make it all work. There is no way Bryson will have come home by three. And even if he does it'll be better if I'm not sitting here looking ready to jump down his throat again. He can play some video games. Bitch to his friends about getting suspended and then by the time I'm home, Rick won't be far behind. We'll talk and figure out what to do next.

Busying myself with cleaning the house, I try to decide how to address what I know now with Daisy. How can I talk with her without sounding upset that she didn't tell me the party was at my house? How can I bring up the video I saw of her and Bryson talking? I wipe down the already clean counter for the third time and feel my knees quake.

I don't even realize I'm hyperventilating until my breaths grow so loud I'm gulping for air. It's been ages since my body has been paralyzed by my mind. I've fought this. Bargained with a beast that resides in my chest and kept him at bay. But that's over now. I'm not in control anymore. And I'm not sure how to get it back.

My phone chimes. The alarm I set. I'm supposed to meet Daisy.

Me: *You're still coming? I'm on my way.*

No answer. I'm worried now she's changed her mind. I can't deal with that.

Me: *It's important we talk. I can pick u up.*

Three dots. A pending response. It's taking longer than it should. Finally her words appear and I know I was right. She's changing her mind.

Daisy: *Maybe I should just go home.*

Me: *No. Meet me. I'm almost there. I'll get you some food. Hungry?*

Another long pause.

Daisy: *Yeah. K. on my way.*

THIRTEEN

ELIZABETH

The ride does nothing to calm my nerves. I crane my neck to look down every side street and around every corner as I drive to the coffee shop. It's silly. Bryson won't be over on this side of town. But still, that primal maternal connection has me searching.

This distracted state I'm in had me missing something important. On the floor of the car nearly tucked under the passenger seat is a white piece of paper I don't recognize. I wonder if it came from Bryson's bag. If it holds some secret to his new and dangerous behavior.

Leaning down, the wheel jerks dangerously to the left but I correct quickly with the paper in my hand. One eye on the road, I flip the paper open and read.

You are nothing. You mean nothing.

I nearly crash into the car in front of me as I keep my eyes fixed for too long on the paper. My tires squeal embarrassingly, but I stop in time. The font of the letter is a playful kind of swirling type that doesn't match the harsh nature of the message. Gripping the paper tightly I crumple it. I don't know who wrote it or why. I am tired of not knowing. I'm tired of being in the dark. There is a new urgency in me to figure out what is going on and who is to blame for all the chaos that's raining down on my family.

I beat Daisy to the coffee shop, so I try to stay busy by seeing if Bryson has turned his location back on. But he hasn't. My iced coffee tastes bitter and I want to blame the barista but it's more likely the bile rising up in my nervous stomach is ruining the flavor.

When Daisy finally does walk in, she's looking weary. Worse than I've ever seen her before. She's probably thinking the same about me.

"Hey," she whispers, looking around as though she's been followed. "Sorry I'm late."

"Are you all right?" I push the sandwich over to her and try to smile.

"Not really." She looks down at the sandwich longingly and then up at me, apologetically. "I'm sorry you came out here. I really don't want to talk. I should have told you that."

"We need to talk about the party." I nibble on my lip and try to quiet the thunderous pounding of my heart before she hears it.

"Uh, I really don't want to—"

"I saw some of the pictures from the pool party. It was at my house." My hand shakes uncontrollably as I try to casually reach for my cup and nearly spill it.

"Mrs. Meadows..." Her eyes close and I watch a tear trail down her cheek.

"Elizabeth," I correct, wanting to remind her we are not at school. "Bryson threw that party. I had no idea. I'm so sorry that I allowed him to be home alone and create an environment where that could happen."

"We shouldn't talk about it." Her eyes dart away and the flower petal-soft features of her face grow rigid.

"You should eat." I take a sip of my coffee, shaking the ice around as if to remind her this is just a casual chat. We are okay. This is still okay. "I wish I knew when we first spoke that my son threw the party. That must have made you feel even more stressed."

Daisy pulls the plate closer to herself and then finally begins eating. I know that look. The conflicted expression of someone who worries about when they might get their next meal and so even under uncomfortable circumstances, they eat.

In between bites she glances up at me. "I know you wanted to help me, but this does change things. I'm remembering more. You should just drop it. Trust me, I'm not worth helping. If you knew what my life was like, you'd definitely bail. You have everything. Don't jeopardize that for me."

"I think I have a pretty good idea what your life is like. Probably a lot like mine was when I was your age. I'm not going to bail on you, because I understand that hurts more than any of the other things that happen. People leaving when you need them the most is traumatic."

She finishes eating before she speaks again, looking like I might take it from her if she says the wrong thing. I remember that feeling too.

"You don't want to hear this. I really want to leave." Shifting to the end of the booth, she looks ready to bolt. There's multiple reasons now why I need answers. I can't let her go. People in the coffee shop are looking our way. The waitress eyes me closely. The party was at my house. I have a responsibility to know what happened.

"Daisy." I circle my hand around her wrist gently. "Stay."

"Mrs. Meadows," she coughs out. I raise a brow at her and she corrects herself. "I mean, Elizabeth. You have to let me go. Trust me."

"Sit back down. Talk to me. I need to hear what you have to say." I loosen my grip on her and gesture back at the spot she's trying to leave.

"I'm remembering things from that night. I was talking with..."

"Bryson." My voice is flat and unemotional. Just-the-facts kind of approach.

"Yes. He was being sweet. Asking if I needed anything. I was falling all over the place and everyone else was just laughing. I didn't know he was your son. Or I didn't really remember it just then."

"You two walked away?" My grip on my own thigh under the table is so tight I'm sure I'll leave a bruise.

"He asked if I wanted to see the fish tank in his room. I don't know, it was something like that. I was embarrassed by how much I had to drink and so I followed him."

I think of his fish tank. Bought when he was nine. A source of much joy and lots of arguments over responsibility and cleanliness. I can't imagine him inviting Daisy into his room to see it. Everything feels wrong suddenly.

"It's all in little bits and pieces from there." She winds her hand up in her hair and tugs a bit as if she's angry with her own mind. "Just flashes. But I did say no. I didn't even know him, and I wouldn't have—"

Tears fill her eyes and she leans away from me as if remembering I created the monster.

Of all the shit I've endured over the years, nothing feels as horrible as this moment. Literally nothing. I've feared for my life. I've fought for it. I've been in some despicable situations and yet Daisy's accusation against my son wrecks me in a way I can't explain. Mostly because I've worked so hard to make sure he is untouchable. Perfect. Protected. And suddenly that bubble has burst. I nearly shriek, but I swallow that down and begin instead to fix this.

Shaking my head, I try to serve her the reality. She's misre-membering. "Bryson is a kid. He just turned fifteen three months ago. He's not even—" I clear my throat, fighting the tears back myself. "Maybe you're remembering wrong?"

The look of shame that fills her face crushes me. I believe women. I know the harm men can do. I advocate. Support. I believe. And here I am, telling this girl she must be remem-bering her own assault wrong. But Bryson is not one of those men. I've raised him differently than that. He would never.

"Probably," she gasps out, looking quickly out the window and blinking the tears out of her eyes. They stream down her face and she uses the sleeve of her sweatshirt to swipe at them quickly. "I drank a lot. Like I said, we don't need to talk about this. I'm going to be fine."

I squeeze again at my thigh, the pain the only thing I can seem to control. "Daisy, you remember Bryson being there?"

Her eyes are wide, searching my face for some kind of direc-tion on what she should do. She won't find an answer, because I have no idea what I really want from her.

"I remember." She gulps. "I'm really sorry."

"You don't have to be sorry about anything. You're the one who was hurt. I need to sort this out... I need some time to..."

"I won't tell anyone," Daisy rushes the words out. "Really. I'm just glad you know so that you can maybe talk to him. But I won't report it. This was my fault for getting that drunk. I mean, I did say no, like a lot of times, but I won't tell anyone. I know he's young and maybe he just got carried away. You could explain to him how bad that is and make sure he doesn't do it again." She's looking at me like we're a team. Accomplices, and that bonds us.

This child is saying all the words I'd never let a victim say. I'd counter them. Tell them bold action and the truth is what would set them free. Secrets only eat away at you like a cancer. But the temptation to make this all go away is too strong.

I say something I can hardly believe I'm saying. "We don't need to do anything right now. This is a very complicated situation and it's important that we handle it correctly. I'm not asking you to bottle all this up, because I know how harmful that can be. I'm just asking you to be patient with me while I sort it out." If this were any other situation and I heard myself talking about an assault as if it's a chore list that needs to be finished up before vacation, I'd scream. But everything is different now. The world is upside down. I can't swear some undying allegiance to Daisy when my son is on the other side of this. He's who I need to protect now. That's what a mother would do. Should do. Right?

FOURTEEN
DAISY

"What's with you lately?" Stacy P. is talking through stiff lips as she applies another coat of some gloss that is meant to plump them up as much as possible. She's glancing at me in the mirror and looks a bit paranoid. We're in the bathroom at the mall taking a break from doing laps and trying on clothes I pretend I don't like but actually just can't afford.

Leaving the coffee shop in a rush was all I could think to do. Elizabeth wanted to ask more questions. She needed some kind of answer from me that I cannot give. I needed to get away from her. The mall is always the best kind of escape.

"Nothing. Why?" My cheeks pink and I look away. There is a hole in the sleeve of my Proenza sweater and I'm trying to cover it with my free hand.

"You're all jumpy lately. You've been blowing off plans. Plus you're doing something weird with your hair."

That weird thing I'm doing with my hair is trying to survive off of dry shampoo and ponytails. Stacy cannot relate to a single thing in my life. Not what I've been through or what kind of hell is coming my way. Her problems orbit around the petty little inconveniences that befall her charmed life.

I wave her off and roll my eyes. "I'm not jumpy. And my stylist is trying to get me to go more days between washes. It's much better for your hair but I have to work my way up to it. It's a process."

"You're definitely jumpy," Veronica says as she flings herself out of the stall. They both laugh when I do jump.

"I'm fine. Seriously. You two are just looking for drama. I'm trying to keep up with these classes and make sure I graduate. Why are the teachers piling on right now?" They seem convinced this might be my problem and their posture relaxes. Veronica is in the mirror now, washing her hands and checking her eye makeup.

"You have to know how to play the system. In history, you let Mr. Rivers look down your shirt when he's walking around pretending to look at what we're writing. That always bumps my grade up. Science you just have to ask a bunch of questions and act like you've never been so excited to learn anything in your life. Mrs. Delstone gets all worked up and happy when she thinks kids love science. For forty minutes a day, I fake being a nerd. Math is a little trickier. Mr. Kline is a stickler and I'm pretty sure he's gay so looking down my shirt does nothing. The key in math is to copy off one of the smart kids. I use Jason Muns, so you need to find your own kid to copy off of. Mr. Kline is usually too busy walking around trying to explain everything he just taught to everyone again to notice."

"And English?" I ask it while trying to look busy tying my shoe, but this is the answer I want most of all. Their assessment on Mrs. Meadows. If she passes the vibe check or not.

Stacy P. shrugs as she thinks it over. "We don't have to worry about English. Meadows thinks we're all obsessed with her. She's fine and all, but she's kind of a try hard. Our clique always gets decent grades if we just include her in our conversations and shit."

Veronica cuts in. "I like Mrs. Meadows. English has been

my worst nightmare for the last three years. This is the first year I actually get it. She explains things in a chill way. And she totally listens to us. Takes us places. Don't hate on Mrs. Meadows."

"I'm not," Stacy P. yelps back as she throws up her hands defensively. "I'm just saying she tries a little too hard. And her son is the same. Did you hear he's suspended for fighting? He should have stayed in his own lane. He's a sophomore and is trying to hang out with seniors. I have no clue why Allison dated him for that long. He thought he was hot shit. Throwing parties. Trying to crash our bonfire last month. We told her she needed to just break it off. He can't even drive yet. It's weird."

"Bryson?" I ask. The sound of people spilling into the bathroom makes the word catch in my throat.

"Yeah, or whatever his name is," Stacy replies as she pulls me by the arm out of the bathroom and back into the busy mall. "Just snap out of whatever your problem is. Grades. PMS. Whatever. And wash your hair. That stylist isn't doing you dirty."

My hand instinctually flies to my hair and my face burns red. "I know, I'm going to quit going to her."

"Use mine," Veronica chirps. "She costs an arm and a leg but her salon is to die for. She even gives me a glass of champagne every time I go in. Very posh."

"I'll give her a try." I pull my arms around myself and listen as they turn their conversation toward some skirt in a storefront that has caught their eye.

I won't be going to Veronica's swanky hair salon. I won't be letting Mr. Rivers look down my shirt just so he adds a few points to my next test. It's stunning how bad their advice can be and yet how deeply I care about their opinions.

It's more of that duplicity. Or maybe an example of the dichotomy of life. Success and failure. Sorrow and joy. Acceptance and alienation. I latch onto Elizabeth's English lessons and pretend they can be some kind of roadmap out of this hellscape that is my mind.

We've read the tragedies. The sonnets. The classics. The memoirs. Every word means something. Every bit of punctuation tells its own story. That's what she teaches us. Everything has a meaning. Everything matters. What I know for sure is things between us have changed now. That conversation has put into motion something powerful enough to wreck us all. Skipping out and going to the mall was just my way to claw and grab onto some normality before everything changes. Before it all falls apart for good. Because I know Mrs. Meadows, and I can't ever meet like that again. I have to make sure of that.

FIFTEEN

ELIZABETH

The ride home is a blur. One of those out-of-body experiences where you arrive to your destination and can't recall any of the twists and turns it took to get there. I drove. Obviously, I navigated the roads just fine, but it's not until I'm entering the four-digit code to the front door keypad that I'm fully back in my body.

The potted plant that usually sits by the door is a mess. There is a bit of soil on the wood planks of the porch and the flowers at the back look like they've been knocked around and stood back up. I linger there for a moment, not hitting the last digit of our code. Waiting for the red car, the notes, the knocked-over pot to make some sort of sense.

"I found him," Jules announces breathlessly, opening my front door before I can even get my hand on the knob.

"Bryson?" My eyes are red-rimmed from tears but Jules doesn't seem to notice. She's too caught up in her own role in this. Her ability to sweep in and save Bryson means the world to her. No matter how often I tell Jules she owes me nothing for the years I spent raising her, she still feels the debt.

"Yes, were you out looking for him? He called and said you two had a fight. He was at the mall. I went and picked him up."

"You drove an hour," I gulp out, emotion throttling my neck. "Weren't you working?"

"My nephew calls, I'm coming. No matter what. He was pretty upset, but he's in his room now chilling out. I told him I'd stay and try to mediate a little bit. But I'm really on your side." She winks and smiles. I'm too caught up in every catastrophic scenario that might come of this and I can't smile back. She doesn't know what I do yet. I envy that ignorance.

"Jules, it's worse than just a fight he got in at school—" My words are cut off by the front door opening again and Rick charging in, bumping his briefcase down on the table loudly.

"Uh-oh, the trouble twins are here. This can't be good." Rick's bubbly expression makes my heart sink even lower. This will deflate him in a way he's unprepared for.

"It's not good," I agree somberly. "It's Bryson."

The wash of fear over his face is instant. "Where is he?"

"In his room," Jules chimes in, clearly trying to lighten this heavy moment. "He got in a fight at school and is suspended."

Rick's hand flies to his chest. "You scared me to death." After a beat of deep breaths he's steady again. "Did he win?"

"Rick," I scold, annoyed by the levity he always tries to inject into everything.

"Listen, I don't want him fighting at school but if he's going to, I'd like him to win." The chuckle is sweet and for my benefit. Rick is letting me know this is not as big of a deal as I'm making it. He sees my red-rimmed eyes and the way my hands are shaking. He must think this is just motherly hysteria.

"It's more than that." I gesture toward the table and we all sit down. I feel like this is a conversation you need to be seated for even though Rick and Jules seem unconvinced.

"He ran off." Jules sighs casually. "But he called me right

away and was safe the whole time. And he's got a girlfriend. Or had one. They broke up. I know it seems like a big deal but—"

"Bryson has been lying about everything," I blurt out angrily, pounding my hand on the table. The candlesticks rattle and their eyes widen. "He had this girlfriend for over four months. He threw a party, there was drinking, and—"

"What party?" Rick asks, twisting his face up in confusion. "He was invited to a party?" His brows shoot up with the hint of pride.

"Don't glamorize this, Rick. It's really bad. He threw the party. Here. In our home." I'm grinding the words out through my teeth, straining my voice to try to keep from yelling.

"A party?" Again he sounds almost proud before lowering his voice and clearing his throat. "Kids screw up," he reminds me gently. "Obviously, Bryson is going through something right now. He's pissed off and trying to assert some kind of independence. But we're his safety net. We need to do a reset here. That's all. It'll be okay."

"It will not be okay," I sob.

"He had a party here?" Rick looks around as if he might find some hidden clues.

The skin over my eyelid begins to twitch. I can't believe what I'm about to say. The hellscape we are falling into. "I saw videos from the party. Right here in our kitchen. It looks like Bryson was drinking. And do you two remember the student I told you about? She was here too. That terrible thing she's going through, it happened in our son's bedroom."

Rick makes some kind of grunting noise as he waits for more of an explanation. In his defense, I'm being vague. But in my defense, I can't bring myself to say the words. But I'll have to.

"I met with her again today. That's where I was this afternoon. I saw, on the video of the party, she and Bryson were talking and then went up the stairs together off camera. I told her I'd seen the video and she said she remembered some of what happened at the party. That it was Bryson that assaulted her. She said no to him, he didn't stop. She remembers. She just told me."

Jules gasps and covers her heart with her hand. I know she, like me, can't fathom this reality. Not our Bryson. It can't be.

Rick slams his hand down on the table as he stands. The chair he was sitting on spills backwards and hits the floor. "Dammit, Elizabeth. What are you— I just don't understand why you would interject yourself into something like this. I warned you. Why?"

"Why?" I bellow back. "The better question is, why after we spent his entire life teaching Bryson about parties and alcohol and consent, he would still do something so terrible?" I don't for a moment believe Bryson would do something like that. Not the Bryson I know. But for some reason I feel compelled to dig in here with Rick. To rattle him by this news the same way it's hit me. Our son has been accused of assault and I want him to sit with this nightmare. To take it seriously.

The look of disgust on Rick's face is seared instantly into my mind. Not only has he never looked at me like this before, I'm not sure anyone has. "He didn't do this. Are you out of your mind? Our son didn't rape a girl at a party."

"She said—"

"I don't give a shit what she said," Rick screams. I feel a chill run up my back. Rick doesn't raise his voice. Not like this. "This is Bryson. Our son. We know him. A year ago he spent Saturday nights up in his room asking you to help him reorganize his baseball card collection. He's not out raping girls. The fact that you'd even consider what she's saying to be true is disgusting. What kind of mother would do that?"

I deflect his words. I am not the villain here. He is the one who insisted I was being overprotective. I was smothering our son. He was ready to be left home alone overnight. In some way, he was responsible. Rick never stopped until I would finally cave. He got his way that night and this is the mess we have to live with now. "On the video you can see them. They clearly walk up the stairs together. Daisy remembers being in his room and his fish tank."

"Stop talking." Rick points his finger at me and Jules stands up too.

She tries to slow this down. "Everyone, just take a second. I know this is emotionally charged but we can't get crazy."

"No." Rick shakes his head. "This isn't emotional at all. It's a legal matter. And that's my world. What I do. So I am telling you to stop talking. We drop this now. This girl didn't want you to report it to anyone. You said so yourself. You are to have no further contact with her."

The order leaves no room for interpretation but I feel something unfamiliar boil in me. Rick has never minced words when it came to big decisions he felt were in the best interest of our family. He's always been the one with the final word. It made more sense. He knew more. Saw the big picture. But in this moment his demands make me furious. "She is my student."

"Then teach her. That's your only job. Don't call her. Don't text her. Don't meet with her after school. I want you to drop this completely. No one says another word about it and we move on. He did not do this. It's her word against his. We lock this down now."

"Rick, we can't just—"

"We have one job, Elizabeth." His eyes pulse with fury. "One. We protect our child. That's it. You have not been right lately. It's been months. Just like before, you're off. You're restless and distracted. Your judgment is unreliable and I will not have whatever you are meddling in come back and hurt Bryson."

"What do you mean?" Jules asks, looking to me for explanation. "What's been wrong?"

Rick answers for me. "The same shit that has been wrong

since you two were children. Because, heaven forbid, she go and deal with her issues with a professional" He paces, unable to even look in my direction.

"What issues?" Jules is worried. Confused.

I wave her off, shooting her a look to drop it. "I'm fine. This has nothing to do with me or how I feel."

"Tell me." Jules looks from me to Rick, her hand propped on her hip. "What are you talking about? What do you know about us when we were kids? These things are not connected, are they?"

Rick groans loudly as though it should be painfully obvious. "Jules, we all walk around here like you two just came into existence when I met you. You were ten and she was nineteen. We pretend you didn't have a whole life. A terrible life. And we never talk about it. Yet it clearly still affects you, Elizabeth. It's why you could actually sit here and think our son would do something so terrible. Because of how you grew up. Only a completely broken person could think that way."

"No." I chuckle humorlessly. His arrogance and assertions are grating. "I can imagine something terrible happening like that because it happens all the time. You know that. And I don't think any parent believes their son would be involved in something like that. But it happens." I want to tell him that of course Bryson did not do this. But I'm not ready to let Rick off the hook.

Jules's mouth is agape as if she can't believe what I've just said. Rick is just as flabbergasted. I want to press on and make my point further but Bryson comes shuffling his way into the kitchen and grimaces at all of us.

"No one died," he groans as he grabs a soda from the fridge and cracks it open. "I know I screwed up. I'll take my punishment, but can we stop acting like I'm getting the electric chair. It's a suspension."

None of us speaks. It's as if we were about to enter the

codes to launch a nuclear war and someone just came in to get our coffee order. His energy is all wrong for the situation. Rick is the first one to find his voice and it's clearly because he's worried what I might say if I beat him to it.

"Bryson, we need to finish our conversation down here and then one of us will be up to talk to you." Rick points back to the stairs.

"I'm not five years old," Bryson snarls, slamming the soda can down hard enough on the counter for some to splash out.

I capitalize on his arrogance. This kid has no idea what is about to crash down on his head. "I asked you if you knew what was going on with Daisy and you said you had no idea."

"Elizabeth, don't." Rick doesn't want answers. He's afraid of the truth. Silencing me has always been easy. It's killing him that I'm not backing down.

Bryson gulps nervously. "Uh, I don't know what her problem is. I barely know her." Bryson's entire posture shifts. The bravado and annoyance melt away. I can't tell if that's a good sign or bad.

"She had plenty to say about how she knows you. I guess that's what happens when you throw a party and give out all the alcohol and pizza you can get your hands on. You two were talking."

"I talked to a bunch of people." Bryson shrugs as I scrutinize his inflection and nuanced facial expressions. When he was young, I'd honed the lie detector test that could catch him with his hand in the cookie jar. Now, it's not so easy to tell. Or maybe I stopped looking so closely. Wasn't that what we were meant to do? Start to let them go.

"I want details on everything that happened that night. I want to know who was there. What went down. I want to know everything. And don't think I'm going to let you just play dumb."

"Elizabeth," Rick yells and we all jump. I feel his voice

rattle in my chest. It's so uncommon for him to raise his voice that I'm startled to the core. Today he's done it more than he has in the last year. "Now is not the time."

"What's going on?" Bryson asks, his hand over his heart, still recovering from Rick's commanding shout. I wish Rick shouted like that more often. If he'd have disciplined Bryson with some consistency our talks about parties and drinking might have stuck. Why did dads always get to be the fun ones? They rile them up at bedtime. Sneak the candy before dinner. They wrestle in the freshy cleaned living room and play the music in the car a little too loud.

It's left me having to say no far more than I say yes. I had to think about the importance of sleep and the well-balanced breakfast. I had to argue my way into getting my son to do the basic things he needs to survive. Logic and rules are my department. Jokes and treats are Rick's. Is that why we're here now?

The anger is rolling through my gut like bingo balls being spun in the church basement on a Saturday night. I don't let Rick and his booming voice silence me.

"Daisy is accusing you of rape. She said she went into your room and even though she said no, you didn't listen." I don't let my voice quiver. I know he did not do this, but he has to understand what lying and partying can do to ruin so many lives.

"What?" Bryson falls back on his heels. "I didn't. We didn't. Nothing happened. She got completely wasted and I told her she could go lie down in my room. I made sure no one messed with her and that she was all set. I never touched her." He looks from me and my angry face to Rick and then Jules. They offer him the sympathy he's desperate for.

"We know you didn't," Rick chimes in reassuringly. Just the same way he'd slide him a few pieces of chocolate after I'd said no. Or let him watch the rest of the baseball game even though I'd said we were out missing bedtime. It had been fifteen years of this. Of him being good cop to my bad cop. I love my son deeply and it is that love that makes me hold him to these standards. Those rules and fights I've had to keep him in line were to keep him safe.

"Do you understand how serious an accusation like this is?" I ask, and can feel Jules and Rick glaring at me. I don't look back at them.

Rick takes two steps forward, as though I am a bullet and he's saving Bryson from me. "Bryson, this is very important. An accusation like this can be incredibly disruptive and dangerous. How we handle it is paramount. I've discussed this with your mother. She won't have any contact, besides teaching, with Daisy. You're not going to say a word of this to anyone. Not your friends. No one. There's a good chance if we don't give this any oxygen, it'll just put itself out."

The jargon always bothered me. The corporate legal metaphors used again and again. They turned my stomach. In the context of my son, it was even worse. "Things like this don't go away," I caution him. I turn toward Jules, knowing she'll agree with me. "Do they?"

"Usually, no." Jules hums apologetically. "You should be prepared in case Daisy does decide to go to the police."

"Police?" Bryson yelps, his face crumpling like he'd just let go of his favorite balloon and lost it to the endless blue sky. "I didn't do anything wrong."

"How long were you in the room?" Rick asks, not reacting to Bryson's emotion. He'd sat across from enough crying witnesses in his life to be able to tune it out. Just the facts. That's how Rick approached things.

Bryson's voice is high and scared. A tone I haven't heard from him since he was a little boy. "Like five minutes. Maybe a little more. Not enough time to—"

"Did anyone see you leave the room?" Rick presses impatiently, his back arrow straight. "I need you to really think about this."

"I don't think so. By the time I came out everyone had gone to the pool. Ally was over but we got in a fight and she left before that. So I think people were just trying to leave me alone. I hung out in the kitchen for a while, I was texting—"

"Us," I say, with a knowing expression. "You were texting us and saying everything was good and you hoped we were having fun in the city. You wished us a happy anniversary."

"I did hope you were having fun." He furrows his brow as though he's frustrated and confused. "The party was just supposed to be a couple of people. It got way out of hand. I didn't want to ruin your night and ask you to come home and fix it for me. I was trying to handle it myself."

I open my mouth to argue against his point but Rick cuts in, furious that I'm derailing things from the clinical legal approach he thinks is best.

"So no one can account for your time? Did anyone walk into the kitchen and talk with you?"

"No. It was a big blowout I had with Ally. No one wanted to get in my face really. They figured I'd be pissed off and might kick everyone out if they did. None of them really liked me. They were just looking for a place to drink and party. Then they wouldn't listen to me at all. They broke the vase. I'm so sorry."

"Did you see anyone else go upstairs?" Rick presses on, ignoring his apology.

"No, I don't think so. But if she said that happened to her, someone else must have. They could have gone up when I was in the kitchen. I didn't hear anyone but..."

"Who would have gone upstairs?" Rick doesn't finish the question. He doesn't ask who would have gone upstairs to his room and taken advantage of a drunk girl. That's too crass for this conversation as far as Rick is concerned. But for me, he's missing the point.

Bryson shrugs. "There were some kids I've never met

before. They were friends of friends. They go to another school. I don't even remember their names. Any of them could have, I guess."

I tick things off on my fingers as I try to get this straight. "You threw a pool party at our house with kids you don't even know. You were drinking and smoking to the point where Daisy needed to be put to bed. And you don't know if someone else went up there? You left her completely defenseless."

Bryson shakes his head as though he could make what I'm saying untrue by sheer will. "It wasn't like that. Or it didn't start that way. I had no clue Daisy was going to drink that much. I didn't know how bad it was until she was falling all over the place. And I didn't invite all those other kids. They just started showing up."

"It never starts that way," Rick finally shouts again. "The liability that you have opened this family up to is astronomical. It was our alcohol. Our house. This is exactly what happens at parties like this. We've talked to you so many times about the consequences of your actions."

"I'm sorry," Bryson cries, the crowd turning on him. I feel vindicated by the agreement, but my gut aches for his tears. I've always comforted him when he's cried. From skinned knees to failed math tests, I'm the person he reaches for. Now, I take a step back and Rick is the one who pulls him in for a hug.

"We're going to figure this out, kiddo. I promise. I'm not going to let anything happen to you. Just stop with the lying and the risky behavior. Promise you won't talk about this with anyone. Let me handle it."

Bryson only nods as he buries his head into his father's broad shoulder. They're the same height now and it's alarming. They are both the size of men. Grown men. Dangerous men.

I lock eyes with Jules. I want her to raise her brow in a way that speaks a million words. Or the flare of her nostrils that means something important. Instead, she looks blankly at me.

Gives me nothing to latch onto. For the first time in a long time, I cannot tell what my sister is thinking. I can't understand what my son has done. In this kitchen, in this moment, I'm on the outside looking in. The family I've made, designed perfectly, fought endlessly for, is not quite so solid as I'd imagined. Rick can't look my way as he finally lets go of Bryson. We're not a united front. We're not in agreement. And I can feel in my heart nothing will ever be the same.

SIXTEEN

ELIZABETH

"You should call out sick today," Rick says flatly as he sits up in bed and checks the messages on his phone. "I'm staying home. I didn't have court today and Willow was able to move the rest of my meetings. I think we need to take a day to regroup."

"I can't. I don't have a sub lined up and I've got kids presenting their projects today. I need to go in." I know my voice is icy and I don't attempt to thaw it out for him.

"You don't." He's curt and glances up from his phone to watch me grab my clothes from the hook behind the door and head for the shower.

"This isn't going to just go away if we bury our heads in the sand, Rick. What do you think Daisy will assume if I stay out of work today? She told me last night that our son sexually assaulted her. That she is distraught and has no one to turn to. Then I just don't show up at work. If you don't want her to say anything about this, then maybe use your head. Me cutting her out only makes her more desperate."

"You cannot discuss this with her any further. You've already put yourself in a precarious position by interjecting yourself to begin with. Now that she's lying and saying it was Bryson, we're at even more of a disadvantage."

"Obviously, it wasn't Bryson. He would never. But someone in this house did. And we have a responsibility in that. So does Bryson."

"You have no idea how these situations work, Elizabeth. This is my job. This is what I do for a living. Let me protect him. Work with me. As a teacher you should have—"

"Yes, Rick, I'm aware of the rules of my job. I also know that when someone is hurt the way Daisy is, there is a loneliness you can't imagine. A desperation. I'm going to do the right thing by not completely abandoning her until we can sort this out."

He groans loudly enough to strain his voice. "If you talk to her about this again, you'll be putting Bryson in danger. You're risking his entire future. This is your son. Your loyalty needs to be to him."

"It is." I'm shouting now and I can feel the blood rushing to my cheeks. "Talking to Daisy is not betraying Bryson. It's protecting him. Right now she believes he did this. I can't just ice her out now and hope she doesn't say anything. I need to help her until we find out who really did do this. Bryson put himself in this position."

"How could you possibly think this is in any way his fault? She is the one who drank herself into oblivion around a bunch of people she hardly knew. He didn't force her to drink and he moved her into his room so she could lie down. He was being a gentleman. He had no idea this would happen. Even considering this as his fault is a complete—"

"Wake up, Rick." I turn my back on him and turn toward the bathroom. "You've been a man your whole life. Look at your friends. Look at your clients. Look at the world. Stop acting like these things don't happen, or they don't happen to people like us. Of course they do. Bryson is old enough to understand that. We've always been open with him about what can happen. He knew better." The rattlesnake bite in my words likely stuns him, but I don't turn to check. Instead I spin the handles of the shower and lose myself in the steam.

This is not how things like this normally go in our marriage. Maybe that's because there has never really been anything quite like this to happen in our family before. But any kind of conflict normally ends the same. Rick and I might bicker and debate for a little while but eventually he gets his way. He reasons and spins and talks until he's badgered me with facts and statistics that might sway me over to his side. If I'm passionate about something I put up a good fight and occasionally we find a lopsided compromise. A way to make me feel like I got a win without him having to give in. It's worked for us for years, but lately I've felt stifled. Steamrollered.

I'm not playing along this time and I know my husband well. He won't be sitting in our bed when I get out. That would be too casual. Too weak. He'll have gone downstairs, made coffee and retreated to his home office that's off the dining room. He's regrouping, strengthening his argument like a good lawyer does.

Just as expected the bed is empty by the time I emerge from the bathroom, makeup on and hair dry. Jules stayed over at our house last night, but she knows enough to sleep in, or at least pretend to. We all lived together long enough for her to sense when space is needed. This leaves only Bryson sitting in the kitchen when I come down to fill up my travel mug and pack my bag.

I nearly laugh, thinking of all the years I've had to drag him out of bed and practically throw him in the shower every morning before school. But now that he's suspended from school, here he is, up with the sun.

"Morning," he croaks out, the bags under his eyes deep and dark. He hasn't slept. That's obvious. But I suppose none of us got much rest.

"No school today. You should go back to bed." I'm not being cold to him. My voice is exactly how it's always been. Maybe even a little sweeter than usual. But there is a filter in the mind of a teenager that hears a tone when there is none.

"Do you hate me?" Bryson asks, his voice breaking with emotion.

"Hate you?" I parrot back, my eyes wide. I've told him every day of his life there was no way in the world to lose my love. That he had me in his corner no matter what. Now, he's not so sure.

"Do you really think I would ever do that to a girl? If you do, then you must hate me." The tears well in his eyes. "It's not what you think."

"You've been keeping a lot from us, and it's hard to know what to think. I wish you'd have told us about you and Ally dating. We needed to know what was going on between you two. We needed to know what was going on in your life."

"Just another reason to hate me right now. I'm a liar. I'm a screw-up. Of course you hate me."

I turn toward my son and give him an earnest look. "Bryson, I don't hate you. These things are complicated. It's why we've always spent so much time talking to you about dating and parties. It's never just sex. It's never just a few drinks. Not at your age and—"

"I didn't have sex with Daisy. I didn't touch her. If you brought her here right now, I'd make her tell you the truth. She's totally lying."

"Or she's remembering wrong," I offer, feeling the sting of him tossing around the word lying so easily.

"Why are you taking her side?" He runs his hands over his head in exasperation. "She's a liar."

"Don't say that." I point my finger at him angrily. "You have no idea what she's going through, and the only way to make it immeasurably worse is to call her that. She's been through hell and it was in our home. At a party you threw."

"And you blame me." He looks at me defiantly, daring me to be disloyal. To have to take back all my talk about unconditional love.

Drawing in a deep breath, I try to reframe things for him. "The most likely scenario is that you left Daisy in your room and someone else went in and hurt her. She's confused but she's not a liar."

"You don't know what it's like to be accused of something like this."

He's still spitting out his last syllable when I unapologetically counter his point. "You don't know what it's like to be the victim of something like this."

"You do?" His face flashes worried and then confused. Children can't fathom the idea that their parents had lives and experiences separate from them. That there might be a whole host of pain that existed before they were born.

"We're talking about Daisy, and I won't allow you to call her a liar just because you're uncomfortable with the consequences of your actions."

"My actions," he shouts wildly, sounding eerily similar to Rick last night. "You do think I did it."

"No, Bryson, but you need to face the fact that none of this would be happening if you weren't lying, drinking, and taking these risks. The reason we didn't want you in adult situations is because you aren't prepared to handle what might happen."

"I get it," Bryson says, still an unwarranted air of irritation in his voice. "But you do know I wouldn't hurt a woman, right? Ever. I'm not that guy."

For some reason this argument infuriates me. There is no monsterlike villain lurking in the shadows down alleys perpetrating all the horrific crimes against young women. It's a culture. It permeates every facet of our society.

"Who is that guy?" I press, pouring my coffee and putting the pot down a little too hard. "Who is the big bad wolf of a man who would do something like that?"

"I don't know." Bryson shrugs and looks away.

"You've got a lot of friends, Bryson. Surely you know at least one or two of them who talk like that. Who brag. Who would hurt someone just to get what they wanted. This playing dumb act doesn't work for me. It's not naiveté that has you unable to answer me. You don't want to face the fact that you know people who would harm women. Right?"

"I guess." He shrugs again and his confusion frustrates me. "Maybe Roy or Danny. They can get kind of gross in the locker room when they talk about the people they sleep with. And they don't really respect girls. They could probably do something like this. They were here that night for an hour. But both left before I brought Daisy upstairs."

"But they have it in them? They're your friends," I counter. "You are friends with guys who would hurt a drunk girl at a party?"

"I don't know if they would," he replies quickly, his words running together. "I'm just saying they have that vibe."

"And who else? Not just people who were at the party. Teachers? Coaches?"

"I guess," he says again, his nostrils flaring. "The girls say Mr. Rivers is kind of a perv in class. And Coach Wakner from lacrosse pays way too much attention to the cheerleaders during games. He always makes comments about them too."

"And how about people at church?" I wave my hand around animatedly. "Any pervs there?"

He looks pensive as he conjures up the name. "Tray's dad is a creep. I think he's actually hooking up with one of the senior girls who volunteers at church. That's a rumor, I guess."

"So all these people who work and live totally normal lives, and yet they're pretty well known for disgusting or predatory behavior? They use their power or their size or their wits to get what they want and hurt who they can."

"I don't know what this has to do with me. I'm not like any of them."

"The world is full of terrible things, Bryson. You're either a part of that or you're fighting against it. There is no in between. If you try to live in the middle, you might as well march yourself over to the side with Mr. Rivers and Roy or Danny. Because best-case scenario right now is you threw a party with copious amounts of alcohol, and left a girl in a bedroom who was completely out of it."

"I thought she was safe."

"You just listed a bunch of people who you think could be dangerous. You're not an idiot, Bryson. You left her there in that room for someone else to come along and hurt her." My voice hardly feels like my own. I know I'm being harsh to Bryson, but my anger is too powerful to bottle up. I can't seem to soften this horrible message.

"I had no idea—"

"You had every idea, because I've made sure you understood how the world worked and how people act. I taught you better than whatever the last six months has been for you."

"I'm sorry!" he shouts, the tears coming back to his eyes. "I screwed up and I'm no better than some scumbag coach who lurks around the locker room. I get it, and—"

"Go to work, Elizabeth," Rick says as he points to the door. "Just go to work."

I watch as he plants a stabilizing hand on Bryson's shoulder. He's letting him stay up late again. Ice cream before dinner. Rescuing him from me and my big bag of rules.

I don't say goodbye. I don't offer any kind of absolution. I love my son beyond measure. It is that love for him that has me taking this stance. These are the moments in people's lives where roads diverge. Where he has to choose to see his role in this and resolve to be better. Try harder. Speak up more. This is where character is built. And he can step into the power he has in this world. Or it's where he will see himself as a victim. Where he will blame and argue. And the cycle just continues.

As Rick drapes his arm over Bryson's shoulder, I know the window has closed. I'll save this conversation for a quieter moment.

Grabbing my keys from the counter, I step outside and let the light, sprinkling rain prickle against my hot cheeks.

I hear the word pulse in my ears.

Liar. Liar. Liar.

I can feel my skin crawl. My mind race. And it's not until I look in my rearview mirror that I'm broken from the past. Because right here in the present, I'm almost positive that's the same red car trailing behind me. I speed away and take a sharp turn hoping to lose them. A cold chill runs up my spine. I've run for my life so many times. I thought those days were behind me, but I'm starting to realize there are two things I can't outrun. The past and danger.

SEVENTEEN

ELIZABETH

Then

I've practiced keeping my voice steady even when my chest is filled with thudding nervous energy. I do for Jules what I wish anyone in my life would do for me. Keep calm and project confidence in the idea that everything will be all right.

"Jules, we can't go home tonight. Mom and Dad won't be there and it's better if we find somewhere else to stay until one of them gets back." I deliver the message with a cool smile and pretend I'm fascinated by something out the dirty window of the burger place.

Jules looks up from her cheeseburger, her eyes wide with confusion. "Did something happen?" She wanted fries too but the burger was all I could swing with the change in my pocket this afternoon. I need the rest to make a call. I pretend, like usual, that I'm not hungry. She believes me and doesn't question why she's the only one with food in front of her.

Ignorance really is bliss. I'd give anything to be in the dark about what happened today at our house. My father, drunk and enraged, couldn't tolerate my mother, high and delusional. It's a toxic combination that becomes violent in a flash. She was going on about the people on the street who were stealing her hair. A more creative delusion than usual.

I can't bring myself to tell Jules the truth. I can't tell her that our father has been arrested again for beating our mother. That our mother, who has always been fragile, is now alone in the hospital with no one there to explain what she really needs and likes. That's usually my job.

Instead, I just say, "They're not there. And we can't stay there either. We have to go to a friend's house for the night."

Jules nods, taking a ravenous bite of the burger and then a sip from her free glass of water. She shrugs in agreement. It's shocking how blindly she'll follow me. Her trust in my plans is misguided but I'm the best bet she has for staying safe, even if I'm shitty at it.

The quarters in my pocket will be enough for the pay phone and I have to hope Keith is home and picks up my call. The knot in my stomach tightens as I squeeze us both into the phone booth and dial. He's the only person I can think of who might be able to help us, but I also know this might be what my grandfather used to call jumping from the frying pan into the fire.

Keith is practically a stranger, though he talks as though we have some kind of special connection. Quick with compliments, something I rarely get, and I like how he looks at me. How he says I'm more than the other girls my age. I know I am, because I've had to grow up faster than them.

I think he's about twenty-one or maybe twenty-two. He can drink, and he's got a good job working for the city doing some kind of maintenance work. I know he's out early every day because he hangs out by my register at the Glam Closet. It's a retail store geared toward women over seventy. The clothes are mostly a lot of fake gems glued to ugly sweaters, and polyester pants they wear halfway up to their necks. They like having me around though, claiming I keep them all feeling young. My praises about how trendy they look have them coming back for more. And something about me has Keith coming in again and again.

When my boss comes around, he claims he's shopping for his grandmother and we giggle to ourselves. Every once in a while, he does buy something, and swears it really is for his nana. I think it's just so he doesn't get kicked out. He's sweet and brings me fries from the food court sometimes. Now I'm going to be asking for a hell of a lot more than fries.

"Hey, Keith," I say when he answers. "This is Elizabeth, from the mall. The Glam Closet." The burning in my cheeks is sheer embarrassment. I hate asking for help, it's mortifying but I look down at Jules and know I have no choice. If we get put into foster care and they get a chance to really see how screwed up things are at home for us, then we might not be able to stay together.

"Lizzy girl," Keith replies with a cheery laugh. No one calls me this but him. It's not my favorite but he thinks I like it and I let him. "What's up?"

"I need a favor. It's fine if you don't want to but—"

"Hey, I gave you my number so you'd call if you needed anything. I meant it. What can I do for you?"

"My sister and I need a place to crash for a couple of days. We won't be any trouble at all. I can bring food for us. We don't need anything special."

"Of course." He's quick to answer and it shocks me. I've been a burden my whole life, and it's always surprising when someone acts like I'm not. "And don't worry about food or anything. I have plenty. Do you want me to pick you up?"

I feel guilty for asking this much out of someone who really doesn't even know us. He owes me nothing. But we're friends and maybe this really is what friends do for each other. "We could probably walk to you."

"No, it's late. Just tell me where you are and I'll come get you." I can hear him shifting around like he's ready to jump in his car. I tell him where we are and apologize again for the trouble.

"Lizzy, you're no trouble at all. You and I have a connection. I've always felt that. I want to be the person who can help you out when you need it. I'll be there soon."

I hang up the phone and try to keep the tears from falling. I don't want to rely on Keith, but I have no other choice.

As we make our way to the park, where I've told Keith we'll be, Jules clings to my hand, her eyes following the swooping birds and the leaves waving on the wind-blown trees. That's where her glance goes. Mine is darting around. Checking for police who might be looking for us. Or a creepy guy lurking in the bushes. Jules daydreams while I fight off waking nightmares.

"Where are we going?" she asks.

"Keith is going to pick us up here." She doesn't know Keith and yet she doesn't probe for more answers.

When we reach the park, Keith is waiting for us, leaning against his car with his arms folded. He's got a tall and lanky build that makes him stand out in a crowd. His dark hair is cropped close to his head and his smoky-colored eyes are almost always lit with a smile.

Despite his easygoing demeanor, there's a sense of resilience about him that suggests he's faced his own share of challenges in life. He moves as if he knows exactly where he's going in life and how to get there. I'm envious of that confidence.

When he speaks, his voice is soft and reassuring, with a hint of gravel that gives it depth and always has me listening intently.

"This must be Jules," he asks, tousling her hair. She beams up at him and nods, feeling special that she's been recognized. I settle her into the back seat of his car and then turn to see he's still standing there. Waiting. Expecting.

He pulls me in for a hug and to my surprise, I melt into his arms. I'd been holding it all together but now, I could feel myself falling apart.

"That bad, kid?" Keith asks as he squeezes me a little tighter. I don't answer. I just sniffle and get myself back together.

"Thanks for doing this. It'll just be a day or two. My mom will be in the hospital for a little bit but won't press charges. Once she's home or they let my dad back out, we'll be fine. If the cops or child protective services catch us home alone while both my parents are dealing with their half of this shit, they'll split Jules and I up."

"It's no trouble. You hungry?"

"I'm okay," I lie.

"I'm starving. Let's get pizza on the way home."

Home. It's ridiculous. The way he says it as if we all live together in some happy little place and getting pizza is just what we do. I should call him on it. Remind him that his home is not mine. That I'm not interested in some pretend life. But the way the word hits my ears, I don't fight against it. I just smile and nod because I like how casually he calls it home.

There are some subtle wrinkles around Keith's eyes that I haven't noticed before. He takes my hand in his and we ride that way to the pizza place. It's awkward but he doesn't act like it is. So I don't either. Jules is half asleep staring out the window, eyes getting heavy.

I want to ask Keith how old he is suddenly, but I don't. It would be rude. I owe him at least some manners. He looks over at me and smiles, squeezing my hand. Is he just trying to make me feel better? Comforted?

We're in his apartment, a third-floor walk-up, twenty minutes later, and I make the couch up into a bed for me and Jules. She's snoring already and I lay her down once the blankets are in place.

"You can't both fit on there," Keith says with a shrug. "You can sleep in my bed."

"Where will you sleep?" The stones in my stomach turn to boulders.

"With you." His grin is odd and he says the words as though they are obvious. "Come on, Lizzy. That's why you're here, right? So we can be together."

"I, uh—" My face falls and I can't hide my worry. "We needed a place to stay for the night and I thought that maybe you'd—"

"And I totally did, right? I came and got you. Got dinner. I'm making sure you and your little sister are safe. Now I know you don't have any money or anything. I'd never ask you for that. I just thought maybe this was also a good way for us to finally get to know each other better."

"Better?" I gulp out.

"You're no little girl, Lizzy. Don't play dumb. I've been coming around your work for months. Bringing you things. I took care of you tonight. Men don't just do that for no reason. You know that."

I think I did know that. I think that's the worst part. In my gut this was all too good to be true. I knew what men expected. Keith is not my hero, he's just my next villain and I'm the idiot who followed him into his house. Now I need to figure out how to get me and Jules out of it.

EIGHTEEN

DAISY

Hot coals fill my shoes. Sand clogs my throat. The skittering of a hundred spiders crawls across my scalp. My senses have me hostage. I can feel my bracelet strangling my wrist. My sweater itching my neck. My hand swelling against my rings. It makes it impossible to hear what my friends are laughing at. Or what my teachers are droning on about all day. There is only one teacher I hear and right now, she's looking directly at me.

"Can I see you after class?" she chirps casually as she hands back our latest essays. I can't understand how she is here today. How she is so calm and acting so normal. "Great job on this, by the way. I loved your take on the poem."

I nod at Elizabeth... Mrs. Meadows, and cannot fathom how she's looking at me so gently. I wonder if everyone is staring at us. If they know. If my jittery reaction has them whispering and wondering.

"Thanks," I croak, cramming the paper into my bag and jumping again when the bell rings.

Mrs. Meadows hurries to get the last few papers handed back as the class rushes toward the door. "Don't forget to do the reading tonight. We'll be discussing it tomorrow, and I want everyone to weigh in."

The room is silent a moment later like a battlefield with no survivors. The cannons quiet. The dead still.

"I have to get to chemistry," I say, slinging my bag over my shoulder.

"I'll write you a pass." She shuts the door and gestures me back to my seat. I awkwardly plop back down. Walking to the classroom window that overlooks the faculty parking lot, she props a hand on her hip. Lingering for a minute, she hums curiously.

"I think we have a quiz," I say, clearing my throat. My leg shakes in that nervous way that always gives me away. Slamming my hand down on my thigh, I force it to be still.

"Do you see that car out there?" She waves me over and I slowly shuffle her way. I don't know what she wants from me.

She lowers her voice as she points. "The red one. Do you know who drives that car?"

"Uh, what car?"

"That red one over there." She points again, this time more impatiently, banging her finger against the glass of the window. "I swear I'm seeing that car everywhere. That's not Jenelle Reeves. Hers is similar but it doesn't have that same kind of thing on the back."

"I don't know." I take a step back and know that my face reads confused as she finally turns and looks at me.

"The quiz." I point over my shoulder toward the door.

"Daisy, it's all right. Don't worry about chemistry. We need to talk."

I gulp. "Okay. About that car?"

"No, about you. About what you told me. Are you doing all right?"

There was no easy way to answer that. The way my eyes shift around, she clearly understands I'm uncomfortable.

"Forget I asked that." She sighs. "That's a dumb question. Of course you aren't. You've been through something traumatic. You're overwhelmed. Also I get the impression you don't have much support at home. Are things not good there?"

"Home?" I ask, remembering with a great ache that she'd seen where I live and the obvious conclusions someone could draw from that.

She doesn't wait for me to elaborate. "I don't talk much about my past, Daisy, but it gives me a unique perspective on things. I know what it looks like to be ravenously hungry. I understand that access to things like water or soap can be limited sometimes. That's a painful reality most people in this school would never understand. But I do."

I feel seen. Not in that validating kind of way but that naked and embarrassed feeling of being found out. After everything we've talked about I don't understand why she's even interested in hearing about my problems, let alone trying to get to the bottom of what might be going on at home.

"I'm fine. You dropped me off at my grandmother's place. I'm just living there for now. It's not a big deal. I don't want people to know." The way I wrap my arms around myself must be a dead giveaway because her face washes with pity.

"They don't have to know. I'm not going to say anything to anyone. I understand what it's like to try to keep your head above water in school. Let alone with all the added pressure of being different. Now with what happened at the party it's a lot to handle. I just want to know how I can help. What are your most urgent needs right now? Let me solve them for you."

Why was she talking about this? Why does she care whether I'm hungry or can take a shower? How is that more important than—

My thoughts stop abruptly like a seen-too-late red light that requires the squealing of tires. She's helping me, to help herself. As if this fixes everything. My stomach sours, but for the first time all day I feel something other than terror and hunger. I'm reminded everyone has an angle. Something to protect. Self-preservation.

When I don't speak, she plows on, clearly trying to steer us both in one direction. "Having all that stress can make your mind play tricks on you. I had a chance to speak with Bryson." She eyes me very closely for a reaction but I don't give one. I can't. "He does remember bringing you to his room but he said he just helped you to bed and left. I'm worried someone else from the party may have gone in there after him. With the amount you drank, perhaps..."

"Right." I nod and stiffen my back. I know what she needs. What she's asking of me. "I had so much to drink."

"We should think about who else was at the party. Maybe that would jog your memory."

"I really don't want to." I step back and look at the closed door. It's all that stands between me and freedom but it feels suddenly so far away. Maybe I'm missing an opportunity here. Overlooking a chance to actually change my circumstances.

"Food." I edge the word out slowly. "And our water is turned off. I came in early this morning to shower in the locker room but I can't keep doing that. We need the water turned back on."

"Of course." Elizabeth scrambles to her bag looking slightly relieved that I've given her something tangible to work with. "I have cash. Do you know how much you need to get it turned back on?"

I think back to the last past due bill and round up by a hundred. "Three fifty, I think."

Elizabeth looks entirely different now. Harried and frantic as if she's a doctor on the verge of solving some medical mystery. This can all be fixed. She can fix it.

"I have five hundred here. Take it. Get the water back on and get some groceries. I know it's a drop in the bucket. None of this is really a solution, but if it gets you ahead just for now, that's good." She smiles but her eyes are too wide to be natural.

The money is fanned out in her hands, just a foot from my face. The desperation in her eyes is unmistakable. She needs me to take this. She needs this to happen. Conflict rages in me. My need to survive is more complex than this cash. Nothing this bad can be fixed with some money. Yet, it can't hurt. She knows that.

"I can't take your money." I bite my lip, understanding why she's offering it to me. "I don't want to get you in trouble."

"You don't want people here to know you need the money, and I don't want people to know I gave it to you. That seems like the perfect scenario for no one finding out." Her voice is a low whisper and it feels conspiratorial. It is conspiratorial. We are going to hold each other's secrets. A dangerous game.

Her voice drops even lower and she crouches a bit to look me in the eyes. "Sometimes it's important to come to an understanding on things. I know there are rules. I understand the school's perspective on all of this, but if I were to report what's going on with you at home, your world would be turned upside down. Your family could be charged with neglect or abuse. You could be put into foster care and end up who knows where. I don't want that for you. Trust me, it's hell. I always wished when I was your age someone could swoop in and help me without all the strings attached. All the red tape of working within a very broken system. You can feel like—"

"No one is coming to save you." I whisper the words out with a ghostly breath.

"What did you say?" She leans away from me as if I'd uttered some ominous curse that would hex her for life. "Where did you hear that?"

"I don't know," I reply with a shrug, protectively covering my heart with my hand. "I guess it just feels like I'm on my own."

Seeming to relax, Elizabeth blinks slowly at me. "I completely understand. You don't have to be. Let me do this for you."

"And what do I do? You don't want me to tell anyone about—"

"About the money," she cuts in breathlessly. "That's all. That's all this is about. And I'll help you as much as I can. Utilities. Maybe some new clothes if you need it. We could go to the mall. You've got your scholarships lined up, but I could help you find stuff for your dorm room next year. That would be great, right?"

"Yeah," I say, glancing up at the clock considering if everyone in chemistry is questioning where I am. If the kids who heard Mrs. Meadows ask me to stay are starting to whisper about why I'm still here. "I really need to get to class."

She waves the money closer to me and I finally reach out and take it.

"Keep it in your bag so it's safe. If you need more, just let me know. Otherwise, let's just figure out a day to go to the mall."

"Yeah, okay. That would be good." I look down at the money. "Thanks. This is really going to help. Not having water at the house has been—"

"I remember exactly how it was. I remember."

I grab my bag and tuck the cash away. The only thing I know for sure right now is Mrs. Meadows does know how bad it can be. It's written on her face in an unmistakable way.

As I walk out into the hallway, I don't look back at her. I don't try to sort out how she's feeling. I clutch the hall pass in my hand and try to make sure no one in chemistry can tell what's going on. I practice my smile. Play my cover story about extra credit I need and stayed after class to sort it out. That will work. They'll believe it. Because Mrs. Meadows is nice like that. She helps everyone she can. She's one of the good ones. Right?

NINETEEN

RICK

Missed opportunities were blasting through the walls of my mind like hastily lit sticks of dynamite. I could have done more. I should have done something sooner. She'd been off lately. I knew that. I saw all the familiar signs and yet I did nothing. I thought it would be different now that Bryson was older. Elizabeth was older, too. But it wasn't better. Maybe it's worse than ever.

"It's going to work out," Jules says, her voice high and unfamiliar in its fake optimism. I'd known her since she was a child, practically raised her as my own. And I know for a fact that it is the voice she uses when she's nervous. When she doesn't really believe what she's saying.

I'm always the one to dash everyone's hope with my reality. I understand it about myself but being rational and logical is a vital part of life. Sometimes people need the blunt truth in order to move forward. "Jules, this is bad. I should have told you sooner but Elizabeth has been shaky lately. Something has been off with her. Have you noticed?"

Jules looks away and wrinkles her nose. "I guess she's been a bit different lately. Kind of distracted. Nothing too serious."

"This happens," I report somberly. "She has these spells. More headaches than usual. Some crying when she thinks no one is watching. She'll be low and then she gets sort of..." I choke on the word. It feels clinical and extreme but also true. I know it will worry Jules. But this entire situation warrants worry.

"What?" Jules leans over her fourth cup of coffee and presses for me to finish my sentence.

"Manic."

"Rick." Jules frowns and leans back suddenly. "She's not mentally ill. Elizabeth is one of the most organized, compassionate and energetic people I know. She's a wonderful sister, mother and wife."

"I'm not saying she isn't. Trust me, I'm reluctant to even bring it up considering everything that's going on right now, but I'm worried that volatility might make the situation with Bryson worse. I have to protect him."

Jules rolls her eyes at me and I'm transported back to her teen years. How we all made it work I'll never understand. On paper, our situation looked like it would implode. Me and Elizabeth getting so serious so fast. Moving her and Jules into my place. Turning into this quasi family and then very soon after, Bryson came along.

"Elizabeth will always protect Bryson. There is nothing in the world my sister loves more than that boy. She's not going to let anything happen to him. Even if she's been off lately or whatever, she'd never put him in danger."

"She already has. And I'm not even talking about this situation with Daisy. Things happened when Bryson was born. You were still so young and we didn't want to scare you. It was difficult to keep it from you, but I did."

"I don't remember anything happening after Bryson was born. Things were great. We were all so happy to have a baby in the house."

"You went to stay with my parents for two weeks, do you remember that?"

"I, uh—" She nods, wincing at the memory as if she understood it was a precursor to something tragic she'd been blind to.

"That's because of how volatile Elizabeth was. She was saying crazy things. Hallucinating. Imagining terrible scenarios about what might happen to Bryson. It got very bad. Eventually her ob-gyn had to insist on treatment. It was postpartum psychosis." I run my hand over my head and grimace. "It's my fault."

Jules looks unconvinced but I try to explain more bluntly. "I know you don't remember this. And like everything else in Elizabeth's past, we don't talk about it. But this happened. I let it happen once and I'm not going to do that again."

"You let her have postpartum?" She's annoyed with me. The way she gets when anyone has something negative to say about Elizabeth. I understand the loyalty. Jules owes her entire life, the wonderful way it's turned out, to Elizabeth and all the sacrifices she made for them to stay together.

"I'm not saying I could have prevented the postpartum issues, but I waited too long to intervene. I saw how bad it was but I wanted to protect her. What would people think? What would happen to her job and her degree she was working so hard for? But then one night I came in when she was giving Bryson a bath and I swear she was filling the tub up dangerously high on purpose."

"Stop." Jules cuts her hand through the air, looking like she wants to strike me.

I try to reassure her. "It wasn't her fault. It happens to women. She needed treatment. That's when I knew beyond a doubt that protecting Bryson was the most important thing. That's where we're at now. I have to do the same."

"She's not in some postpartum breakdown, Rick. There is a serious accusation against Bryson who lied, threw a party and allowed people to drink here in your home. He created a dangerous situation and Elizabeth is in a very precarious position because of that."

"I know Bryson screwed up, but if you could have heard Elizabeth this morning, you'd know I was right. The things she was saying to him were just awful. Not at all what a mother should be saying at a time like this. It was out of character and from such an angry place. It was venomous. That's not her."

Jules sets her jaw as she finally considers my argument seriously. "This situation would stir up a lot of feelings in any mother. She's processing. I'm sure she didn't mean to say anything hurtful." Jules fidgets with a loose string on the sleeve of her sweater and tries to believe what she's saying. She saw it last night. She knows I'm right.

"You don't understand. These spells or bouts of depression or whatever she has are always rooted in some deep pain. Something or many things that happened to her when she was young. We've never talked about them, but I know when she gets that shadowy look in her eyes and this quiet seething anger just below the surface that she's unstable. It's been coming on, and this will push her over the edge. You've seen it. I know you have."

I'm imploring her to agree with me. It all feels so subjective. Like I'm trying to hold smoke in my hand. A magic trick. But I can see Jules is coming around.

"I guess I've seen her struggle. She shielded me from so much when I was a kid. She saved my life. I've always known she'd weathered some terrible things, and, sure, I've seen her get a little down and distracted over the years but it always passes. I've never seen her manic." Jules waves her hand at the idea as though she's swatting away a fly.

"Because I help her through it." I pound my chest. "I keep it quiet. Do you remember five years ago when Bryson had his tonsils out? Elizabeth was having one of her episodes and I had to keep her home for a week. We told people it was because Bryson had some issues with recovery and he needed her around. That wasn't true. Elizabeth was freaking out. Crying uncontrollably one minute and then angry the next."

"I don't remember that."

"We didn't tell you."

"You should have called me. I had no idea."

"You'd just moved out and I didn't want to worry you." I shake my head and correct myself. "No, if I'm being honest, it's more than that. I didn't want you to think differently of her. Elizabeth is so strong. Strength is important to her. I never wanted to take that away."

"What triggered it for her about Bryson getting his tonsils out?"

I groan nervously. This has a *can of worms* kind of feeling as if we won't be able to go back to how things used to be once she knows. "Elizabeth had gotten stuck in the hospital elevator with a man. He was a janitor. I guess he was cracking some jokes and then hit the emergency stop button to tease her or something. She lost it. I couldn't calm her down for a week. She was completely untethered. I just circled the wagons here and tried to wait for it to pass."

"Clearly she's experienced some kind of—"

"Yes, but she's never talked about it." I can't even let Jules finish the sentence. "There is no world in which I can seem to accept my wife is a victim of any kind. She doesn't want that label and I don't want it for her. She doesn't want to discuss it. Not with me. Not with anyone. And she's had other issues, too. Hyper fixations and obsessive behavior. She plans things to death, so worried we won't have what we need somewhere. That we'll be hungry or stranded. You've seen all the junk she has in her purse. Like she's packing for an emergency every day."

"That's hardly something to be sounding the alarm about.

She's got some coping strategies. That's all." Jules is nodding her head with every syllable she speaks as if that might sway me. But I've seen too much now. I can't pretend any of this is normal.

"I'm not explaining it right." I rake my hands down my face and try to gather my thoughts. "Elizabeth is hot and cold. She's laser-focused and then extremely distracted. She's triggered and afraid and then fiercely angry. She has some trauma that she has to process, or I'm afraid of what might happen. I'm seriously scared for her, Jules. I have been for a while, but I've always just tried to downplay it. Not bring attention to how bad it can get. But now, I don't have a choice. This situation with Bryson will be a trigger. Any kind of harm against women or children always seems to unnerve her. Something this personal could break her. And I have to protect Bryson."

Jules stands and stares at me skeptically. "Why hasn't she told me any of this? I've asked her if she's okay. I've asked if she wants to talk about the past."

"Her entire life, since the day you were born, has been focused on shielding you from your family's crap. She fought for custody of you. She's done everything she could to make sure you don't suffer whatever fate she had to. Not telling you is just an extension of that protection, I think."

With a hint of anger, Jules shifts the guilt she's feeling over to me. "You're married to her. How do you marry someone and not know what fate they suffered? How do you not ask about all the things she's been through?"

"It's not what she wanted. I allowed her to keep her secrets and have some privacy because I thought one day she'd seek some professional help, but she hasn't. And now I'm really worried. We have to do something."

"What do you want me to do?" Jules raises her brows in disbelief. "She obviously doesn't trust me with any of this, considering I had no idea she was even struggling. At best I thought she was a little depressed, maybe sad about Bryson being so busy all the time. I had no idea it was so serious."

"That's my fault. I shouldn't have worked so hard to keep it all a secret. I just wanted to shelter her and not let these swings impact her life or her job. I thought it would get better over time. I didn't see this coming. I didn't think our son would be accused of..."

"He obviously didn't do it, Rick. It's Bryson. He would never."

I don't answer. I know he would never. But that doesn't solve the problem at hand.

"Rick." Her voice is sharp. "You don't think he could have really done that?"

"He didn't do this," I say, nearly chanting it, like it'll become our mantra. "Of course he didn't. But I know the justice system and our belief in his innocence won't be enough to save him. If Elizabeth can't get herself together and do what I know is right for Bryson, we could lose him to this. We need a clear plan and to be completely united. Which is why you need to talk to her. You're her sister, she'll listen to you."

"Dad," Bryson croaks nervously as he shuffles into the kitchen. He's still in his pajamas but he's finally got bed head from getting some sleep. That's a good sign.

"Hey, bud. You hungry?"

"Not really." He holds up a crumpled piece of paper and winces at it. "I just found this in my backpack. I don't know why she would..." I can see a large typed message across the front. "She really thinks I'm evil. My own mom thinks I'm evil?"

My eyes jump at the words out of order. There is no left to right at the moment. My brain can't manage that. It's just jumbled letters forming clearly hurtful words. Finally, with great effort, I put it in order.

For those who reject the truth and follow evil, there will be wrath and anger.

I cross the room and pull the paper from his hands and tear it in half with great affect. "I don't know what that is." There is apology in my voice. I haven't protected him enough. "It's not true. You aren't evil."

He sobs out his words. "She left it this morning. It was in my backpack. It had to be Mom. She hates me. This wasn't there yesterday. I went to get my book out to read and this came out. She thinks I'm evil."

"No, she doesn't." Jules is quick to Bryson's side. "I don't know what that paper was all about, but I know she loves you. We all do. I'll talk to her this afternoon. We'll figure this out."

She locks eyes with me. Any doubt she had evaporates now that Bryson is slumped over and so hurt by the note Elizabeth left him.

She'll talk to her sister. We'll all be united on how to move forward. This will be settled. My wife will be healthy and happy, the burdens of her past lifted finally once she gets help.

Before I can celebrate the step forward my phone chimes with an unfamiliar sound. Not a text message but an alert. One from the bank.

"Shit," I breathe, rubbing my hand over my brows.

"What is it?" Jules asks, leaning to try to catch a glimpse of my screen.

"She took five hundred dollars out of the ATM this morning." I take care of the bills. It made Elizabeth too anxious to keep up with that stuff. I always just assured her there was plenty of money to do whatever she pleased, but I took care of the mundane bill paying and investing. These alerts always felt a bit intrusive into her spending, but keeping the accounts straight was important.

"Maybe she needed to pay a bill or something?" Jules lowers

her voice and nibbles at her lip. Bryson, lost in his own pain, woke for a second and looks at the phone screen as well.

"Is she okay?" he asks nervously.

"She's fine. It's nothing. I remember now. Your mother was hosting something for a friend's birthday party and she was going to pay cash to the food vendor. It's fine."

Both Jules and Bryson look relieved. It's the only small gift I can give them in this disaster we're all living through. At least they can breathe easier for a minute, because I can't catch my breath at all.

Five hundred dollars.

She'd stopped on the way into work for five hundred dollars. What kind of mess could she be making with that cash? What the hell did she do with that money?

TWENTY

DAISY

"Can you just come down to the utilities office with me and get the water turned back on? They won't let me do it without you." There is a new smell in the apartment. Something altogether different and worse than before I left for school. That's shocking, considering how bad it was already.

The source becomes apparent as I see a pile of garbage spilled over in the kitchen.

"Where did this come from?" I work hard to make sure all trash gets tossed outside as often as possible. I can't afford to make my unwashed clothes smell like lingering trash.

"I had it in the bedroom," my grandmother answers between puffs of her cigarette. "It was starting to smell. Take it out."

I shake my head. "We need to go pay the water bill. Can you please come? I have the money but it's in your name."

"You have the money?" This has my grandmother's head turning my way, her matted hair unmoving and stiff.

"Yes. So, please. We need to get the water on."

"Where did you get the money?" She grinds her cigarette

into the ashtray and narrows her eyes. "Dirty money. That's why we're living here in the first place."

"It's just money. Money that we need. Can we not fight about it?"

"Your father was always messing with dirty money. That's why you have nothing. That's why you're here. No parents. Nothing to your name. I'm stuck with you because he couldn't help but be a filthy man with filthy greed. Filthy needs. Taking the easy way out."

The rage that bubbles up in me feels enough to make me homicidal. Shame fills me when I realize how often I consider killing my grandmother. How unworthy she is of life and yet how much mine depends on hers right now. Any talk about my parents sends me into a blind rage. Any thoughts of the life I had before this. How idyllic and comfortable it was. How much food I threw away. How many clothes I tossed to the side because I didn't *love it* anymore. It makes me crazy. My father is her son and yet she has no loyalty to him. Perfectly comfortable talking shit about her own child. I want to pick up the ashtray and smash it over her head.

But prison might be worse than this, so I talk myself out of it. She is all I have. I am broken and alone. Even the five hundred dollars won't matter in the end. The water getting turned back on might be a small victory. Some food in the fridge a stopgap. But I'm destined to live in the scum until I can claw my way out. To deal with the curse my family cannot escape. We are always going to be nothing, even if Elizabeth thinks she can change that. There is no saving someone who the world has given up on.

TWENTY-ONE

ELIZABETH

Now

I met Jules at the ice-cream shop down the street from our house. She texted. Not really asking but telling me that's where she'd be and I should meet her on my way home.

She'd gotten more like that in the last few years. Not quite demanding, but assertive. There was something disorientating about raising your sibling. I struggled, switching between parent and sister when I was basically a child myself. It's made these adult years sometimes awkward.

Selfishly, I wanted to have someone to confide in and giggle with, but also knew Jules needed structure and stability. Now, as we're both adults, we slip in and out of those complicated roles with a disconcerting ease, like two actors trapped in a dysfunctional play, unable to break free from the suffocating script. Some days I'm mother hen. Other days I'm silly sister. And more recently, as she's found her own footing in the world, she was becoming the voice of reason.

I push open the sticky door of The Wild Scoop. The entire place is decorated with murals of jungle animals and tropical plants. I let my mind slither back through our memories here. The way Bryson had learned to roar like a lion and pretend to swing like a monkey as we waited for his favorite flavor to be scooped into a cup.

Truth should really be easier to believe. I've always thought that. I can hear the cacophony of voices warning me how I would miss those days. And still I longed for them to be over. No matter how much I planned, how nicely I dressed him or how carefully I tried to parent him, Bryson would still melt down. Maybe no more or less than any other toddler, but it crushed me. Was he being bad because I was bad at mothering him? Were his failures just a reflection of my own? Now, those questions feel even heavier.

Jules has her face buried in her phone as I step in. I did pretty good with her. She's successful. Runs her own investigative firm. Rick and I helped her with the funding and getting a few clients he'd worked with in the past to use her. She has a solid reputation. Some really strong skills in her field. And she's a good person. Unimpeachable, really. So at least I did that.

"I ordered your favorite." She beams as she tucks her phone away and slides a root beer float over toward me.

She's worried. I can feel it enveloping me like a thick mist. This demand on me to do things their way was getting louder. To pretend as if I don't have a voice or an opinion was unfair.

"Is this a one-woman intervention, because I can save you some time. I'm fine."

"Fine is relative. You always used to say that when I was struggling," Jules reminds me, her voice gentle and empathetic. Too sticky-sweet like the spilled glops of ice cream on the table near us. It feels fake and I want to call her on it but I don't. I give her the chance to explain why we're here.

"Things are complicated. I'll admit that. And maybe Rick and I don't agree on how to handle them. But we'll work it out."

"This is not fine." She slid a ripped-up piece of paper over to me and her nostrils flare. "Why would you put this in Bryson's bag? It upset him. It scared him, really."

I look down at the paper and read the message. It's familiar to me, I admit that. I wouldn't write that to him. There were days in my life where those types of things would have been scribbled in my journal or a repetitive thought looping in my brain, but not to my son. But I didn't put anything in his bag. I'd remember doing that. I know stress can make you crazy, but not that crazy. "This isn't from me."

"I'm worried about you," Jules edges out, hiding behind her own milkshake for a long moment. "Rick is worried about you. He thinks you need to take some time off work and talk to a therapist."

My skin prickles at the thought of the two of them sitting around my kitchen table. The one I'd labored over picking out and making sure it was perfect. I can picture them, coffee in hand, discussing everything that is wrong with me.

I roll my eyes. "You two had a nice chat about me while I was at work, I guess? Now he's got you here trying to butter me up with a root beer float while you team up. I am telling you, I didn't put anything in Bryson's bag." I don't tell her about the note I found in my car or the threatening phone calls. We aren't coming from a place of trust right now and the less she knows the better.

Jules attempts to be assertive and while I love that she's found her voice in the world, I wish she wasn't using it on me. "I want you to hear me out, because this is coming from a place of concern. I think you need to take a break. A couple of days out of work, and maybe try to find someone you can talk to."

"About what, Jules? What is so broken in me that I need emergency intervention of some kind?" The problem with this question is that I know the answer. Maybe she does too. But when you go so long without talking about something it becomes this odd taboo. As if the passing of time makes it somehow impossible to translate into the language you know.

There are well-worn paths we've cut through the jungle of our childhood. We don't step off them. We don't venture out. If she remembers flashes of how terrifying something was, she's kind enough not to recount it out loud. Jules doesn't probe for me to fill in the sordid details or slide missing puzzle pieces back into place. That's how we've always done this.

The curiosity she has is not equal to the reliving of the memories I would have to face again. Vivid. Undying. Relentless. Her interest cannot be worth more than my self-preservation. And luckily, she decides to follow the old script.

"You've been through a lot in your life. It's okay not to be okay." The generalities and platitudes are gentle and easy to bat away.

I shake my head. "I don't need help. I can handle this. All those things I've been through have made me strong. Prepared."

"I'm not sure it's reasonable for anyone to feel prepared for what's happening right now. The accusations against Bryson, the note you left him, the fight he got into at school. It's a lot to deal with."

This damn note. There is something unsettling about being in the dark. Literally and figuratively. I still sleep with the bathroom light on and Rick has never asked me why. He's never tried to turn it off either. It's one of those things he understands without having to know every detail. But this other kind of darkness, the sense that people know something I don't, bothers me more than the monsters lurking in the night.

"Can you stop bringing up the note. I didn't leave it for him."

Jules looks at me, her eyes searching mine. God, she wants me to be okay. She wants this to be a blip. A mistake. I am her brave, fierce, fight you in the street if you come too close, sister. I am a pillar that holds up her life and I can see her begging me

with every word to be solid. But there are cracks and she's notic-
ing. I want to tell her to stop looking then.

"You don't remember leaving him a note?" She's staring at
me. Trying to sort out what to believe.

"I didn't leave him this damn note, Jules," I snap, slamming
my hand down on the ripped paper. Other patrons turn our
way but I don't care.

"You either don't remember writing him the note, which
means you need to take a break and slow down. Or you are
lying, which also means you need to take a break and slow
down. You can't possibly believe leaving Bryson some ominous
message in his bag was a good idea? Or yelling at him this
morning."

"I wasn't yelling at him. Is that what Rick said? I was talking
to him about how serious this is. How upset I am. Bryson has to
realize what's happened and how to do everything he can to
make it right. Rick characterized it as me yelling at him?"

She grinds her teeth in anger and it shocks me. "I know you
wrote this. It's the same stuff you used to put in that purple
fuzzy journal you stole from the lost and found at school. Bible
quotes. Dark and creepy lines about death. Justice. Evil. All
sorts of stuff. This note today was the same. So do you not
remember doing it, or are you lying?"

I pause, searching my brain for the right answer. Am I cruel
or going crazy? That's what she's asking me.

"I don't know. I didn't write anything." This time I'm less
assertive in my innocence.

"You remember that journal?" She raises a brow at me.
"The stuff you put in there was messed up. It was just like this."

"That journal was just..." I consider explaining myself but it
wouldn't matter. Jules knew nothing of that boiling kettle
feeling that required the whistling steam to shoot out. What I
wrote was a manifestation of all the darkness around me. It was
a release. Nothing more.

"That's in the past," Jules jumps in, knowing this will put me at ease. "You needed the journal then for whatever reason. We have to be talking about what's going on right now."

"There isn't anything to talk about. I'm sorry that Rick put you in this position, but we aren't going to sit over a couple of milkshakes and fix what's going on. You don't understand how complicated this situation really is. There are layers to it. And I'm very good at dealing with that. Maneuvering. Cajoling. Smoothing over. You've never had to do that. I've always done it for you. From the outside the answers might seem very straight-forward but for me, it's a chess game. Let me move the pieces."

"The five hundred dollars you took out this morning. Was that one of the pieces you were trying to move? Rick got an alert from the bank."

My heart drops. "Why is he discussing our finances with you? This is ridiculous. Please, objectively, can you tell me if this feels pretty damn strange that he's got you talking about this with me? He wants to control this situation just like every other aspect of our marriage and for the first time I'm not letting him."

"He's worried." She pauses and plants her palms on her knees. "But yes, it definitely feels odd to be having this conver-sation. Are you calling Rick controlling? He's always been so good to us."

"Two things can be true." I fold my arms across my chest. "Rick is a good man and our lives turned out great. But most of what works in our marriage is because I don't challenge what he says. What he wants. He thinks he's always right and I usually agree. It's easy and he's never really steered us wrong. But I know that abandoning Daisy right now will be worse in the end. I know how these things work from the inside out. He doesn't."

"But two things can be true," she parrots back to me with a tiny smile. "Maybe you are right about this and he is right that you need to get some support for other issues."

I nod in agreement, tired of trying to make my point.

"I gave the money to Daisy. She needed her water turned back on and some groceries. Her situation is dire. I felt..." I trail off as I watch Jules crumble before my eyes.

She's horrified. It's as if I just told her I'd committed some global atrocity. "Elizabeth, you can't do that. It looks like hush money. What do you think people will assume when—"

"She's not going to tell anyone."

"Yes, because you gave her hush money. A bribe."

"It's none of those things," I cut back quickly. "You always had food because I made sure of it. You always had a roof over your head because I fought to make that happen. I was fifteen, working at the mall. Do you really think I made enough money to do those things? No, of course I didn't. I had to find other ways to make sure we could survive. There were never people showing up in our lives to give us the one thing we needed."

Jules looks confused.

"Money. No one handed us over cash just so we could survive. I had to twist myself into pretzels, forgo every better instinct I had, and pander to evil people so that we might have a chance at making it one more week. Our entire lives could have been different if the people showing up to help us weren't all fueled by their own selfish agendas. I gave the money to Daisy, with no strings attached."

"There is no possible way for her to believe that. Not after accusing your son of a crime. Of course she'll assume you're paying her to stay quiet about Bryson. I know that you suffered and—"

"You know nothing." I hiss the words out in a far-off and angry voice. "Jules, you don't know a damn thing about what I've done. What I had to do. I'm in a position to help Daisy. I can't change what she remembers or what might have happened, but she deserves help no matter what. Helping her is helping Bryson."

My sister is speechless. She doesn't ask me to tell her what

I'm alluding to for the same reason Rick never has either. They don't want to know. They can't handle the details and haunting truth. They pretend they are being kind by not pressing, and maybe there is some of that, but they also enjoy living in a world where they don't know how bad it was.

After a while Jules stands up and fishes her keys out of her pocket. "You need to go talk to someone. Please. I'll help you find a therapist. But you're not thinking straight. If you ever trusted me in your life, if you believe I love you, then listen to me. Or..."

"Or what?" I'm genuinely curious if Rick has given her some sort of ultimatum to pitch.

"Don't do that," Jules pleads. "Can you just look at this impartially? What's the big deal about going to talk to someone who might be able to help? We did it when we were kids."

"It was court-ordered and it was horrible."

"You went after you had Bryson, too? That must have helped."

"He told you that?" My knees crash together under the table as I try to stand abruptly. "Rick had no right to share that with you."

I look at my watch and think of Rick sitting at home waiting patiently for an update. I'm outnumbered now. He and Jules have never looked so dug in together about anything. "He's really never going to drop this, is he?"

"He loves you. He loves all of us." There are tears in Jules's eyes. I want to tell her that love isn't about demands and control. It's not supposed to be about bending people to your will in order to "save" them. But I know what a lost cause looks like. Sometimes surrender is the only play.

"Fine. I'll make an appointment. I can't take time off school right now but next week when I can line up a sub and some lesson plan alternatives, I will."

The relief on her face makes me sad for her. She's trying to help me. Trying to do what Rick expects of her. He's wound her tight with worry and then unleashed her like a top.

"I'll help you find an appointment if you want. This is all going to be okay."

I nod and smile, doing what I've always done for Jules. Giving her what she wants in spite of my own needs. I might be losing this battle but for the sake of my son, I'll win the war.

TWENTY-TWO

ELIZABETH

Three hours and seven minutes until I have to don a thick mask of cheery relatability and get a therapist to accept the little bits of information I'm willing to share. Rick and I have barely spoken in the last two days and Jules has gone back to her apartment. Bryson has been avoiding me at all costs, and though I've told him multiple times I didn't leave him any note, I can tell he doesn't believe me. Three hours and five minutes to go.

The mere thought of it is enough to make my stomach ache. Until then, at least I get to be in a place where I know what I do matters. Where people listen to what I have to say. My class is staring at me intently.

"*The Lies of the Night*. You all finished it yesterday. I am so excited to hear your take on it. Let's open up the discussion." I hold up my copy so they can see how well loved it is. There are a million little notes in the margins and the cover is worn from being carried around in my bag for the last decade. This book is more than just a fiction story. To me, it reads like a playbook. A memoir, though the characters never really lived.

It's not on the approved curriculum list but every year I make a case, have the parents sign off and get it into my lesson plans. All so I can talk it through and love it out loud with people who are experiencing it for the first time. Something I wish I could do again.

"I hated the ending," Carly moans, crinkling her face up in disgust. "Honestly, it perpetuates the narrative of accepting abuse as some kind of happily ever after."

Carly is a feminist. Something I love about her. Her voice in this class has been grounding and valuable. But I feel instantly defensive. Not this book. This book is not problematic. It's beautiful. I wait for one of the other vocal students to chime in and correct her. Instead, people are nodding their heads in agreement.

Stacy P., who rarely looks up from her freshly manicured nails, calls out her opinion. "Seriously. Are they really trying to make Andre look like some hero? He's the worst."

"The worst?" I can't hide my shock as they tear down the character I loved the most. The man who I'd seen as the hero in my own story. I try to make my case. "Andre comes into Valerie's life after an enormous amount of pain and trauma. He helps her." I am careful not to say he saves her. That trope won't land well in this generation and I'm glad for that.

"He exploits her," Mike chimes in, tossing the book on his desk like he doesn't want to be associated with it. I can feel my mouth drop open and I leave it like that for a long minute so they can sense my disbelief.

Stacy P. claps her hands once. "Exactly. I read this article about the blank canvas phenomenon."

"She watched a TikTok," Bo chokes out, pretending he's coughing to cover up his dig at her. They have a love-hate relationship that causes way too much drama.

"It was a TikTok about an article," Stacy corrects, smiling playfully at him. Apparently, they're on good terms today. That won't last. "Anyway it was about the blank canvas phenomenon. Do you know that one, Mrs. Meadows?"

I run my hand protectively over the cover of my copy of the book and shake my head, indicating I hadn't heard of it.

Stacy beams with pride to know something I don't. "It's about how older men and men with power or wealth seek out young women because they are looking for someone who hasn't yet found their identity."

"A blank canvas," Carly chimes in. "It's super messed up. They want to find these young women before they've formed their preferences, their beliefs and moral compass. That's what Andre was doing in the book. He wasn't rescuing Valerie. He was creating this toxic parent/child relationship. He's trying to raise her, not date her."

I hold up my hands and pump them in the air. My defensiveness over this book is disproportionate to what my students might expect. When we debate as a class I am almost always the neutral facilitator of the conversation. But I love this story. I love every page. Every word. The student's new age opinions feel like an attack. But I draw in a deep breath and try again. "Valerie was literally at rock bottom. She had been abused. Left behind. Tossed out in the world with nothing. Andre could have easily passed her by. He stopped. He helped. How can we say that's toxic?"

"Right," Bo agrees, generously trying to keep me from being alone in this. "Everyone was messing with her, and Andre is the first one to come in and actually help her. What do you want him to do, just leave her on her own?"

Kelly, with her pierced nose and winged eyeliner, raises her hand. We don't really do that when we're in an open discussion, but for all her fashion rebellion she's a stickler for the rules. I point and indicate she's free to speak.

"Abuse is way too often boxed into the old idea of just a punch or something physical. I agree with the others, Andre had power and money that Valerie didn't. Bo, you asked if he should have just left her, and the answer is no. He could have still helped her in many ways, like helping her become stable and independent."

"He did do that," a boy from the back calls out, sounding annoyed as if men are always the villain these days. "You guys are just men bashers."

Stacy P. snaps her head around. "And he should have done all those things to help her without sleeping with her. You can support someone without having sex with them or starting up a relationship."

The class rumbles with waves of agreement and I step in. "I'm confused here. I understand what you're saying about the power differential. But Andre clearly loves Valerie. It's in every word he says."

"That's love bombing." Carly rolls her eyes. "He's laying it on thick at the beginning so she gets blinded by all of the affection and attention. But it won't last."

Stacy P. puts her pencil contemplatively to her chin. "That's what happened to my aunt. She married a guy fifteen years older than her when she was like twenty. Then when she hit her thirties, she realized she had no clue what she liked or believed. He spent all his time grooming her. That's what happens when the woman is young. It's creepy."

They're throwing around every buzzword and I pick up my book and clutch it to my chest. "You are all being so harsh. This is a love story with a happy ending."

"It's not the end," Bo says, grinning at Stacy P. and then looking over at me. "I get what they're saying. I guess that's the point. It might be working now but I think they're right. At some point Valerie isn't twenty anymore and she's going to realize maybe Andre took advantage of her. Look at how he tells her how to dress. Buying her all those clothes wasn't just some kind gesture. He was trying to get her to look the way he thought was right. He had control over a ton of things to make her a certain way."

"And then the gaslighting starts," Carly says, leaning forward. Under any other condition I'd love this debate. My class is thinking critically and really considering how this book applies to the world today. I guess perhaps I need to consider it through a new lens myself.

Carly continues her point as I come to terms with what I missed in these pages. "Valerie is going to wake up one day in her thirties after she's had a couple of kids and realize she has no clue who she is. She'll start asserting herself and trying to find her voice and Andre will tell her she's crazy. Changing. Dramatic. Gaslighting her into staying under his control."

"Oh hell," Bo shouts, covering his mouth with his arm like he would for a cough. "I just realized you're throwing shade at Mrs. Meadows. Isn't your husband old?"

I laugh and shake my head. "He's ten years older than me. Not old."

Carly shifts nervously in her seat. "And your son is a sophomore. You must have been really young when you had him. Were you still in college?"

"This isn't about me," I deflect. I've been an open book to my students and they all shoot me looks of concern as I slam that part of my life shut. "This is about Valerie and Andre. I like to believe there can be a happy ending for two people with good intentions and love in their heart. I'm not saying those other issues can't arise, but do you believe Andre was consciously seeking out a woman he could mold into what he wanted?" I use that term rather than the creepier grooming accusation.

"Intention is not enough anymore." Carly leans back and crosses her large black boots at the ankle.

"Well, this book is fifty years old," I remind her with a chuckle. "Andre was probably pretty progressive for his time."

"I guess." Carly shrugs. "How old were you when you had your son?"

"Twenty," I reply flatly as I look up at the clock. "But my

situation was different and my husband is a kind, amazing man who has always encouraged me to have my own thoughts and feelings." The words are thick in my mouth and I pray they can't tell. Rick is a hero. My hero. He saved my life and took care of Jules without a second of hesitation. That is a good man. And he has encouraged me in many ways over the years. Many. As long as he agreed they were right. As long as I was moving in the direction he wanted me to go.

"Good," Stacy P. replies as she begins to pack up her books. "There are too many assholes out there preying on girls."

I let the colorful language slide as long as it feels relevant to the conversation and not gratuitous. It goes against the code of conduct rules at school, and my students know it's not something they can do in front of other teachers or if anyone is observing my class. But I find curse words pertinent to some discussions. And in this case, it works. Men who prey on younger women to control and harm them are assholes. But that's not what happened with Rick. Our marriage is totally different.

"Okay, you guys can leave early. Just please be good in the hallway. Don't get me busted again. Hit the vending machines and the bathroom, but don't be loud."

They gathered up their things and stayed mostly quiet as they spilled out of my classroom four minutes early. Another thing that sent my colleagues into a fit if they noticed. Usually I do it for the benefit of my students, but today it's for me.

Lifting the book I've loved for years to my chest again I hug it like I'm saying goodbye to an old friend I'll never see again. Because I certainly will never look at these pages the same way. They aren't a fairy tale that mirrors my survival and happy ending. They are suddenly a cautionary tale.

My mind flashes through the arguments Rick and I have had over the years and how quickly I acquiesced to his opinions. Why did I do that? He's older. He's lived. He knows how the world is supposed to work. Not the feral, wild existence I'd been calling life. I think about how he helped me pick clothes to wear. Pick classes to attend. How he encouraged me to be a teacher so I could have the summers off with our child. How I like the same music he does, because he told me it was good. How he's shaped my faith, my values, my personality. The way I think. The way I talk. My entire life with Rick I've been grateful to him for being the guardrails that taught me what was right and wrong. Now as my head spins with old memories I worry those guardrails were more like prison bars.

Is that why he sent Jules to talk to me? Is that why he's demanding I comply with what he thinks is right for Bryson now? Or this damn appointment with a therapist in a few hours that I didn't even want. Am I finding my voice and he's trying to silence it?

TWENTY-THREE

ELIZABETH

"Knock knock," Cherry Wilson sings as she pretends to knock on my open door. "Do you have a minute?"

She's a first-year teacher with the bright expression of someone who thinks the world is a wonderful place just waiting to welcome her with open arms. Her long fake lashes flutter at me expectantly. I don't want to invite her in but I can't think fast enough to turn her down.

She's sitting on the desk in the front row of my classroom sighing loudly. "Can I get your advice? I've got a student I'm really worried about."

"Daisy?" I blurt the name before I think better of it.

"Who?" She narrows her eyes. "No, she's not a student of mine. Why, what's going on with her?"

"Sorry, nothing. My head is in the clouds. I just had a good discussion with my students. They hate my favorite book of all time and I think they made me hate it too." I wave off her look of concern and laugh until she chuckles.

"I'm sure they were just giving you a hard time. They love to do that." She looks suddenly defeated. I remember how hard it was to manage a classroom and figure out how to reach the kids when I was first starting out. I wasn't much older than the kids in my classroom at the time and they knew it.

"What can I help you with?"

"Jessica Parker has been one of my top students and now she's falling apart. She's stopped turning in assignments. Won't participate in class anymore. I was going to send an email home but then I worried what if the problem is home?"

"That can be tricky," I reply gently. "Have you asked her what's going on?"

"Only casually on her way out the door. I guess I should have her meet with me during study hall. And have Mr. Digson sit in too, right?"

Every mention of Digson makes my skin prickle. I don't understand why school districts keep men like him around. They could have a guidance counselor on staff that could actually help kids navigate these impossibly difficult times. I try to mask my feelings as I answer. "That's protocol."

"You don't have him come in when you meet with students?" Jessica asks this question in a whisper as though the school rule police might bust in and arrest me.

"He's a dinosaur. The kids hate him and always clam up when he's around. I don't find it necessary to have him sit in when I talk to my struggling students." I pause and take in her worried face. "But you're a new teacher. You should follow the protocol. But you're right to wait on sending a note home. Sometimes, if home is the source of the problem, you can make it worse with an email."

"So I don't send one?"

I think about all the nuances in teaching. How impossible it is to do everything right every time. "When you're meeting with her, mention you're considering sending an email home and watch her reaction. If she seems disproportionately scared or anxious, take note of that. You have to do a lot of reading between the lines."

"There is so much they don't teach you in school about actually supporting your students."

"You're on the right track," I reply warmly. "But the problems they're facing can be very serious. Dangerous. Life-threatening. We really are their first line of defense. It's so much more than the grades and curriculum. We have to be someone they can trust and depend on. We're their confidantes. Their protectors."

"But everyone is always warning me not to be their friends. That was the focus of my last evaluation with Awasa. He was laying it on thick about boundaries and authority. I guess I was giving a vibe that he thought was problematic."

"Awasa thinks kids have no business needing anything besides an education. If he knew half of what they're going through he'd be a lot more empathetic."

"Aren't you worried about getting in trouble?" Jessica nibbles her fingernail nervously.

"I lose more sleep about what might have happened to the students I didn't help than what might happen to me for helping them."

The bell rings and we stand up, ready to face the next period. I think of what I've just said. My proclamation. Something I truly believe in. And my next thought is how much Rick would hate that. How he'd reel me in. Caution me. Remind me how things really worked and why. Ten years ago, I would have agreed with him. Five years ago, I would have seen his point of view and backed down. Now, as the anger bubbles up in me, I'd use my last breath to argue my point and prove him wrong.

So many revelations fall on me at once. Andre wasn't the hero in that book. He was just more polished and savvier than the people who had controlled Valerie before.

Now the question lingers in my mind like a man at the bar who ignores last call. I can't seem to get it to leave. Do I have a grasp on who I am and what I think? Or did the people I let into my life shape me into whatever they thought was right? And, maybe more importantly, is it too late to find myself?

TWENTY-FOUR

DAISY

There is a wild kind of look in her eyes as Mrs. Meadow catches my arm in the hallway and asks me to step into her classroom. The day is over. I'm supposed to be getting the bus right now, but I can tell she's not going to take no for an answer. I've been avoiding her as much as possible the last couple of days, but she snatched me up this time.

"Are you okay?" I ask, licking my dry lips as she closes her classroom door behind me.

"I've been thinking a lot today." Her voice is quick and breathless. "I've been feeling so torn about what the right thing to do is. Then I realized, that's not true. My gut tells me exactly what to do, it's everyone else's voice in my head that's confusing me. So I wanted to tell you, I'm going to help you. I'm going to be here for you whatever you need."

I blink slowly as she paces the room. "You've helped me a lot already. We got the water turned back on. I got some groceries. You've done plenty."

"I can help more. There is something you need to know about me. We've talked a little. I've alluded to things we have in common. But, Daisy, my childhood was awful and I just constantly prayed someone would come help me. I fought and suffered and sacrificed. No one showed up for me when I was your age. I can be that for you."

"I— Well, can you do that?" My mind races toward every aspect of my life that has been teetering on the edge. About to fall off. Always hungry. Never enough money for anything. Fighting to make the kids here think I'm normal. I'm tired.

My hesitation sends her further into a fit. "I can do whatever I want. Because there is right and wrong and it's not always what the rule book says. They say you should be the person you needed when you were younger. That's where the healing starts to happen. So that's what I'm doing. I'm going to be that for you. I'm shutting out everyone else who is trying to convince me that some complicated bureaucratic messy path is the right way. I have the resources and experience you need and I'm going to make sure you can benefit from that. It's simple."

"I don't know what I need," I stutter out, taking a step back from her. "I think I'll be okay. But right now I'm going to get the bus."

"I'll give you a ride home. You don't have to know what you need. I know. I know because I was there."

"The bus is fine. I think I should just take the bus."

Two more steps back from her have me at the door. "I really do appreciate what you're doing but I think I've asked too much of you already. I know that you feel bad about—"

"No." She blinks so fast I wonder if she's on drugs. "That's not what this is about and it's not too much. I've been thinking back to how hard it was. How much I had to fight and scrape and even break the law just to survive. I don't want that happening for you. Talk to me about your family. About what you've been through. I can see it. It's in your eyes. That brokenness. That party at my house wasn't the start of your problems. It was there before. Don't do what I did. Don't try to bury it.

There is no hole deep enough to keep it from rising up. From coming back."

"I am going to go." I sling my bag over my shoulder and put my hand on the door handle. It turns from the outside, someone else pushing their way in as I step aside.

"Mrs. Meadows, can I get the notes from yesterday when I was out?" Stacy P. is flipping her perfect hair off her shoulder and barely looking up. When she finally catches a glimpse of me, and then Mrs. Meadows, she twists her face up in confusion. "Oh sorry. I didn't know anyone was in here."

There is a vibe. An unmistakable coolness in the air that Stacy feels instantly. Mrs. Meadows has beads of sweat gathering on her forehead. My eyes are damp. My hand shakes as I pull the door open more and step out.

"Woah," Stacy yelps as she follows me out. "What's that all about? Are you in trouble with Mrs. Meadows? You must have done something pretty bad because she's nice to everyone. Lets everything slide."

"I'm not in trouble," I gulp out as I remember to cover the small stain that I couldn't get out of the secondhand Armani shirt I'm wearing. "It's nothing."

"Oh, it's something. That was a really creepy vibe in there. She looked all messed up."

I shrug. "Not sure. I have to catch the bus."

"Is your car still getting fitted for custom wheels? That's been forever. I'll give you a ride."

"No." The words snap from my mouth like a twig. "I mean, no thanks. I'm good. I can do some work on the bus."

"Daisy." She tugs my arm until I stop. "Is everything all right? Did something happen with Mrs. Meadows? Tell me."

She wasn't saying 'tell me' as in, you can trust me. Or let me help you. She was demanding it as if the latest gossip was owed to her.

When my phone begins ringing it feels like being saved by the bell. An excuse to have to leave this situation.

"Oh God, she's calling you." Stacy points to the screen of my phone and gasps as Mrs. Meadows's name scrolls across it. I click the button to send it to voice mail and a second later, it's ringing again.

"Holy shit." Stacy blinks slowly at me. "Stalker, much?"

"I have to go."

"The buses are long gone." She laughs and points again to my phone. "Why don't you have your bestie take you home. She's calling again."

"She's not..." I pull away from Stacy and run down the hallway to the doors that lead to the student parking lot. I don't have a plan for how to get home, I just know I need air or I'll choke and die. Or I'll hit Stacy. Something will happen that I can't take back. That's what this is. The unraveling of things I will never be able to put back together. My life is in tatters and Stacy is an eyewitness. The whole school will know soon enough.

TWENTY-FIVE

ELIZABETH

"When is your appointment?" Rick is trying to look chipper and unbothered but it's coming across as something new. Fake. I've been cold to him since the moment I stepped back in the house today. I see him through new eyes suddenly and it's not in his favor. I know I came on too strong with Daisy but I felt compelled to say all the things I wish someone had said to me. It would be so much less complicated if not for her misremembering what happened that night with Bryson. I know that's what has her conflicted about my help.

"I'm not going to the therapist appointment." My back is to Rick now as I search the fridge for something I can throw together for dinner. This is my specialty. I can make something out of nothing and make it quick. Following a fancy recipe is great but turning leftovers and half-opened bottles of condiments into a meal is better.

"I thought we agreed—"

I cut him off but continue riffling through the fridge. "You agreed and then sent my sister to fight your battle. I've had a long day. The last thing I want to do is go talk to a stranger about what you think is wrong with me. We have enough going on without having some doctor poking around and trying to cause more drama."

"That's not what therapy will do. Having so much going on is what we need to deal with. The damn phone is ringing every night with mysterious phone calls. The notes. Your car being keyed. Something is not right."

"Yes, and a therapist isn't going to magically unlock the key to who is doing all of that. It's obviously linked in some way to Daisy's assault, so that's where we need to focus. We need to get to the bottom of who was at our house and hurt her. The rest will sort itself out."

"Elizabeth." His voice booms and I think of the students in my class. The characters in my favorite book. Is this really what happens when a woman decides to find her voice?

"Don't yell at me." I spin on him and jab my finger through the air. "You don't get to bully someone into therapy just because we disagree on something. I've made my choice for tonight. I'm tired, and I'm not going to the appointment."

I've been waiting for this. Anticipating his anger. Playing through what he might say. For a moment I think he might walk away, but instead he's moving closer to me.

"Elizabeth, I love you so much. I just want you to be okay. Jules told me you gave that girl five hundred dollars. You left a very alarming note in your son's bag that hurt him deeply. You had more contact with this girl again after I told you that doing so could put Bryson's future and freedom at risk. Do those actions seem like something a healthy person would do?"

"I'm unwell?" I laugh off his accusation. "You told Jules I'm manic. How strange that over the last fifteen years I've raised our son, kept our house running, and built a career. Do those sound like the actions of a crazy person? Or is it more likely that you don't want to be challenged and the best way to invalidate me is to call me crazy?"

"Invalidate?" He closes his eyes and tries to draw in a centering breath, but I don't give him time to.

"Why did you marry me?" I deliver the question with a wave of my hand.

"What?"

"I was a broke, out-of-work, defeated young woman with custody of my sister. I had nothing to offer. I wasn't particularly beautiful or witty at that point in my life. Things were quite bleak. What attracted you to me?"

"I'm not playing this game. You're intentionally changing the subject."

"This should be a fairly easy question." I raise up a challenging brow. "What could a man possibly see in a girl that age who had nothing to offer and no prospects of a future? The only attractive part of that situation is the idea that you could turn me into whatever you wanted. And you did." I gesture around the gleaming white kitchen and the fancy appliances. "You raised me into the woman you wanted and someone you could control. Because, what the hell did I know? You were older and wiser; if you said something I should just agree with it. I was a blank canvas you could paint any way you wanted. And you being my custody lawyer—"

"I was never your lawyer. What are you saying?" Rick takes two steps back and spills into one of the stools that sit at the kitchen island. He's aghast at my accusations. There is this wild blink he does when he's formulating an argument and it's in overdrive right now.

"I wasn't your custody lawyer for Jules. You do know that, right? I'm worried about you." He whispers the words in a ghostly tone. "I fell in love with you because you were tenacious. There was this determination in you I'd never seen in anyone before. I loved that you didn't wallow or even look back on the bad stuff that had obviously happened in your life. You might not have had a plan but you had the most intense belief in your own future. That's what I fell in love with. You questioning that breaks my heart." Rick clutches his chest and winces in pain.

The mistake makes my cheeks burn pink with anger. I know Rick wasn't my custody lawyer. I know we met at the doctor's office when he came in with his niece. I know that. But my anger is blurry. Bleeding together. It is the melding of all the people who hurt me and Rick is not absolved from that. But me misspeaking and misremembering will only fuel his opinion of me being unstable.

"Elizabeth, please. Just sit down and talk to me." He looks as though he's in pain.

I don't like to see him hurting. I never have. But I know what I'm feeling is real. I know that before any of this even started, something in my soul had shifted. Dislodged. And he didn't like that.

"I brought pizza," Jules sings as she pushes her way through the screen door. We'd grown used to this over the years. Jules was a precocious little girl when Rick and I started dating, and I was insistent that I wasn't going to ditch her just so we could go out and have fun. So along she came. And there have since been a million moments like this, where her bad timing interrupts the highs and lows of our marriage.

"Now isn't a good time," Rick grumbles, dipping his head low. This is telling. If he thought he was right in this moment, he'd be welcoming Jules in to take his side.

"Is Bryson here?" Jules asks, looking past us, worried whatever we're doing might impact her nephew.

"No, he's over at Mikah's catching up on the work he missed being suspended." Rick clears his throat and looks away from me.

"What?" I slam my palm to the cold countertop. "You let him go out? He's suspended. Grounded. With everything we just found out, how could you let him go?"

Jules puts the pizza down on the table and moves to get some plates. I appreciate her ability to pretend everything is fine and we should all just grab a slice. But that's not happening.

"Don't you have your appointment?" she asks casually, grabbing a stack of napkins. "I thought the pizza might be easier before you left."

"She's not going." Rick folds his arms over his chest and waits for me to make a case for myself. I don't.

"I'm not hungry. I'm going to go grade some papers. Thanks for the pizza, Jules. Save some slices for Bryson."

"Sis," Jules calls out as I walk away. "Wait."

It's the doorbell that has me stopping, not her plea. It's the front door, not the side that everyone who knows us uses. It could be a salesperson trying to sell us solar panels or roof repairs. Or it could be something important. I pause, waiting as Rick answers it. I can't see who's there, but I can hear Rick's worried tone.

"Elizabeth," he calls and a shiver rolls up my spine. "The police are here."

TWENTY-SIX

ELIZABETH

Then

Foster care had been the looming threat that hung over our heads for years. Dodging it had been my most crucial responsibility. Propping up whichever dysfunctional parent was not in prison or a psych ward was hard work. Making whatever rundown apartment we had look decent enough to keep us from being taken away was a full-time job.

I just had to keep Jules with me long enough for me to turn eighteen and prove I could take care of her. Now it's time. My birthday was no real celebration but I could feel the handcuffs of never being old enough to really help Jules finally unlocking. I can do this now. Three jobs. An application on an apartment that looks promising. And a letter mailed to a bunch of lawyers that maybe might help me get custody.

Life has taught me not to get excited. Getting my hopes up is a habit I broke before I was ten years old.

My pager beeps with an unfamiliar number and I pick up the phone behind the counter of the pretzel kiosk at the mall. Of all my jobs, this one helps the most. It pays shit, but I work shifts that are usually pretty quiet and because of how we manage the food, anything that doesn't get eaten during my shift I can take home with me. Jules and I have been living off of slightly stale pretzels and mini hot dogs for months.

"Hi, I just got a page?" I try to duck down a bit so that any passing customers don't come to order.

"Miss Winkler, this is Tucker Rutherford. I received your letter and am returning your call. This is in regards to a custody case?"

"Oh, Mr. Rutherford. Yes. Thank you. I need to get custody of my sister. Someone I work with at the community center said you may be able to help."

There is a long pause. "Well, I do work custody cases. How old are you?"

"I just turned eighteen last week."

Another long pause. "And how old is your sister?"

"Eight, nine next month."

"And your parents currently have custody of her?"

"My father is in prison for domestic abuse. He won't be out for three years at least. My mother has been in and out of institutions for the last ten years. The only reason she's out right now is because I've been taking care of her. She's not fit to care for Jules, that's my sister."

Mr. Rutherford hums out a concerned noise. "Have child protective services documented your case?"

"They have, but for the most part I've kept things together well enough that it's rare we've had to go into foster care and it's never for long. Really, I've just been waiting for my birthday so I could make this all official."

"It's a bit more complicated than that. The state needs to terminate the parental rights. Then you need to be deemed fit to care for her. That's a process. It's not enough to just be better than your parents."

"But you can do all that? Or help me do it?" I hate people

who lead with pessimism. Who talk about how much I can't do instead of what I can. If I lived that way, I'd probably already be dead.

"I can try. You understand this process costs a great deal, too? There are a lot of hoops to jump through and fees to be paid. Are you sure you're in a position to do this?"

"I'm sure that my sister is going to live with me and have a good life. I don't need to hear about how hard it's going to be. Life's already hard for both of us. At least we'd be together."

He clears his throat. "Can you come in for a meeting?"

My heart flutters with relief. This is better than being hung up on or immediately told no. "I can. I just have to work out my schedule. I have three jobs and I take care of Jules, getting her back and forth to school and making sure my mother isn't hurting her. I'm in the city on Tuesday and Thursday nights working at the community center. I could come by then. Like seven o'clock."

"I'm not in my office at seven o'clock at night." He laughs gently. "I could meet you at the coffee shop near the community center around then. This Tuesday?"

"Sure. I'll be there. Do I need to bring anything?"

"Everything." He answers flatly and draws in a deep breath. "Bring any records of abuse and reports to child services. Any testimonies from people in your life who could make a statement on your behalf. Your financial records. Living arrangements. Future plans. And anyone in your life who might be able to help and support you."

"There's no one like that." I clear my throat nervously. "I can get all the other stuff but it's just us. Me and Jules."

"Make a list of things the court would use against you too. Things in your past that might look disqualifying or questionable. Intimate partners who might be a problem for your reputation. Trouble you've had with the law."

"There's been a little of that."

"As an adult or a child?"

"I turned eighteen last week."

"And have you been good this week?" He chuckles again and I laugh too.

"Very."

"Okay then, we can work on getting anything on your record as a minor expunged. This is going to be a fight. An expensive fight. Hopefully your parents are willing to give up their rights and you're able to prove yourself fit."

"Hopefully," I parrot back. I'd always just envisioned after I was old enough, Jules would be mine. I'd already been taking care of her for so long. We'd just make it official so I could sign papers for her and make decisions and stuff. But I guess it's the official part that will be tough. Hope was a funny thing. I didn't like pessimism, but I also wasn't foolish enough to be an optimist. I lived somewhere in between. Cautious and motivated. Now, with the real process starting, I had to believe I could do this. I had to win this fight. If I didn't, what the hell would happen to Jules?

TWENTY-SEVEN

ELIZABETH

Then

I usually wear jeans and a T-shirt to the community center where I work with kids who don't know how to read. Of all the jobs I've ever had, this is my favorite. There are no free pretzels but there is something more rewarding. I'm doing something real. Teaching someone something they'll use for the rest of their lives.

When I go in later, the kids will tease me for being in my fancy black pants and fuzzy pink sweater. These chunky-soled sandals are the nicest I have but I've been coloring in the worn-out spots with a black marker for a year now. My full face of makeup and straightened silky hair will also get some laughs from the kids. But I need this to work. I need this lawyer to believe in me.

The coffee shop is quiet this time of night and I spot Mr. Rutherford in the corner. I recognize him from the picture on his law firm's website. I'd stared at it for most of the afternoon, trying to figure out if he was as kind as I needed him to be. Many men before him had duped me, but my gut told me he was different. Why would someone at the community center suggest him if he wasn't a good man?

Before he sees me, I take him in fully. He's sitting at a table with his laptop and a stack of legal papers in front of him. He's well-dressed in a tailored dark grey suit over a crisp white shirt and a deep-burgundy tie that complements his dark brown hair. Focused and absorbed in his work, occasionally sipping on his coffee as he reads through the legal documents on his laptop screen. I wonder why he smiles as he reads over his work. It's giving off a warm and welcoming vibe as if maybe he can find the lighter side of anything.

"Mr. Rutherford?" I paint on my biggest smile and dip my head like I'm an obedient girl. For some reason I feel like that might help.

"Miss Winkler." He gestures at the large wingback chair across from him and I try to sit down delicately. "I wasn't sure what to order for you, but I can get you something now."

He half stands up but I wave him off. "I'm fine. I don't drink coffee."

"Are you hungry?"

I nearly laugh at the question. I can't remember a time when I wasn't walking around at least a little hungry. I just shake my head and wave him off again. "I'm fine, really."

Handing over the stack of documents I have, I wait patiently. He places them down on top of the others he has and begins flipping through them. He winces at a few police reports and I take comfort in his humanity. There's a chance he's seen much worse in his career, and maybe his reaction is just for my benefit. Even if it is, I appreciate it. He's bearing witness to how terrible things had been in our home.

"This is pretty compelling stuff. You've got a very good case to make sure your sister doesn't stay with either of your parents. That's a good start."

"But there's a lot more?"

"There is." For the first time he looks up at me and I feel the weight of his gaze. The intensity of his blue eyes takes my breath away, but I quickly gather myself. He's handsome. Tall. I can tell even though he's sitting down. There is no ring on his finger but he's got to be married. A man like this wouldn't be single.

"I'll do anything. Just tell me what to do." I lean in and bump the table, nearly toppling over his coffee. Catching it just in time, he smiles warmly at me.

"You need to be the best option for Jules. A judge will want you to have an established and safe home. They'll expect you to be able to provide everything she needs. At your age..." He looks sympathetic.

"I've been taking care of her for her entire life. My age is irrelevant. And I'm working on a better apartment. The house we are in now with my mother is rat-infested and falling down around us. Once I have the money for first and last month's rent, I'll have a good place."

He nods, but looks unconvinced. "And employment?"

"I'm very employed. I work three jobs right now."

"That's the problem. A court will perceive that as an unhospitable schedule for caring for a school-age child."

"I can't exactly change that right now. I've just graduated. The only places I've worked are the mall, the community center, and delivering pizzas until my car broke down. I don't have a lot of experience in anything else, and any one of those jobs doesn't pay enough."

He jots down a few notes. Then sets his jaw as he stares intently at me. "I need you to answer this question honestly. Really think about it."

"Okay." I draw the word out and my eyes dart away, not able to hold his gaze.

"You're a beautiful, young, determined woman. Do you

really want to suddenly become the sole guardian of a young child?"

"She is my sister." I'd be lying if his words, his assessment of me didn't make my body swell with pride and some kind of anticipation I can't name.

"That's not what I asked. You have your whole life ahead of you. Without any outside obligations it's clear a woman like you could thrive. Excel. You're adding undue obstacles to your life. It will be hard."

I lose my breath again as, for the second time, he calls me a woman. Hits every syllable of the word as if he wants me to really put it on and walk around in it. Model it for him. There is a heat here. I recognize it because I've wielded it like a weapon since my body first became something men turned to see walk by. Usually, I'm the one creating this feeling in someone so I can get what I want. Now, it's organic. Just happening outside of my control.

"Hard is relative," I reply, trying to sound smart enough to sit at the same table as him. "I've had it hard since the day I was born. Jules hasn't. I've made sure of that. I've put food on the table. Fought the rats every night so they don't jump onto our bed. She goes to school clean. Clean clothes. Clean hair. She doesn't remember how violent our father was and she doesn't know how sick our mother is. I've insulated her from all of it. Hard doesn't scare me. Jules realizing how awful life could be, that terrifies me."

He draws in a long breath and closes his eyes. "Shit."

"What?" My heart leaps to my throat as I wonder what I got wrong. How I screwed this up.

"You are completely unprepared for this. No support system. Not enough money." He flips through my bank statements and old police reports. Even my arrest record. "There is no possible way you'll be able to pull this off, and yet you've got me. I'm invested now. That speech worked. We've got to get this done."

Like an elevator that just plummeted to the basement and is now soaring to the penthouse, I can feel my equilibrium swirling wildly. "Really?" The tears well in my eyes but I blink them away. "I will do anything, Mr. Rutherford."

"We're in this now. You might as well call me Tucker." He looks down at one paper I brought and grimaces. "We need to discuss your prior criminal history."

"You said it might not matter? I was a minor."

"I will be unlikely to get all of this expunged, but I'm a great lawyer." He smiles wryly. "With enough context, I can work to make it irrelevant to a custody case. Tell me about these arrests."

"There isn't much to tell." I shift uncomfortably in my seat and wish now I had a drink as my mouth goes dry.

"I'm seeing a lot of theft. Starting at around thirteen. Men in hotel rooms claiming you stole their wallets. It's concerning. You're going to need money to make this process work. I need to know that when you say you'll do anything that doesn't include—"

"I am not a prostitute." My voice is so loud it rattles my teeth and has a few heads in the coffee shop turning my way. To quiet me, Tucker reaches his hand across the table and covers mine. The warmth. The softness. The size. Everything about his hand sends shockwaves through my body and I'm immediately quiet. His plan worked, but probably not for the reason he thought.

"I'm sorry," he whispers, his head low to catch my eyes. "I wasn't trying to insult you. It's just important that desperation doesn't create any new problems. I wasn't trying to imply anything about you."

"I was thirteen. I couldn't work a normal job yet. I wasn't sleeping with men. I was conning them and then robbing them. And every single vile one of them deserved a hell of a lot more than just getting their wallets stolen. Any man willing to go to a hotel room like that with a child—"

"I'm sorry," he says, louder this time. "I'm sorry you had to do that. It must have been terribly dangerous."

"I always felt like not eating or being taken away from home and put in foster care was more dangerous. Men are simple creatures. They have a one-track mind. When they think they're about to get some kind of instant gratification, the rest of their brain shuts off. I had some close calls but most of the men never pressed charges because they were worried they'd have to explain why they were in a hotel with a child. But they shouldn't have been so worried. The men who did turn me in were never even questioned."

"The legal system fails all the time. You've been failed again and again." He gestures to the papers in his lap. "But I won't fail you. I promise."

Men made promises all the time. They said what they needed to get what they wanted. But Tucker was different. I was sure of it. He saw something in me. Something I'd been trying to attain for years. Strength. My ferocity wasn't lost on him. It didn't scare him off. I could tell by the look in his eyes, it drew him to me.

"Just tell me what to do." I blink away the stray tears and realize his hand is still on mine. "Please. I need a break. I need something to finally go my way."

Releasing me from his grip, he leans back and nods his head as though he's putting all the pieces of a riddle together, determined to solve it. "Brian Stilton needs a receptionist for his office. He's a child psychologist. A good man. And lucky for us he owes me a bunch of favors."

I hang onto the way he says the word us, filled with relief to be part of some team. "I like kids. My favorite job has been here at the community center."

"Good. I'll make sure he has you somewhere around twenty-two an hour."

"Dollars?"

"Yes. That should allow you to quit your other jobs. After three months you'll have health insurance. Benefits. Six months working there should be compelling for a judge. Now an apartment, what do you need for that?"

"I have some money in the bank. Just enough for first and last." I feel proud I've been able to put that much together but he's not impressed.

"You'll need the utilities on. Furniture. Food. It has to be a real home that Jules can come into and be safe and be fed."

"I can start with the apartment and figure the rest of the other stuff out."

"We won't have time for that. You need to start having home studies soon. Visits. Some mandatory classes. Having the apartment set up will need to be a priority."

"Um, I can maybe—"

Without skipping a beat he interrupts me. "I'll lend you a thousand. That should get you what you need. I'll work with Brian, your soon-to-be boss, to have him take fifty dollars out of your pay monthly until you're settled up with me."

"You're going to give me a thousand dollars?"

"Lend. I'm lending it to you without interest."

My brows crash together. For the first time in this meeting I feel the prickly heat of skepticism claw up my back. "Why would you do that?"

Tucker laughs. "You've really been through it, haven't you? Has anyone ever helped you without any strings attached?"

"No."

His face falls sad, then he clears his throat. "I understand if you don't trust me, but I'm not looking for anything in return. I do this kind of work when I can. Pro bono. When I meet someone who deserves a break and I'm in a position to give it to them, I do. Just about every system in our country sets a person like you up to fail. You didn't pick your family. You didn't pick your circumstances. But getting out is hard. I want to make it easier for who I can, when I can."

"Shit," I whisper back through a smile.

"What?"

"I actually believe you too."

TWENTY-EIGHT

DAISY

There are two of me now. The before and the after. I miss the before version of myself. I mourn her. She was so dumb and simple. Her biggest problems are now laughable to me. And yet, I don't really laugh anymore.

I stare at the article I'm supposed to be reading. I'm supposed to turn this boring text into a posterboard project that will teach my classmates something. But the words all jumble together. And I know my classmates won't learn a damn thing from whatever I stand up in front of the class and try to teach them. Because the real lessons are out in the world. You only remember things in a real way when you are terrified. When you nearly wet your pants because someone says something so horrifying you think you might forget how to breathe. That's when the brain really kicks into gear. You can recall the smell of a cologne even when it's no longer in the same room as you. The little noises stay humming in your ears for ages.

That's how people learn and remember. That's what becomes impossible to forget.

I've turned my phone off for the last five hours and I know that's a crime in the teenage world. My friends are likely blowing up my texts. Asking me to meet them somewhere. Texting each other about why I haven't answered. They'll have all the juicy answers soon enough.

"Girl," my grandmother shouts, sending a hot lightning bolt up my spine. "Get out here and fix this damn television. You did something to it."

"I didn't," I yell back, the rage in my voice surprising. If it shocks my grandmother she doesn't let on.

"Get out here and fix it now. My show starts in ten minutes."

I throw myself off the creaky bed and march angrily out to her. "I don't care about your show. I don't care if you screwed up the television again. I am trying to do my schoolwork so I can graduate and get the hell out of here."

"You've got some nerve. I make one phone call and you're gone. If I don't want you, there is no one. You better remember that."

"It doesn't matter," I shout back, slicing my hand through the air. "This is done anyway. It's all over. I don't care where I end up."

"Fix the television." She purses her lips and her matted hair shakes with her angry posture. "You don't want to cross me now."

She has no idea. It would be shocking to her to find out she is the least of my problems right now. Her call to child services which I had to fear for so long, wouldn't even register now on the list of the worst things to happen to me this month. Her vile fearmongering can't compare to the laundry list of shit I'm dealing with now.

"Call." I take two steps back from her and stick up my middle finger. "I'm done with you. I'm done with all of this. I can't take any more." I walk back into the tiny room I'm supposed to be grateful to have and slam my door.

There is no point in fighting with her anymore. There is

nothing left to fight for.

TWENTY-NINE

ELIZABETH

Then

"Today's the day." Tucker ushers me into his office with a wide smile and the bouncing energy of a child who has just been told they're going to the zoo.

I need this. I'm not sure if he knows how important his upbeat energy is, but it's everything. My nerves are shot. The last six months have been a blur of learning a new job, trying to placate my mother and make myself into the perfect guardian for my sister in the eyes of the court.

"You look optimistic." I fall into the chair across from his desk and look expectantly at him. There are always two kinds of people in any sort of relationship that works well. A person who thinks the sky is falling and the one who tells them everything will work out. In my life I'm always the latter. I'm always chanting phrases of comfort. Tucker has allowed me to become the worrier. The one who needs to be assured. And without skipping a beat, he's been there.

"I'm very optimistic. You've pulled this off in spectacular fashion. I have no doubt after today, you'll be the sole guardian of Jules. You'll be living together in that apartment you've busted your ass for. You'll keep excelling in your job and maybe build a real career for yourself. You've done it."

"The credit should go to you." I wave in his direction and swallow past the emotion threatening to clog my throat. "I couldn't have done any of this without you."

"You'll be without me soon." He licks his lips and furrows his brow the way he does when he's debating something. We've spent so many days and late nights in this office. He's done more for me and Jules than any lawyer normally would.

I love him.

Love.

It's childish and shortsighted, but I don't care. Mostly because it doesn't matter. Tucker is a good man with a wife and a baby on the way. He's kind. Generous. I can love him even if he can't love me back.

"It's not like I'm going too far." I chuckle and wait for him to reassure me that we'll still see each other.

"Can I tell you something?" He folds his hands and leans on his desk. "I shouldn't say this but it's killing me. This is all going to be over soon. The thought of not seeing you again keeps me up at night." He drops his head as though he's fighting with himself. "I know this isn't appropriate. I can't believe I'm even saying it, but you keep me up a lot at night. The thought of you, it..."

This is not completely shocking. I'm no fool. Our hands have brushed, we've leaned over the same documents, he's looked at me too long over a dinner meeting. I know what the male gaze feels like and Tucker's has fallen on me plenty of times before. But in the same breath he speaks glowingly about his darling wife. About his amazing life. His home. Everything he's built. Wanting me doesn't make the pro and con list work out. I know that. He knows that.

"We can still hang out sometimes." I reach my hand across his desk and touch his. "I'm not dying."

"I am." His head shoots up. "Or I feel like I am. Do you know what it's like to question everything in your life? To wonder if you picked the wrong path. I sit here with you and I'm in awe. You are powerful. You are smart. I look at you and I can see your future. And I can see myself in it. That's so screwed up. That's not right. I have a life. I can't just step into yours."

The words spill from him at an alarming rate. Tucker is a composed man. He's measured and calculated. I've never seen him like this.

"But I'm just—"

"Don't you dare." With a nearly frightening urgency he takes my hand that had been resting on his. His eyes dance wildly as he drinks me in. "Don't you ever say you are just anything. You are incredible. The most incredible woman I have met. I bet against you when you first came to me and I knew within ten minutes that was a mistake. You are everything."

"Tucker." I squeeze his hand back, worried for him. Sorry for making him feel this upset. Conflicted. "You're married. You have a baby on the way. We've spent a lot of time together and maybe you're just feeling confused."

"Tell me you don't feel the same way?" He stands and rounds his desk. He's towering over me, pleading with his eyes. Lying to him would be a gift. Telling him that I don't love him would be the most generous thing I could do for him. I'd wound him now but, in the end, I'd keep him from imploding his life.

Two trains of thought run in tandem in my mind. Tucker is the kindest man I've ever met. He's spent money, time and energy saving my life. Saving Jules's life. I would be a fool to turn him away. The second thought is darker. Murky like the bottom of a lake. If I say no, will he still come to court with me today? Will he work as hard as he can to make sure I get custody of Jules? Did he know I would think of that before he asked how I felt about him?

"I know how I feel about you," I say, standing and holding my breath for a long moment, hoping he would say something more. When he doesn't, I give him the two things he's desperate for. My answer and my body. "I feel the same way."

It is a permission granted. In this moment it doesn't matter that he is thirty-seven and I am eighteen. It doesn't matter that he is married. The only thing that matters is that I am what he wants and he has what I need.

The kiss is rough and hungry but soon turns tender. His urgency is ever present but his kindness seems to rise to the top. I can tell with every move of his hands on my body it matters most to him that I feel safe.

What he doesn't realize is, while my desire for him is strong, my mind only knows one response to these moments. Leaving. Separating. Shutting off. I want to be present with him but I am like a robot built of broken parts. Assembled from heaps of trash. I am made up of every bad experience. Every boundary broken. Every consent not given. Maybe he doesn't know he is traveling down a path that has previously been stomped and trampled.

"What is it?" Tucker pulls away, bringing his hands up to my cheeks. "What's the matter?"

"Nothing." I smile and raise to my tiptoes to start our kiss again. That's all I know. That's my job. You can't stop once it starts.

"Oh, babe." Tucker pulls away again and laces his fingers with mine. "I shouldn't have done that. I can't just kiss you like that."

With a hand over his own heart he looks down at me and shakes his head. I feel suddenly like a failure. Like I've let him down.

"I'm fine. I want this." I try to pull him closer.

"You haven't told me everything you've been through, but you've told me enough. I should have known better than to just spring this on you. Men haven't treated you well." He shakes his head again. "That's an understatement. I'm sorry I came at you like that. You deserve better."

"I'm totally fine," I lie again, this time with a few tears in my eyes. "You're not like those other men."

"I'm not." He kisses the crown of my head and pulls me into his arms. "But right now I'm not acting any better than them. I'm so sorry. The way I feel about you, it's not just about a physical attraction. By kissing you like that it makes it seem like I just want one thing. That's not true. That's not what I want at all."

I speak into his shoulder as he squeezes me tightly. "But we already started. It's not like we can just stop. It's fine we can—"

He cuts me off, his hands bracing my shoulders and leaning me backwards so he can look me in the eyes. "We can always stop. We can always wait. You get a say. Not just with me. With anyone. You know that, right? Anything that doesn't feel right, you get to stop."

I nod and don't bother explaining to him how far from the truth that was. Shock fills my body as he begins to cry.

"Dammit, Lizzy, I'm so sorry. I didn't plan this. I didn't mean to ambush you and just thrust myself on you like that. It's awful. I'll never do anything like that again."

"You'll never kiss me again?" My face crumples as I wipe the tears from his cheeks.

"Do you want me to kiss you again some day?" he gulps, clearly trying to get himself back under control.

"Yes." I plead with my eyes. I don't want to sleep with Tucker in his office with his assistant outside. I don't want to wonder what would have happened to my court case if I said no. But I do want him to kiss me again. I want him to kiss me when nothing is on the line. When he's not my lawyer and I'm not his client.

The relief that washes over him feeds the part of my soul that is desperate to please him.

"The next time I kiss you, it'll be different. You'll know you're safe. You'll get a say. You'll feel as good as I do."

There were layers of subtext in his words. Sensuality. Promises. Desire. The moment he lets me go I feel exposed and cold. Being out of his arms now that I've been in them feels like a letdown I couldn't possibly brace myself for. I don't know when he'll kiss me again. But I'll be ready when he does.

THIRTY

RICK

The police are wearing suits and ties. Detectives. Not some beat cops here to talk with us. They mean business. I welcome them in and settle them onto the couch in the living room as Jules and Elizabeth come to stand, hovering around like worried-looking moths too attracted to the flame to leave.

"What can I do for you, detectives?" The blood is charging through my veins, thudding in my ears like a marching band. I know the answer to this question already. Everything is about to change. My son will never be the same after this. I don't believe for a second that he assaulted someone, but I know truth is subjective and the criminal justice system is unforgiving and broken.

"We're here to talk about an incident report that's been made." Detective Cole is a tall man with slicked-back blond hair and a permanently smug expression. I've had many officers like him on the stand over the years. The other detective, Laurence, is the good cop. Or at least that's the expression he's holding. Gentle eyes, open body language, relaxed posture. I'll try to connect with him.

"Can you tell me what the report is about?" I lean back in

my chair and cross my legs casually. "We'd like to help in any way we can." I pray with every fiber in my body that Elizabeth will stay quiet. I need her to let me handle this. It's the only shot to protect Bryson. She's done nothing but make it worse.

"We know what it's about," Elizabeth cuts in. She's tucking her wild hair behind her ears and looking like she's ready to jump out of her skin.

"You do?" Cole furrows his well-sculpted brows and gestures for Elizabeth to hang herself with the rope he's handing over.

"We don't really. Can you tell us more?" I shoot Elizabeth a scolding look. I want to take a gentler approach, but nothing is more important to me than Bryson right now. It can't be.

Laurence kindly saves me from the catastrophe that's about to happen if my wife keeps talking. "Mrs. Meadows, a student at your school has filed a report and we're conducting an investigation. We wanted to come and hear your side of the story."

"My son isn't home right now so—" Elizabeth waves them off.

"This isn't about your son." Laurence gestures for Elizabeth to sit down but she ignores him. "The student has accused you of harassing her, attempting to initiate an inappropriate relationship among other things. We would like to hear what you have to say about that."

The air leaves the room; the only two who seem to be able to draw in breath are the two detectives. Jules holds the door frame to steady herself as she asks the question Elizabeth can't seem to vocalize. "Wait, what?"

Laurence goes on explaining. "The student claims you initiated communication with her via cell phone, then pressured her to meet with you outside of school on multiple occasions. You've made her feel uncomfortable and she's found your behavior obsessive and worrying. Could you tell us more about that from your perspective?"

"We don't have anything to say," I cut in, holding up a hand to Elizabeth. "I'll be acting as her counsel right now and we won't be making any statements."

Cole claps his hands loudly together once and clears his throat. "Well, that would be a terrible idea considering how much evidence we've already gathered."

I don't fall for that ploy. "And we'll address that evidence when the—"

Elizabeth takes a step forward. "There is a lot more to the story than you know. Daisy is struggling. I, as her teacher, have been offering her support. The situation is complex."

"Why do you think she'd make this report then?" Cole is loving this. There is nothing better for a detective than a suspect talking.

"Elizabeth." I stand and put my body between her and the detectives. "It's very important that you stop talking right now. I am trying to protect you. Let me see them out and then we can discuss it."

"No. This is crazy. Daisy is living in squalor and I think there is abuse at home. She has a lot going on and you two cops should be over there helping her."

Laurence tries to gesture again for Elizabeth to sit down. "We're aware of the student's living arrangements and the challenges. You said you were concerned about possible neglect or abuse. Did you report that?"

Dammit. They are setting every possible trap and she's walking directly into them. "Elizabeth, don't answer that."

"I didn't report it because I understand what it's like to be tossed into foster care. The last thing she needed was to be thrust into a system that would traumatize her more. I was working to help her. I was supporting her."

Cole looks like an animal about to leap at his prey. "By giving her five hundred dollars?"

"She was struggling with food insecurity and her water was turned off. I gave her money to help with that."

With an arrogant smirk Cole folds his arms across his chest. "Do you think it's appropriate to give cash to students?"

"Do you know what I think is inappropriate?" Elizabeth's anger is growing. I want to tackle her, drag her into the kitchen and cover her mouth. I know nothing short of that will keep her from talking. She ignores my pleas as she continues to make her point.

"It's inappropriate for a student not to have basic needs met like food and portable water. It's inappropriate that the artwork we have in the corner over there cost three times as much as the cash I gave her. The red tape and bureaucracy that stand between the people who need help and the ones who want to give it is what's inappropriate."

Laurence is trying. I can see it in his eyes. "Mrs. Meadows, I really appreciate your passion for wanting to help a student. What I'm telling you is that your help and attempts at communicating and meeting with that student made her feel unsafe. Apparently to the point where she was willing to come into the police station and ask for help."

With a gruff laugh Cole chimes in. "And there are other people who witnessed this behavior too. People at the restaurant you met at who said they saw the student crying and looking very uncomfortable. They heard you insist on her getting in your car even when she didn't want to."

Elizabeth dismisses their accusation. "She wanted to take the bus. It was late and she was alone. You would rather I send her out into the night by herself? This is ridiculous. You're missing the whole point."

"What is the point?" Cole asks, pretending he cares.

"She was assaulted."

"Elizabeth, don't do this." I don't try to hide the desperation in my voice. Turning to Jules I can see the shock in her eyes.

The lack of ability to process. But I need her. I need her to help me. But she does nothing as Elizabeth continues.

"That's what this is really about. She was assaulted and was completely unraveling. I approached her and tried to offer her support. In doing so I discovered her living conditions. All of this has been me trying to help her. Now she's afraid of people finding out and she's changing her story to try to save face."

"In my experience," Cole bites out, "people who are afraid of someone finding something out don't go to the police. She came to us because she's afraid of you."

"That's ridiculous." Elizabeth tosses up her hands. "The assault—"

"She told us about that," Laurence corrects firmly and my heart drops. "She said that you did approach her after class when she was having a rough day due to her current home life. You exchanged phone numbers and then the text messages and meetings off campus started. Then she said you became obsessed with the idea that she was assaulted. You introduced the topic and then eventually accused your own son of being her attacker."

"Elizabeth." I can only say her name. There are no other words.

"No." Elizabeth laughs without a hint of humor. "I saw video of them talking."

"Yes, she told us you kept bringing up your son. Asking if she knew him. She told you they'd chatted once recently at a party here at your house. Then from there you obsessively latched onto the idea that he'd assaulted her."

My stomach lurches, threatening to send up my last cup of coffee. I've dealt with an array of complex cases in my years as a lawyer. I've sat across from many clients and witnesses who were living with mental illness. I know exactly how vulnerable they can be in a justice system always so hell-bent on meeting quotas and closing cases.

"I need to stop us here," I announce, straightening my back and tucking my hands into my pockets. "I believe that Elizabeth is a danger to herself and others, including my son. She needs to be evaluated immediately by your crisis assistance team and likely involuntarily committed for an emergency psychiatric assessment and inpatient treatment."

"Rick," Jules and Elizabeth say my name in unison with the same level of shock.

Cole looks disappointed, deflating at the change of direction. "I'll call in the mental health crisis team to come." He stands and steps out of the house, leaving Laurence to deal with the new scenario.

He shifts uncomfortably in his seat. "Does she have a history of mental illness?"

"Can you not talk about me like I'm not here?" Elizabeth is enraged.

That's part of the playbook for mental health. The person suffering is sidelined and everyone talks over and around them. I usually try to change that when I'm involved but for her own good, I need Elizabeth to be quiet. I speak for her even though she will see it as a betrayal. "She was hospitalized and treated for a serious case of postpartum psychosis. Also she's been addressed at work for behavior with other students that's crossed the line. This is an escalation."

"This is a mistake," Elizabeth corrects. "I need to talk to Daisy. If she realizes what she's done and that she needs to tell the truth about the assault then she can clear this up. Bryson didn't do it, but it did happen."

Laurence leans forward and his face falls gravely serious. "You cannot have any contact with her. None."

"I can clear this up with five minutes in a room with her." Elizabeth runs her hands through her hair again.

Laurence looks to Jules, furrowing his brows. "You're her

sister? Do you agree she needs to be evaluated and possibly committed for an involuntary hold."

"I, ah—I'm not sure that's necessary."

"I found another note in Bryson's bag," I cut in. "Jules, this one was worse. Angrier and more ominous. You know something is wrong."

She only nods, looks over at Laurence and then nods again. Elizabeth spirals into panic, pacing around the room in disbelief.

"You're going to have me thrown into the nut house?" Elizabeth grabs my arms and I feel her nails digging in. "I need you to believe me. I'm not making this up. I know what happened. Don't you trust me?"

"I do." Years of practice at not getting too close to my clients allows me to compartmentalize this. There is right and wrong. There is what must be done and what we wish could be done. They are rarely the same. "I believe that you believe this is what happened. But right now you aren't thinking clearly. I need you to trust me. I love you and I don't want anything to happen to you. You need to go talk to some doctors and let them help you."

"Ma'am, we're going to ask you to step outside with us." Laurence is gesturing for Elizabeth to follow as Cole peeks his head back in, indicating the mental health team is on their way.

"Jules," Elizabeth moans, eyeing her sister desperately. "Please don't let him do this. I fought so hard to make sure you were safe, to make sure no one ever took you away like this. Don't let him do this."

I put my body between the two of them. If Jules falls apart now she could compromise this completely. "I promise it's going to be okay, Elizabeth. I won't let anything happen to you. The moment I can come to you, I will."

Her expression changes like an animal who'd just had a cage close in around them. Gnashing her teeth and speaking through tight lips, she jabs her finger in my direction. "Don't. Don't you dare come see me. I'll never forgive you for this."

I steel myself against her threat. No one wants to be in this position. No one wants to be the person who has their wife taken away for her own good. I see in her expression a fear I've always tried to save her from. And now I'm the one causing it.

"How could you?" Jules cries, covering her mouth with her hand to smother her sobs.

"Jules, we have to do this. We have to. Elizabeth needs help. We both agreed she's not well. The notes. She made up an accusation against our son. Do you know how dangerous that is to his life? If that student hadn't gone to the police to report Elizabeth, Bryson could be going to jail right now. You know Elizabeth would never want to hurt Bryson, so her doing this proves she needs help. A lot of help." I've lost all semblance of a calm and measured argument. I am wild with anger. Enough so that Jules steps back, stops crying for a moment and looks frightened.

"I'm sorry," she whispers. "You're right. I just can't believe this is happening." Falling to her knees and crying again, I kneel beside her. We're in a heap of tears, trying to form sentences to comfort each other when Bryson walks in through the kitchen.

"What happened?" His brows are so high with fear they disappear in his shaggy hair. "Where's Mom?"

There is no emotion or feeling in my body that is more important than my son knowing everything will be okay. That's my job. I will make this all right. Nothing will stop me. Not even Elizabeth.

THIRTY-ONE

DAISY

People know. Of course they would. The network that connects high school students to each other when it comes to rumors is intense. I knew the moment I walked into that police station this would be top news at school.

Stacy P. grabs my arm and I have to juggle my books to make sure they don't spill onto the floor.

"Girl, what the hell? Why didn't you tell me what was going on?" She pulls me into a corner between the rows of lockers and looks expectantly at me. When I don't answer she goes on. "I knew when I walked in on you two that something weird was happening. I told my mom and she called the school. So even if you didn't go to the cops, they were going to bust her anyway."

"I'm not supposed to talk about it." I stare down at my shoes and feel every eye on me as people walk by.

"Says who? You're the victim here. Telling your friends what you're going through is not against the law." Stacy is a wiz at finding loopholes and making a case for why rules shouldn't apply to her.

"The police told me not to talk about it."

"I don't see any cops." She glances around coolly and rushes me with a gesture to say something.

I comply finally. "I don't even know what happened. Mrs. Meadows is really nice. She just kind of snapped, I think. I heard from the officers that she's in a mental hospital now and she has to stay there until they say she's okay to leave. It's totally screwed up."

"She's in Bayview?" Stacy says this so loud a gaggle of other girls passing by stop and join our conversation as if they'd been invited. Peppering me with questions, they are hungry for more gossip. The worry that's been needling me relentlessly for all this time is subsiding briefly as I realize they are not honing in on me, but fixated completely on Mrs. Meadows. They don't have any idea about how poor I am and how disgusting my home is. It isn't me they want to tear down, it's Mrs. Meadows. The temptation to keep their feeding frenzy going is too much to resist.

"I guess she completely lost it on the cops, and her husband said he wanted her committed. She's totally nuts." My shoulders lift a little as the girls focus on me with undivided attention. The way it used to be at my old school. I could hold court like this whenever I wanted. Because I used to matter. And right now I matter again. "She was stalking me. Calling me all the time. You can't believe the things she wanted me to say. What she wanted me to go along with. I knew she'd lost it but I thought she was nice and pretty harmless."

"Yeah," Stacy agrees frantically. "But then I walked into Mrs. Meadows's classroom and something was so sketchy. I was totally there. Daisy ran out of there and I followed. Then Mrs. Meadows was blowing up her phone. It was creepy as hell. I actually told my mom. She called the school."

Another girl with a soccer jersey and a mouth full of braces leans forward to add her part to the drama. "My sister said Mrs. Meadows got in trouble after a field trip three years ago where some kids were vaping and she didn't report them. I guess she actually told them they could do it if they wanted."

Mary, the tiniest girl in our grade who rarely spoke, seemed eager to jump into our gossip. "Mrs. Meadows told my brother the answers to a test once so he could still play football that season. She totally let him cheat. What kind of teacher does that?"

Stacy nods at me. "I knew she was weird. Why does she let us swear in class and act like she's one of us? Probably just so she can get close to students and make it creepy. What a whack job. I bet we're going to hear some pretty crazy stuff now. It'll all come out. She will never teach again. That's if they ever let her out of the loony bin."

The bell rings and everyone reluctantly breaks away from the giggling gossip and toward their class. I have more to say. Important context. But the rumor mill is in unstoppable motion now. It wouldn't matter what part of the story I corrected. These things take on a life of their own, and have a habit of ruining the lives of others. That's not my battle. I've got enough problems of my own to try to deal with. At least for now, no one knows my secrets.

THIRTY-TWO

ELIZABETH

Now

I'm contemplating a hunger strike. Or maybe I'll just stick with staying silent. It seems to be frustrating the hell out of everyone here at Bayview and I'm glad because I'm pretty pissed off myself.

The person I'm currently icing out is Dr. Margarite Harlow. Because she's trying to build a rapport with me, she's insisting I can call her Maggie. I know that trick. I understand how to build bridges with people, but I'm not interested in becoming pals with Maggie.

Firstly, we have nothing in common. She's a psychiatrist in her late sixties. With her silver hair neatly tied back in a bun she forces a warm smile that's meant to reflect her genuine compassion. Her goal, with her thick-rimmed red glasses, is to exude a sense of wisdom and professionalism but show she's still got some spunk and humor under that exterior. Her vibrant blue eyes sparkle with intelligence, offering a sense of reassurance. If I wasn't sitting across from her as a patient, I'd likely think she was fine. But right now, she's the enemy.

I take in her space as if it might give me some advantage. Some clue as to how I could outwit or outwill her.

The entrance to Dr. Harlow's office is marked by a sturdy wooden door adorned with a discreet nameplate. There are locks that remind me I'm here against my will, but the rest of the room is designed to try to put me at ease. I'm greeted by a cozy, earth-toned armchair that's clearly for me. Hers is directly across. The walls are adorned with serene artwork and inspirational quotes, fostering a sense of tranquility within the space. Juxtaposed by the yelling down the hallway from an angry patient demanding more blankets.

I read into the setup of her personal workspace and see that it reveals a meticulously organized and thoughtfully designed area. A large desk made of polished mahogany takes center stage, adorned with a few family photographs, a small potted plant, and an elegant brass desk lamp. Behind the desk, a bookshelf lines the wall, filled with an extensive collection of medical textbooks, psychological literature, and personal mementos.

Dr. Harlow is doing everything right and yet this is all so wrong. I nibble on the inside of my lip to keep from speaking.

"Elizabeth, I know you've not felt comfortable enough to speak with anyone on staff yet. I can understand that an abrupt change like this can be very jarring. I just want you to know that my goal is to get you healthy and get you home. If that's a similar goal to what you want for yourself, our best path toward that is talking to each other."

"I am healthy." I fold my arms across my chest and they itch against the polyester, hospital-issued top I'm wearing.

"But you do want to return home?" Dr. Harlow knows better than to look too excited by the fact that I've decided to speak. She only cocks up a brow and challenges me to go on.

"I don't belong here. This is a big misunderstanding. I was

helping a student through a difficult time and it got completely misconstrued."

"Tell me more about that." She puts the back of her pen to her lips pensively and waits for me to explain. Instead, I look at the stack of papers behind her that have my name on them.

"You've gotten a whole file on me, I'm sure. So why would I rehash it all? What do you know about why I'm here?"

She nods, her eyes moving toward the same stack of papers. "I've read your medical history, the report the police made and the notes from your husband and your sister upon intake. But none of that is in context. I need to know how you feel and what happened from your perspective."

"It's all there," I huff and point to the papers. "I'm not foolish enough to think I'm going to convince you my perspective matters. I know what I heard and saw. I know what happened."

"Do you understand that the student—"

"Daisy. Her name is Daisy. Can we just call her that?"

"Sure." Dr. Harlow jots something down on the pad on her lap. "Daisy is stating that you did come speak with her while she was struggling with some issues at home. She thought it kind and appreciated your concern."

"That's exactly what happened." I lean in to emphasize how insane it is that I'm here considering we're in agreement on the circumstances.

"Can you tell me what you were feeling or experiencing prior to this encounter with Daisy? In the days and weeks leading up to this was there anything new going on in your life?"

"Nothing." I answer it honestly, but with a sharp edge to the word. The nothingness was part of the problem. There was a void and I'd been falling deeper into it. "Things were quiet."

"Was that a change for you?" Dr. Harlow blinks slowly at me. She's like one of those pigs hunting truffles in the wild and she knows she's on to something, even if I'm sure it won't lead anywhere.

"It was different. It's hard to describe how."

"Your son is fifteen?"

"Yes." I prickle at the idea of bringing Bryson into this.

"Parents, especially those who tend to be the primary care-givers, can sometimes feel unsettled when the duties of that role change drastically. That can often occur during these teen years. Parenting can be so urgent and incessant. You're constantly meeting needs just to find there is another a moment later. When that stops it can leave us feeling unsure how to fill that time." I understand she's using the term us to make me feel as though we are the same. But she's not a prisoner here.

"It was a change. I guess I was feeling a bit fidgety. Maybe bored." I think back to how quiet the house had become. How my thoughts wandered further than I'd let them before.

"You have the added experience of having parented since you were a very young child. You took care of your sister, gained custody of her. You've essentially been full-time parenting for the last twenty-five years, now suddenly that responsibility is different."

"Rick is working a lot too. He's on a very high-profile case, and Bryson has been doing his own thing. Rick's been gone. Even Jules, living an hour away, has been an adjustment. But if you're searching for some major stressor in my life that set off me going nuts, there wasn't one. Because that didn't happen."

"I will never use the term nuts, just so we're clear." Dr. Harlow jots down something else. "But a stressor doesn't have to be some traumatic event. It can be the lack of something, too. Can you tell me what you felt when you started to realize things were slowing down in your world? You weren't needed as much. Your career was stable. Your sister was living her own life. How did you fill the extra time?"

"Just thinking, I guess." This is a slipup. I'm oversharing

but there is something hypnotic about the way Dr. Harlow nods her head almost imperceptibly, like you have to squint to see if she's agreeing with you. And for some reason, I want her to.

"And were those thoughts of your past?"

I snap back to the moment and remember Rick's betrayal and how it landed me here. "Rick has no idea what my childhood was like but he's dead set on connecting the dots between what happened then and what he thinks is happening now. He has no clue what my life was like."

"Was it intentional? Keeping all that from Rick, was that a conscious decision?"

"You can't survive something if you keep putting yourself through it." I clap my hands together too loudly and they sting from the contact. I remember in this moment that every move I make impacts how long I have to stay here. I settle and lean back more casually in the chair.

"Can you survive after something if you don't heal from it?" She looks proud of this counterpoint.

"Healing is myth. I'm healed in that I've built a new life that I function fine in. I raised my sister. Got married. Had my son. You know the person you really need to psychoanalyze is Rick."

"Why?" She purses her lips and her pen hovers over the paper.

"He married me when I was twenty and pregnant. We started dating when I was at a very low point in my life. He was ten years older, had a million opportunities ahead of him and he marries me. What do the books you've read tell you about that?" I gesture to the shelf behind her.

"There is no way for me to know what his motivation was then. I'd like to stay focused on you. Can we talk about your mental health history?" She grabs the stack of papers and flips to a page with a yellow flag holding her place.

"It was a long time ago. Postpartum. Something tons of women go through. It's not relevant here."

"Many women do experience it. I'm not saying it's connected to the situation now, I'm just wondering what you can tell me about that time. Your diagnosis wasn't postpartum depression but postpartum psychosis. There is a distinction. Did you experience feeling confused and with obsessive thoughts, hallucinations or delusions? Or sleep problems or paranoia?"

"It wasn't like that. I was having these visions." I catch myself and wave her off. "It was more like daydreams. Rick overreacted then too. I was only in treatment for three days and then they realized I was fine. I took some medication for about six months and then weaned off. I was fine. Just like I'm fine right now."

Dr. Harlow nods but is wholly unconvinced by my argument. A long moment passes as she scans the notes in my file. "I want to be transparent with you." She crosses her legs at the ankle and puts the files back where they were on her desk behind her. "I think that there is something going on here that you need to be treated for. It could perhaps be similar to what you experienced after your son was born. You were able to move past the stressor, and medication supported you through that transition, but I don't believe you were able to get to the root of the problem. Without that, you can likely continue to find yourself experiencing symptoms that will undoubtedly impact your everyday life."

"Tell me how you see a connection between these two things. Fifteen years apart, you think this is related?" I make sure she knows I think she's wrong.

"I think everything tends to be related. Do you agree that your childhood was traumatic? Just as a yes or no response."

"Yes."

"In the children that you've taught over the years, has it

been your experience that their trauma can impact various aspects of their lives?"

"Of course."

"But you don't believe your experiences might have the same impact on you?"

"I don't feel like..." Her argument is sound, which is frustrating as hell. "I still can't see how these things might be connected. When Bryson was born I was tired, not eating, falling apart. The things I was imagining weren't full conversations with people. I know I talked to Daisy. I know I met with her and we ate and she was right there in front of me."

"I believe that happened as well. It's early on in our time, but from all the notes I've read and our interaction here, I believe you to be a pragmatic, kind, honest individual who has dedicated your life to helping the people you care about. Sacrificing a lot to do so."

This doesn't feel like pandering just so we can connect. She seems as though she's being genuine and I allow myself to hope that maybe she'll see the truth and I'll get out of here. Until I hear the next sentence.

"I think it will be important for us to explore how auditory hallucinations might have played a part in your encounters with Daisy."

I chuckle even though it's probably inappropriate. Something she'll scratch down in her notebook about me. Laughing at the wrong time.

"Auditory hallucinations?"

"They can distort and even interject your thoughts into a conversation, and your memory of that conversation would be altered."

"And you think this is triggered by me feeling a little bored?" I shake my head at the absurdity.

"No, I think that the sudden change to your daily schedule and responsibilities may have opened a door to part of your mind and memories that you've otherwise been intentionally too busy to explore. Now as things quiet down those events and traumas of your past are resurfacing. That can also happen when your son has come to the same age you were when you were experiencing them."

"But then why Daisy? Why would I say my son did something so terrible? That makes no sense. I know what she said to me." My mind flips wildly through the possibilities. Daisy is afraid and recanting. She's hurt or feels unsupported and is lashing out. Or I'm the problem. What they are saying about me is true and I can't trust my own mind. It's all a terrifying blur, but one I can't imagine this doctor could possibly sort out for me.

"You may see some of yourself in Daisy. I don't doubt that you recognized she was in distress. There is a chance that you projected some of your own experiences from your youth onto her. Were you ever the victim of sexual assault?"

Again, I laugh humorlessly. "Women have been dealing with this since the beginning of time. Of course I have my own experiences with it, but Daisy..." I trail off as I try to get hold of the right thread. I'm attempting to line up all the memories that are meshing with this current disaster.

"We won't solve this all today," Dr. Harlow says through a smile. "But we've made some great progress. You'll have group counseling tonight and then you and I will meet again in the morning. Will you please give some thought to what we discussed today and consider sharing some of your childhood experiences with me?"

I nod, slipping through time like I'm strapped into an amusement park ride that won't stop jerking and twisting.

The same refrain loops in my mind as I think of Daisy. I know what I heard. I know what she said.

It morphs slowly into a distorted voice. Do I know what I heard? Is that what she said?

THIRTY-THREE

ELIZABETH

Then

I saw it on the news. My lawyer, my savior, my lover. Gone.

I'd foolishly believed when I was growing up that I'd experienced the worst of it. That it was all going to get better the older I was because I would be in control. I would work my way out of the terrible situations and make sure they were a thing of the past.

I only understood that people could be good and evil. I didn't know love could kill you. I didn't think that there could be so many complex dimensions to my feelings for someone. It was like experiencing life in primary colors, simple and straightforward. However, once Tucker entered my world, my emotions transformed into a vibrant blend of greens and purples. It was as if all the shades and complexities of my previous experiences were mixing together while I fell in love with him.

Our last night together was perfect. Unblemished by the storm that was waiting for him. The one he never saw coming. The last night he left my bed there was no sign of problems. I'd found a way to stop begging for his full attention and love, and he'd found a clandestine schedule away from his wife and new baby for us to still be together. It wasn't perfect but we'd given up on the idea of perfection. I just wanted him. This was all I could get. I'd make it enough.

Tucker loved me. Fiercely. Deeply. I was like no woman he'd ever known before. He missed no opportunity to curse timing. To wish he had met me before he'd met his wife.

How could I not love him? He'd given me my life. My sister. The roof over my head. The job that sustained me. There was a hunger in him to cherish me. To make sure I knew how incredible I was.

It wasn't until I'd cried myself sick over his death that the truth began to come out. Not our truth. Not all the things he whispered in my ear as he held me tightly through the night. The nights he told his wife he was staying in the city to prepare for court in the morning. No. This was someone else's truth.

The other girls.

Nine of them. The ones he'd helped so generously win their cases in court for free. He gave them his time and energy. His money. His wisdom. Connections were used to get them jobs. Bribes were paid to drop their charges. Tucker Rutherford was a brilliant predator who used his power and privilege to extort and control young women. Leading them right to bed. The bed I'd found myself in.

This part didn't make the news. His jump from the hotel balcony did, but not the reason why. People spoke fondly of him. They mourned his passing. No one ever spoke out publicly. Not even his wife. She saved everything she had to say for me.

She showed up at my apartment one morning. Spitting mad and fists flying.

The irony was endless. She was at my apartment. The one I could only afford because Tucker lent me the money. I was still living here because he'd gotten me the job at his friend's office.

Tucker had been dead for five days. Five days of me crying and falling to pieces. But on day five she showed up and opened my eyes to the truth.

I'll never forget the slap. The rage in her eyes. It will haunt me forever.

"Enjoying your good fortune?" she asked. The deep circles beneath her eyes were freshly covered with tears and streaks of mascara. The baggy sweatshirt with holes in the sleeves looked like something she'd been wearing for a week. "It cost me my life. It cost me everything. You whore."

I had to ask too many questions. I couldn't keep up. Who was she? What was she talking about? Through hissing anger and sporadic sobs she unfurled the story like an ancient scroll, each tale more horrific than the last. Everything she'd uncovered. All she knew. There were moments I could tell she was taking comfort in the fact that the information destroyed me. She didn't want to be the only one in pieces.

"I'm leaving." She wiped frantically at her wet cheeks. "My husband is buried. My mom and dad are coming to pick me up in two days. I'll start over in California and my life will be great. But I'm going to make sure every single one of you little whores loses everything. Your job is done. I've already made that call. This apartment he worked out a deal for you to have lower rent, consider that over. You'll be back out on the street in the gutter where he found all of you."

"You can't—" This was where the slap came in. It was meant to answer the question I didn't get a chance to ask. She most certainly could and would make good on these threats. I could see it in her eyes.

I didn't have time to feel my heart breaking over my first love. I was too busy finding out he never loved me at all. I was no different than any woman he'd ever met. I was at least the same as the other nine of them.

Tucker's wife had been right. Right about it all. A few of the other girls came and found me before I was evicted. They needed to see it for themselves. Our anger and embarrassment ran together as we compared our stories. The similarities were nauseating. The timelines overlapping. The fact that he'd been able to keep it all a secret for so long would have been impressive if it wasn't so disturbing.

There were dozens of unanswerable questions that were replaced quickly by unsolvable problems. I was fired. Evicted. Custody of Jules could be challenged again if I didn't find us a place to live and a job that could pay for it.

While that should have been all that mattered, when I closed my eyes, I only saw Tucker. I felt his love. It had to be real. If that wasn't real, then I don't know what was.

I would never be able to put myself back together after this. There would be no life for me without Tucker's love. My mind slipped. Skipped like a scratched-up record. I lost time. I forgot things. I saw what wasn't really there. I felt that slap on my cheek every morning. Every night. I saw Tucker. Everywhere.

Then one day I did see him. The lawyer. The older man. The possibilities. The life I'd pretended we might have some day. He walked into the doctor's office where I was waiting for Jules's flu shot appointment. He was doing the same for his niece.

I saw Rick. And I grabbed on as tight as I could and tried to make myself sane again. Tried and tried and tried.

THIRTY-FOUR

ELIZABETH

Now

"I think two weeks would be a reasonable start." Dr. Harlow is standing behind her desk, not settled comfortably in the chair that sits across from mine. "We've made some great progress. I feel I have an understanding of your early childhood. And we've finally begun digging into your adolescence and the start of your relationship with Rick. I believe that's where the projection onto Daisy's situation may have stemmed from."

"Two weeks?" It had already been four days. Bryson's suspension would be over by Monday and he'd be returning to school. Rumors would be flying about me. I needed to be home to support him. "I can't be out of my life for two more weeks."

"This is your life." She gestures at me and then around the room. "I spoke with one of the officers who are investigating the report against you. They wanted an update on your status."

"Why?" I think of the ride to Bayview. The way I shrieked and cried. How insane they must have thought I was.

"Daisy doesn't want to press any charges. There will still be an investigation that will likely end in your termination and loss of your teaching license. As a mandatory reporter you put yourself in some hot water there. But as far as anything more serious stemming from Daisy's complaint, she's made it clear she wants to move on from that if you're receiving care."

"If." I didn't like ultimatums. I could read between the lines. If I didn't commit to this and stay as long as Maggie thought I should, then maybe there would be charges against me.

"Yes. I think it's a reasonable expectation on her part. She's not looking for you to get in trouble, just to be well. Does that make sense?"

I was coming around to it all. The time I'd spent in group therapy and one-on-one with Maggie over the last few days had given her theory credibility. The more I talked, unleashed the venom of my childhood that had been choking me for so long, the more I could see how off-center it was. That's what we'd been calling it. Rather than crazy or illegal, we talked about my parents and the slums they raised us in as off-center. Not normal. Harmful.

"What are you feeling right now?" This was Maggie's favorite question to ask and my least favorite to answer.

"Angry. I'm still very angry with Rick. I'm trying to predict what things will look like when I get home. How we'll ever come back from this. But I just can't picture a life with him."

"What do you wish Rick would have done differently?"

"Trusted me. Believed me. That's what I wish he'd done. We've been together for nearly seventeen years and he was so quick to just act like I'm the problem."

"Now, we've talked about the logical side of this situation, right? I know that you are still hesitant to believe that you're experiencing some sort of mental health crisis that's altered your perception. But when we ground ourselves in the facts, that becomes clearer, correct?"

I only nod and she looks unsatisfied as she presses on. "So you have the police, Daisy, Jules and Rick all experiencing the same reality. This also tracks with your previous mental health history. All signs point to the fact that the people you've trusted in the past along with other professionals are not conspiring to make you seem or feel unwell. There is a real issue here and we're doing the work to get to the bottom of it."

She's said this to me multiple times before, and each time I swallow it down like a jagged pill. I am uneasy with the idea that I cannot trust my own thoughts. That my brain is somehow capable of betraying me so deeply. It's easier to believe everyone else is in on some wild conspiracy than to believe I can hear and see things that are not really happening. My stomach tightens with pain as I allow my mind to travel to Daisy.

I've been a fierce protector of children since I was old enough to do so. Now I'm coming face to face with the idea that I've inflicted pain. I think of all the terror and shocking levels of treachery I'd been through and how I'd now done the same to Daisy. Maybe not as bad, but still, if what they say is true, I impacted her negatively.

If this is all true.

If...

"So two weeks." Maggie clasps her hands together as if she's sealing the deal with herself.

"Okay." I close my eyes and try to will myself to believe this is the best thing. If I am sick, then I am where I need to be. If I was supporting someone else in this situation, I'd tell them to stay here. To get well. To trust the process and the people in it. I just need to quiet the voice in my mind that is screaming to run. To find out what really happened. Because deep down, I know what I heard. I know what she said. But I also know that maybe I'm wrong.

THIRTY-FIVE

RICK

Elizabeth didn't want me to pick her up. It was Jules she requested. The doctors have warned me that there would be some strong emotions. We could find ourselves at an impasse on things and I should do what I could to keep Elizabeth rooted in reality without challenging her too firmly. It would be a tightrope, and I already envisioned the whole lot of us tumbling off.

"Why are we just waiting here for her?" Bryson is sullen and shaking his leg impatiently as we sit at the kitchen table looking out the window toward the street. "Are we supposed to yell surprise when she comes in?"

"I just want her to know we're happy she's home." I lean to see a little further down the road and realize how stupid I look. Jules told us she would text when they were on our road. We didn't need to be sitting here for the last twenty minutes.

"Are we glad to see her though?" Bryson stretches and yawns from boredom. Or maybe exhaustion. I haven't really been paying attention to whether or not he's been sleeping all that well. I know he's playing video games until I fall asleep at two in the morning. He didn't need to get up for school so it didn't seem to make sense to yell at him to turn it off. Online learning had seemed the only viable option once the entire school knew the absolute chaos happening in his own house. I have never been one to hide away from a fight, but Bryson didn't deserve to go in that building every day and face what people were saying about us.

There was only about two hours of work every day for online school and he seemed to be doing fine with it. Or maybe he wasn't. I hadn't checked that either.

In the absence of Elizabeth I realized just how much she'd done for our family. How many little things she handled that made up and greased the gears of our life.

Two and a half weeks without her had felt like a lifetime. But it had been what was needed. It was my fault. I'd let her go too long without getting treatment. I'd let her push down all the pain she was feeling instead of giving her a safe place to bring it. Our lives together started so quickly. We went from strangers to lovers, to spouses to parents at warp speed. When I was finally ready to hear what she'd been through the timing seemed wrong. Like that pain would somehow diminish or even poison the life we were building. But that selfishness brought us here. To this tipping point. And I just have to pray we haven't tipped so far we can't get back.

"Don't take this attitude when she gets here. We are happy she's back. This has been hell without her, and I can't even imagine what she's going through. You're going to get your shit together and make sure she knows you're glad she's home."

"She's ruined our lives, Dad. How can you pretend she didn't? I can't go back to school. All my friends only talk to me to get gossip updates they can spread around the cafeteria. Mom went nuts and she ruined our family in the process. People know what she accused me of. My own mother said—"

"Bryson, shut the hell up." The car was pulling into the driveway just as I realized I'd done it again. This is a conversation Bryson and I could have had dozens of times in the last two and a half weeks. But I avoided it. Let him sulk alone and lose himself in electronics while I buried my head in work and trying to make sure there was food in the fridge and all the little tasks on the to-do list got done.

All the conversations I've never had in my life will end up being the downfall of my family. But I know the choices I've made for them are right. Even if they hate it now.

Bryson huffed. "Fine. You don't have to take it out on me. She's the one who freaked out."

"You have no idea what your mother has been through in her life. You are this privileged little prince who gets what you want when you want it because your mother fought her whole life just to survive. You can't be bothered to look up from your own shit long enough to realize how much pain she was in."

I'm talking to myself. About myself. Bryson doesn't know that. He takes my words like a punch. Winces as they fly across the table to him.

"I got it," Bryson says, looking wounded. "I'm happy she's home."

Jules comes in first, like she's clearing a path through the paparazzi for a famous actress or scoping out a hostile environment to make sure it's safe.

"Look who's home," she sings, and throws her arm over Elizabeth. "She's graduated from the nut house."

"I just put my cap and gown away." Elizabeth smiles wide and gestures back toward the car as though that's where she left it. "I was valedictorian."

It feels too soon for jokes. The hurt still so raw. But the levity brings air back to the room and I see it filling Bryson's lungs.

"Congratulations." He stands up and walks up for a hug. "I told Dad to get you a cake but he thought that would be a little over the top."

"He was right." She pats his back and I feel a swell of relief. I expected fireworks. Anger so impossible to harness that she would be seething at the sight of me. "Cupcakes are much more appropriate for a situation like this."

"Welcome home," I whisper when it's my turn for a hug. I'm shocked by how tightly she grips me. I know her. In our years together I've learned her touch. What it means. This is not how she would hug me if she were filled with venom and misery. This is a hug of forgiveness. Of gratitude. Latching on as if I am the buoy in a dark sea.

"Thank you." She releases me after a long moment and we all stand in the awkwardness of this reunion. There is no road map for this. No instruction manual for welcoming someone home after you had them forcibly committed for emergency mental health intervention.

"Should we order some food?" Jules asks, rubbing Elizabeth's back.

"Hey," Elizabeth replies, lighting with excitement. "Maybe I'll be able to use a knife again. That's a big deal."

We laugh at the dark humor. What else can we do? This is where we are at. The new foundation of our bulldozed life that we have to rebuild on. The least we can do is laugh while we try to survive it all.

THIRTY-SIX

DAISY

I can't. I cannot. I really thought I was prepared for this but my emotions are rubbed raw and I just want to crawl into my old bed in my nice house and pretend none of this is real. But that life is gone. It's been gone for a while.

I've run through every possible scenario in my mind. Everything I can do and say that might change where I'm at and what's happening. That's why I'm here. Where I know she'll be. This is what has to happen next.

"Mrs. Meadows," I croak out nervously as she steps out of her car and jumps at the sight of me.

"Daisy, what are you doing here?" She clutches her chest.

"I remembered you said you used to come here on Tuesday afternoons to get a manicure. I didn't know if you still did, but I wanted to try to catch you."

Elizabeth clings to the frame of her open car door and looks ready to bolt. "We can't have any contact. I'm not supposed to be talking to you at all."

"Don't you want to, though?" I flutter my lashes at her. "You must have a ton of questions. I felt so bad for what happened. I can't sleep. I can't eat. I just needed to talk to you and tell you I'm sorry."

"Daisy." She pauses and looks around anxiously. The parking lot is quiet besides us and she decides to go on. "I'm sorry for what I put you through. I spent some time evaluating what was going on in my life and what has transpired in years past, and that's what caused the problem. No. It wasn't a problem. It was harm to you and I'm very sorry. You have no responsibility in this. You're the victim. I didn't mean to scare you."

"You didn't scare me." My eyes are wide and my breath catches on my words like fish on sharp hooks. "It wasn't you. This was my fault."

I watch her face collapse in on itself with skepticism. "No, Daisy. Trust me. I know it's hard to understand but my mental state was—"

"You're in danger." I shout the words and then quiet myself with a hand over my mouth. When I'm sure no one is looking our way, I try to explain. "We both are."

"What are you talking about?" She is horrified and waiting breathlessly for me to go on.

"All the conversations I had with you were true. You weren't crazy or stalking me. You were right. But your husband came to see me. He was really kind at first but then when I told him what we'd been talking about was true he got angry. He said anyone who would hurt his son would pay grave consequences. No one would believe a girl like me. He knew all the tricks in court to make me look bad and Bryson look like a victim. He talked about how I'm older than Bryson. I've had boyfriends before. Slept with them. He just went on and on. It made me scared."

"Rick talked to you? I don't even know what..." Elizabeth trails off and stares at me with desperation in her eyes. She needs me to go on.

"He swore no one would believe me. But I told him one person believes me. He knew what I meant. He knew I was talking about you and it made him furious. He said he'd ruin us both if I didn't do what he was telling me. He had this plan."

Her face lit with understanding. "To make me look crazy?"

"Yes. He said it would fit perfectly because sometimes you did break the rules to help people. He talked about where we met up and how it might look to other people. This plan was completely mapped out. What I would say to the police. When I would do it. He was meticulous. I just needed someone at school to see it too. That's when Stacy P. came in and I ran off. I let her see you calling my phone. I knew she'd tell her mom. I knew it would make the story Rick wanted me to tell more believable. I'm so sorry."

"Is this real?" She reaches out and touches the hem of my shirt as though I might disappear into a dreamlike fog. "You don't understand. For the last couple of weeks I've had to believe that nothing you said to me was really what I'd heard. That I'd made all of this up in my head. Auditory hallucinations. I'd scared you and become obsessed because my own pain was never properly addressed. I projected it onto you. Is that happening right now?" She runs her hands up into her hair. "It doesn't matter if you tell me it is or it isn't. I could hear whatever I want to hear. My brain can't be trusted."

"I swear." I reach out for her hand. "This is really happening."

"I need you to tell someone else. Someone I trust."

"I can't tell anyone else. I think he'll kill me. Or you. And definitely not the police, he must know some police pretty well because they've been coming around wherever I am. He's trying to make sure I know he's having me watched."

"I just can't believe…" Her face crumples and I know maybe she's starting to believe me. "So your accusation was true?"

"I know that something happened," Daisy whimpered. "It's fuzzy. I wasn't ready to do or say anything, but then Rick—"

"Why would he do this?"

"I don't know. The only thing he cared about was that I shut up and did what he told me. If I did, he promised me my first year's tuition at college and that he'd help me get housing near campus. But only if I didn't tell anyone what he was making me do. But I can't live like this. You were so kind to me. I just couldn't stay quiet."

"Jules. My sister." She closes her eyes and takes her phone from her pocket. "You just need to tell Jules. I promise it won't go anywhere else from there. But I can't keep my head straight otherwise and if this is true, I'm going to need to be able to trust myself again. Please do this for me."

She dials a number, has a very brief phone call with her sister and then goes back to sit in her car. I wait quietly on a bench nearby for over thirty minutes until a car comes flying into the parking lot.

"Are you okay?" a woman asks, barely slamming her car into park before she's hopping out and addressing Elizabeth.

She points at me and whispers something I can't hear. I know I'll need to repeat what I just said. Jules approaches me tentatively and I try to get it together.

"Daisy, I'm sorry if Elizabeth—"

I cut her off with a wave of my hand and explain it all again. This time I'm more composed because I want to be believed. I want the details to really be heard.

"What the hell?" Jules cries, pinching the bridge of her nose and squinting like she's in pain. "How could he do this? Elizabeth, I am so sorry I didn't believe you. I can't believe I let him—"

"No," Elizabeth replies firmly. "He did this. It's not on any of us. Rick is scary and very convincing. We were all doing what we thought was right. He was just playing a sick game to get what he wanted in the end."

"So Bryson?" Jules drops her gaze to the ground and shakes her head. "He actually..."

"I don't know," I sputter out. "It's so blurry. I shouldn't have been so definitive about it while things were hazy. I just remember his room and the fish tank. But maybe—"

Elizabeth cuts me off. "Daisy, I can't do anything to help you right now. I'm not saying that to be cruel. But if I try, I'll just dig the hole even deeper for myself and we'll come out looking nuts. We need to protect ourselves. You stick with the story Rick told you to tell. You take whatever he was going to give and demand even more if you want to. It doesn't make this right but I'm just not in a position where I could do more for you. Take what you can get out of him."

"Maybe if we all go together and try to tell the police." I take a step back and tip my chin up confidently.

Jules looks like she might agree with me, but Elizabeth cuts her off.

"We can't. This is too far gone. Rick is too smart. We're not in a position to go up against him right now. He has a one-track mind. If he thinks this is the best way to keep Bryson safe, there is nothing we can do or say to change that. I've tried plenty over the years to sway him on things and never been successful. Something this serious, you can see what lengths he's willing to go in the name of protecting Bryson. It's crazy, and we can't compete with that by just calling the police."

"What are you going to do?" I look to each of the women wondering if they have a way through this.

Jules and Elizabeth look at each other for a long beat before she answers. "I don't know. For now, nothing. I'll go home, play the part he's expecting me to. I can't do anything rash right now. If I do, they'll just chalk it up to more mental illness."

Jules pounds her fist into her palm. "The three of us are going to go to the police."

I move further away from them in protest, but Mrs. Meadows shuts the idea down anyway. "Rick will not have been dumb enough to leave any evidence of what he's done. It'll be our word against his and he's far more powerful and connected than we are. I just spent two weeks in a mental institution. Daisy is young and poor. Rick would never leave us a way to trace this back to him. The police won't help."

Jules is clearly unsatisfied. "So you're going home to play happy housewife and pretend this never happened? He threatened and extorted an assault victim. He had you committed and convinced people you were crazy."

"I know." The stoic look on Mrs. Meadows's face borders on unsettling. "If I leave him now, it will just look impulsive. Bryson will never come with me willingly and a court wouldn't grant me custody of him. I have to be strategic."

"How are you so calm?" Jules's voice is sharp and unforgiving. "Your husband of sixteen years betrayed you. He tricked you and used you. Lied to everyone. You're not freaking out?"

She bit at her lip and considered it all for a moment. "I've just been waiting for this day, I think. I never let myself believe Rick was better than all the men before him. He was going to cheat on me and run off with a barely old enough girl. He'd gamble away Bryson's college fund. I might not have pegged him for this exactly, but apparently a lifetime of catastrophizing with my every free moment I've been preparing for him to screw this up. That's probably not healthy, but I always knew he couldn't be better than the rest of them."

The sobering explanation seems to end our conversation in its tracks. There is nothing more to talk about. It is what it is.

"We can't have any more contact, Daisy," Mrs. Meadows instructs. "I'm sorry for how this went but I promise I won't put you in any more danger. Take what you can from him. That's the best I can offer."

I don't move. Mostly because I have nowhere to go. They both get back in their cars and drive off. I presume to make some kind of plan of their own. I wonder if it will be revenge or retreat. Somehow, I have a feeling I'll find out soon enough.

THIRTY-SEVEN

ELIZABETH

Jules will want answers from me. Answers I don't have. It's why I ignored her texts about going to her house and instead just head home. She calls but I don't answer. I can't explain to her why Rick would do this. There is no simple answer. It's layered in his need for control. His expectation to get things to go his way. I've always known he would go to great lengths to be the architect of our lives. I didn't realize he would sacrifice me so coldly in the process.

I flash to the ride to Bayview. The fear. The moments I spent questioning my own sanity. Beginning to believe I was insane.

Looking at my hand tightly on the steering wheel I can see my first mistake. My nails aren't painted. Rick will notice. He'll remember I was going out to an appointment. I'll have to lie and say I'd forgotten to confirm and the line for walk-ins was too long. I'm unstable enough according to him. It's a believable mistake.

I'd been busy lately asking myself the wrong question. I just had to know why Rick loved me. I forgot to ask myself why I'd chosen him. If it was a choice at all. It was simply what I needed. Perfect timing. My life was a gaping hole, a busted-up wall. Rick was the spackle. The new Sheetrock. He could make me all shiny and new. All I had to do was follow along. Listen to him. Believe him. I picked Rick because he was like Tucker. Rick saw me. He said all the right things. Did everything I needed.

Therapy had me asking these kinds of questions, and now as I pull in my driveway and look at the house I was so proud to own and move into to raise my family, I can hear the answer in my head.

Rick was just unfinished business. I'd never have a life with Tucker. I didn't heal an ounce from finding out he used me or realizing he'd ended his own life rather than face it. Rick was my way of latching onto the little bits I wasn't ready to let go of. And he was different. He wouldn't betray me the way Tucker did. I laugh at the thought.

Now it's different. I'm not a young woman with my little sister in tow wandering aimlessly through life with a destroyed heart. I'm a grown woman. I know how to make a life out of the ashes. I can survive this. I can do it completely on my own. Rick can't play the puppet master anymore. He can't decide my fate. My sanity.

"Hey, Mom," Bryson calls, his head buried in the fridge. I'd finally gotten things back on track from being away. There's plenty of fresh fruits and vegetables in there and even some meals I made ahead that Bryson could throw in the microwave for lunch now that he was doing school online to finish the year.

"Hey. You finished school already?" I try to keep my voice steady. I had the whole car ride home to get my shit together. To internalize the absolute betrayal my husband has orchestrated. I can swallow it down for the sake of my son.

"Yup. It's pretty easy when you don't have to add in all the drama and the extra crap teachers try to talk to you about. I'm actually way ahead. Maybe this online school is how I should do it next year too."

"Maybe." I shrug and start peeling an orange from the counter.

"Seriously? Dad said you'd never go for that."

"We need to do what works. I think you and I are going to have to figure a lot of things out in the near future. That might mean we have to be flexible on some stuff."

"That sounds ominous." He takes half the orange I offer him and props his elbows on the counter. "Are you starting to feel weird again? Maybe you should call the doctor."

"I'm doing really well, Bryson. I promise. The hospital helped me a lot. I didn't realize how much I was holding in."

"Why didn't you tell us about all the stuff you went through?" He fills his mouth with too much orange and I fight the urge to warn him about choking. He's not a little boy anymore. He's not my little boy anymore.

"You wouldn't want to hear it. Trust me. Living it was bad enough. It would change the way you see me. It would change everything."

Bryson rolls his eyes, not appreciating my deflection. "No offense, but don't you think everything kind of needs to change?"

I laugh mostly because he's right. "Some day you and I will talk all about it. Some might be hard to hear but I do want you to know who I really am."

His face falls as he finishes his half of the orange. "When you left those notes in my bag, were you really pissed off at me? Did you hate me?"

"I didn't leave those notes for you." I want to scream at the top of my lungs that Rick had done it. That this entire thing had been a chess match and I was losing. But Bryson idolizes his father and I am his messy-minded mother with problems. There would be no way to make a case for myself right now. No way to be believed. "I wasn't in my right state of mind," I correct. "It wasn't really me. But I am sorry if those notes bothered you."

"I just don't want you to think I'm some kind of jerk. Or that I deserve some like gothic retribution. We're not even religious. It was really weird."

"I don't think anything like that. Some day, I hope we can get to a place where this all makes sense and we can understand each other perfectly." The desire to scream the truth from the rooftops is strong. But I have to take a page from Rick's book. I have to be strategic. Calculated.

"What do we do until then?" Bryson holds out his hand and takes another quarter of my orange. I give it without hesitation. Part of me understands why Rick would do unspeakable and twisted things to protect our child. The other part of me realizes being capable of that psychopathic manipulation makes him dangerous beyond measure.

I'll help Bryson. We'll be safe. Life will be better. I just need to make sure Rick isn't a part of it.

THIRTY-EIGHT

ELIZABETH

"You seem a bit distant." Maggie offers her warm smile along with this assessment of me. I left Bayview and returned home a month ago and we meet twice a week. It's been two weeks since I found out what Rick did to send me here in the first place.

The hardest part has been going through the motions. Pretending I'm on this slow but steady healing journey. Lying in bed next to Rick acting as though I'm grateful he had me sent to Bayview. That I can see my life getting immeasurably better. Because he's getting what he wants, more control, he's easy to fool. But Maggie requires a more convincing conversation. I spend all my appointments saying what I know she wants to hear and pretending to make incremental progress toward a goal. Today I'm making a big change. It won't be the truth, but it's my next move.

"I feel a little distant," I admit sheepishly. "Things just don't feel right between Rick and I. I've let go of the misplaced anger about how he handled things when I was sick." I hate calling myself sick but I know it's part of the journey Maggie needs to see me on. "I understand now he was worried and doing what he could to protect me. But I think I've come to a place where I realize our relationship is not sustainable. Not because of what happened. That's just been the catalyst to some real introspection. What we have wasn't built from a healthy place and we're so enmeshed in each other that I can't heal this way. I don't know where I begin and he ends."

"That's a lot." Maggie keeps her face even while I deliver this bombshell. I'm using the buzzwords. Speaking her language. "Tell me more about those feelings."

"Rick and I had a very unbalanced relationship for years. He literally raised me. Parented me. We weren't a partnership. I think that put us both in a position to be something unhealthy to each other. I really want to explore my past and be able to get healthy again; I just don't see a way to do that unless I have some space from Rick."

"What does space mean to you?"

"Physical distance. A break in communication." I shrug as though I haven't practiced this conversation a hundred times in my head.

"That seems like a rather seismic change to your life. It can be difficult to refrain from being impulsive when doing this work. I want to caution you about that but also support your feelings."

"I don't think I've been transparent enough about my relationship with Rick with you." I look away as though this embarrasses me. Like I feel bad for hiding this from her. "I've really only begun accepting some of it myself recently. I needed Rick to be infallible and perfect because he's the reason I have the life I do. I would be nothing without him. It never felt right to talk negatively about him. It would be..."

"Ungrateful?"

"Yes." I snap my fingers as if she's brilliant. "Rick dominates our lives. Decisions. Preferences. Plans. I don't really have a voice. I never have. Now I don't blame him for this, I was so young when we met, we were raising Jules, and then Bryson came along quickly. I was in survival mode before we met and didn't have a chance to process any of it. I told you the man I was dating before him died by suicide."

"Yes. And he was older too? A lawyer?"

"He was. Looking back, it's all convoluted. I wasn't ready to be in another relationship. I certainly wasn't ready to be married or have a child. It was all too much and I shut down. That meant Rick had to take over and I think he's been in control ever since."

"Control? What does he control exactly?"

"Everything. I relied on him to literally raise me. Fix me. He controls the money. Our vacations. What field I went into. What school I went to. Where I worked. What we do and when. I'm embarrassed to say I didn't notice it for a long time, and then when I did it was too late. Rick is not willing to change. And it's probably unfair to ask him to."

"How do you know he's not willing to adjust the state of your relationship to give you what you need to move forward?"

"Years of experience with him." I chuckle and feel relieved when Maggie smiles and nods. "I've also asked him directly. I've told him that I want some space to make more independent decisions. Even small ones that are mostly just preference. He's been inflexible. I asked if he would consider coming to some of our sessions and he said no. These are my problems and he's not going to change everything about himself to make me happy. I mean, it's just too much. From the way I cut my hair to how I park in the driveway. There are just rules for everything. I can't live like that. And he can't seem to stop."

"That must have been difficult to hear. When we tell our partners what we need and they aren't receptive it can be very challenging."

"Actually I felt kind of relieved. Him not wanting to change makes the idea of moving on from him seem a little easier. Even like it's the right thing to do. I don't know if it's forever but I do know that it's what I need now. There's only one thing holding me back."

"Bryson?"

"Yes, I can't imagine being away from him right now. He's got so much on his plate and we realize how much he was struggling even before this. Risky behaviors. Lying. The last thing he needs is to be in the middle of a separation that has him picking sides."

"That would definitely be challenging, but he also needs a healthy mother. If you think that some of that healing needs to take place outside of your relationship with Rick, then that has to be considered."

"The affairs have been tough too." I drop my head and bring my hand up to my cheek.

"Affairs?" Maggie looks more than confused. She's worried. Am I making things up again? Are these delusions?

"I've known for a while. I never let it bother me but now, all things considered, it just makes some of my other choices a bit easier." This is not a lie but not something I can prove either. Rick is too smart to be caught having an affair. There will never be lipstick on his collar or a stray hotel receipt. But I've felt the shift before. The difference in his touch. The way he handles his phone more privately. There's a jumpiness that I know ties back to some scandalous rendezvous or flirtatious message. I've never dug deeper, because I never wanted to know. I needed Rick to be better than Tucker. I'd built my life on that truth.

"You never mentioned Rick having affairs before." Maggie looks pensive.

"I know. I'm not sure why I've been so embarrassed about it considering the other things we talked about in here. But that all focused on the past. This feels very here and now. I just didn't want to look like someone who couldn't keep my husband satisfied in my marriage."

"Being satisfied doesn't tend to equal fidelity. But this is an important layer we should be evaluating."

"I think I'm going to talk to him this week. He'll probably freak out, but I feel like I know what I need."

"What do you mean when you say freak out? Expand on that a little." She jots down a few notes. That's good. Get it in writing.

I look away, intentionally not meeting her worried expression. "I just know he'll be very upset with the idea of his life changing so dramatically. He also won't see it coming, which I will agree is unfair to him, but it's certainly not something I'm doing lightly. Maybe just a conversation will give us a starting point. Some sort of catalyst." These are words I know Maggie will love. I've been very insightful and reflective at our last few sessions. Calm. Open. I'd almost forgotten how adept I was at this. I'd mostly used my powers for good in adulthood. It was no longer about manipulating people into getting what I wanted, but instead reading and understanding them so we could connect and I could help them. Now I'm back to my old ways. Rick can't be the only one pulling the strings.

"I think you're on the right track." Maggie beams with pride. I feel bad she thinks she's fixed me. I'm doing what I always used to do. I'm fixing myself. I'm going to save the people I love from the people who don't know how to love. That's my super power. I can fix this.

THIRTY-NINE

ELIZABETH

Jules is pacing. I want to scream at her to settle down but I instead try to repeat the plan in my head again and again. It will work. I know it will. It's just crazy enough to accomplish what we need.

"This is insane," she whispers, her lip quivering with emotion. "We can't really do this."

"Tell me another way. We know that Rick threatened Daisy's life. Bribed her. Had me followed and painted as insane. He manipulated you. He's dangerous. I know we love him but two things can be true. I never let you see that when you were little. One wonderful thing and one terrible thing can take up the exact same space."

Jules is reluctant to accept the reality. "Rick has always been so amazing to us. He's a good father. Maybe he was just feeling desperate trying to protect Bryson and he screwed up. If we do this, he'll be disbarred. His career will be over. Your marriage will be over."

"My career is over." My hushed voice is angry and I can see Jules recoil. "This was my marriage too, but it isn't me ending it, it was his choices that brought us here. Threatening Daisy was not some screw-up. It was unconscionable."

"Is this revenge? If you're just trying to make him pay for hurting you then I can't do this. We can still go to the police."

"A couple of hysterical women plagued by mental illness and loyal to each other. We won't be believed. You know that. We love Bryson," I remind her coolly. "He's going to need us. And I need to get my son away from a man willing to do all those terrible things."

Jules doesn't answer but I know that's the best she can offer in the way of agreement. Her silence is the complicity I need from her.

I remind her of her role. "You'll need to be convincing. He's pulling in now. Go take the trash out back." I gesture to the full bag of trash I made sure was left for this very moment. When she doesn't move, I point again.

When she's finally in motion I know we're on a knife's edge. All of this could implode. If Jules isn't solid, I can't pull this off. Nothing about me right now is dependable enough to believe. I need her credibility.

Rick is reaching for his briefcase and straightening his tie as he steps out of his car. Searching my heart I try to remind myself of the things he's done wrong and not all the things he's done right. Because the charitable decisions he made toward me and Jules were still rooted in his own selfishness. His own seeking of power over us. I block out the memory of the look on his face when he held Bryson just moments after he was born. I stop myself from the old images of endless lessons on riding a bike, or the long talks we used to all have around the fire pit in the backyard. The anniversary gifts. The beach vacations. The nights of passion. The long drives as his passenger. I think only of the expression he must have held while threatening Daisy. The way he placed horrible notes in our son's bag to make me look insane. How he knew those police were coming and feigned shock and awe when they took me away.

When he comes through the door, I slam it wildly behind him. The glass rattles and he lunges forward, clutching his chest and looking stunned.

"What the hell, Elizabeth?" He tosses his briefcase down on the ground and I wind up as hard as I can and kick it across the room. It crashes against a row of crystal glasses and sends them smashing against the floor.

"Stop," I scream. "Rick, don't."

With his mouth agape and his eyes wide he searches for something that might make sense. Before he can ask another question, I scream again and shove him as hard as I can as many times as I can until he gathers my wrists into his hands and backs me to the fridge.

"What's wrong with you?" His voice booms and his cheeks flush with what looks like anger but I know is fear. I fight against his tight grip, crying and begging him to let me go. Turning my head, I lean and bite his thumb so hard he yelps and instinctually slams me against the wall until I release his skin from my teeth.

All at once it falls into place. Jules runs back in from the yard. Bryson's heavy feet come down the hall. Jules slaps and screams at a confused and downright scared Rick, demanding he let me go just as Bryson rounds the corner to see it all.

"Dad," he yells, and I realize how deep and manly his voice is now. "Let her go!"

"I'm calling the police," Jules announces as Rick loosens his grip and I slink down to the floor in a heap.

"What the hell, Dad?" Bryson asks, his voice finally cracking with emotion.

"It's okay." I'm panting and hugging my arms around myself. "Bryson, he didn't mean it. Everything is going to be okay."

"He didn't mean it?" Jules asks, playing her part beautifully. "I heard what he said to you. I saw what he was doing."

"She went crazy," Rick sputters out, each syllable less convincing than the last.

"Bullshit," Jules shrieks. "You've already played that game. I heard it all. You didn't like what she had to say and you lost it. You want everything your way or else. Get outside right now. The police are coming."

I stand with some help from Jules and move toward Bryson.

"We're going to be fine." This finally feels true when the blue lights come streaking down our street. I'd thought that the only way I could ever really have a life that mattered was to be with a man. A man like Tucker or Rick. Now I think maybe the only way to do it is to make sure I'm as far away from them as possible.

FORTY

ELIZABETH

The reports were quickly taken and compared, Rick's the only one that didn't add up. Maggie with all her credible degrees and fancy words was called and consulted, giving me a glowing assessment and confirming, with my permission to disclose it, that I'd planned to talk to Rick about a separation. She used my words. Parroting back that I was worried he'd freak out. And it looks as though he did.

The guilt of ambushing him subsides when Bryson leans his head on my shoulder. I feel for him. The world he once knew is gone and the rosy picture he's always had of Rick is tarnished. But Rick brought that on himself with the hubris to think he could manipulate this situation and bend people to his will.

We're in the living room. Rick's bail won't be set until Monday. We'll have a couple of days of not having to worry about him.

I'm not sure if Rick pieced it together. He doesn't know how much I know. But what I'm certain about is that any man willing to write threatening notes to his son to frame his wife is a dangerous one. Any man who will have his wife followed and manipulate the police to the point of portraying her as paranoid will stop at nothing to have his way. I was locked away from my son for more than two weeks while he pulled the strings attached to every puppet he could find. I won't wait around to see how angry he is on the other side of his arrest.

"We need to pack a bag in the morning. We can't stay here." I report this somberly to Bryson.

"Why?" He doesn't lift his head up to ask this question. He's too tired. "There is a protective order. Dad won't come here, and if he does—"

I cut him off. "It will never be your job to protect me from your father. Or anyone else. But a piece of paper from a judge doesn't keep people safe. Trust me. You, me, and Jules need to leave for a while. We've got plenty of money in the bank. You're doing online school since it turned into a rumor factory and this chaos made it impossible for you to go and have a normal learning experience there. We'll just spend the end of the school year and summer at the beach somewhere and regroup."

I feel him nod in agreement. Shockingly he doesn't argue about how he'll miss home and his friends. He doesn't fight me at all.

But he does have a question. "Can you and Jules finally tell me about your family? About all the things that happened and who you were back then. I really want to know."

"Why?" The answer to this question is surprisingly important to me. No one has ever really given me a reply that made sense. It's usually morbid curiosity.

"Because I want some of this to make sense. I need to know who you were and how all of this happened. There are just too many secrets, and I can't take it."

That was an answer I could work with. He deserved more than I'd given him. "I promise. Once we get out of here, I'll explain everything."

I consider telling Bryson the full truth. What his father did and how I had to find a way to stop him. But we're not there yet.

He needs to see what I allow him to and nothing more. Because the part of the equation I can't solve is his part in it. His night with Daisy. What she thought she remembered. I know he's innocent, but I know she's hurting. As we've come to say too often now, both can be true.

Jules comes in with a black duffle bag on her arm and two puffy black bags of the same color under her eyes. She's exhausted. I forgot how easy I'd made her life. How unfamiliar this territory is for her. She never had to bob and weave her way through precarious situations with grown men to get an outcome she wanted.

"I need to go out for a little bit." I announce this as I gently move Bryson's head from my shoulder. "There is something I need to do before we go."

"It's getting late," Jules worries out loud. "Can it wait until tomorrow?"

"No, I want to make sure I get this done tonight. Bryson, head up to your room and pack some bags. Stuff for the beach."

"I'll go with you. Where are you going?"

"You have to pack, and I need to do this alone." I pat his shoulder and send him on his way.

He slinks off like a zombie drawn in a certain direction with no real thought.

"I know where you're going," Jules whispers accusingly. "You shouldn't talk to her again. Not yet. We need to just go tomorrow and let the rest play out without us."

"The rest that plays out might be Rick taking it out on Daisy when he can't find us. It's completely out of character for him to be violent, but I'm not taking anything for granted now. He's desperate. Things have escalated so much. Even if that's never been who he was before, I can't gamble Daisy's safety on that. I need to warn her about what's happened. She risked a lot to tell me the truth. I owe her this. I can give her a head start if she wants to get out of here too. She's already got money from Rick.

I can give her a little more if she needs it. Cash from the safe. No paper trail."

"Take my coat," Jules insists, slipping out of her jean jacket and handing it over.

"It's not even cold." I don't reach my arm out for it but she just shoves it at me.

"It's supposed to get cool tonight. Plus it looks cute on you." She smiles but I can see the corners of her mouth fighting to stay up. I have worn these people out. But we will rest. We will be safe soon enough. I just need to make sure Daisy is too. I'll never be able to live with myself if I don't.

I use the burner phone Jules picked up to text Daisy. She was smart about those kinds of things. I hadn't even thought to grab a phone like this. I'll ditch it later. We're meeting at the running track by Myers Park. It's close by the house so I won't have to be gone from Bryson too long. We'll do some laps and look like regular people chatting away.

Pulling into the park I see her hunched on the bleachers looking pathetic. I wonder if I am like radiation. Just poisoning everyone in my orbit. Am I the problem here? If I was going back to see Maggie, I'd ask her this. Am I the source of all of this exhaustion and misery? The common denominator? She'd tell me no, but I'd still wonder.

"Want to walk some laps?" I ask, painting on a warm smile. I'm about to uproot her life again. She has no one. It's foolish to believe some cash in her pocket is enough to really be okay. She's a child. She's alone.

I have a flash of a future that is a dream, morphing into a nightmare. A crazy thought that just can't happen, but I must consider. I could take her with us. Save her. Protect her. Make her my own. But for the horrible fact that she thinks Bryson might have harmed her. I could convince her it's not true. Maybe dig in enough to find out who did take advantage of her and show her the truth. But there isn't enough time and the biology that binds me to my son is strong. I choose him.

We're halfway around the track before Daisy speaks. I assume she's either heard what happened with Rick or she feels the tension building in me. She's tentative and scared.

"Why did you want to meet?"

"Rick was arrested," I say flatly. "Not for anything to do with you. I haven't told anyone what you told me. It was a separate incident."

"The whole school was talking about that too." She's looking down at her shoes as we walk at a snail's pace around the empty track. "He beat you up?"

"Not exactly. I had to make it look like he had."

"I wasn't sure how you were going to do it, but you did. It was faster than I thought it would be." She smiles but only for a second. "You really screwed him over. I'm impressed. You did the rest of the hard work for me."

"I, um..." Her words confuse me, as does her odd facial expression.

"You imploded the rest of your life. I didn't give you enough credit. You're exactly the manipulative bitch I thought you were. But you work quicker than I imagined."

"Bitch?" I ask, stopping in my tracks and looking at Daisy full on for the first time since we began walking. There are no tears in her eyes. No worry on her brow. She's happy. Thrilled.

"It feels really good to see a plan come together. I worked hard for this. Now you're out of a job. Your husband will get disbarred. Your son will be all screwed up. This worked out really well. The last part will be my favorite, though."

"Daisy, what are you talking about? Are you all right?" I feel that old worry that maybe my mind is broken and can't be trusted.

"I had a really good life before I moved here. I lived in California. You know that, right?"

"Yeah, I think you told me..."

"We had a lot of money. I was popular at my school. Things weren't perfect but I was getting by just fine. My mother was a drug addict. Not the street junkie that might come to mind. The soccer mom kind. A little sloppy in car pool. Someone who seemed like she just loved a few too many mimosas at brunch. For most of my life, she managed okay. I just always assumed my dad's death messed her up."

"Daisy, what does this have to do with anything?" I feel the words catching in my throat as I desperately try to make sense of the shift in her body language.

"That was very clever what you did to Rick. You're out here framing him for assault. Real nice. I guess that tracks with your reputation though."

"You said he was following you. Threatening you. That he bribed you into staying quiet about you setting me up. I thought—"

"I did set you up." She claps her hands excitedly. "But Rick didn't do any of those things to me. And Bryson, doubting his chivalry. I couldn't tell if you believed what I said about him or not. I only talked to him for like ten minutes. Long enough to make sure someone caught us on video talking. I needed you to have some kind of proof. You chased it down so quick. You're like a dog with a bone. I thought I'd have to find a way to get you to see the video, but you did it all on your own.'

"I never believed Bryson did that." This feels utterly important suddenly, even though part of me could believe this scenario. I'm sick at the idea but it's true. I'd seen enough in the world to know anyone at any time could surprise you in the worst way.

"Good, because he's the only one I feel bad for in all this. He was a complete gentleman that night. A good kid."

"Then why did you tell me he raped you?" I bite this question out between gritted teeth. It feels like the start of this entire thing. The cannon moment that ruined us all.

"I needed you to lose your mind. It's a really important part of trying to distort reality. You know that. Ruining someone's credibility is the best way to make sure no one believes anything they say. Once people thought you were a creepy stalker teacher who lost her mind, it was very easy to put everything else in motion. Is there really anything worse than a mother who would make up an accusation about her own son? You made yourself way too easy a target."

I'm embarrassed how long it's taking for her words to reach my brain. I think of screaming. Of charging back to my car, but I know this runs deeper and I need to know what kind of hell she's thrust me into.

"Once my mom overdosed and my grandfather's Alzheimer's got too bad for him to be my guardian, I was going to be put into the system, unless there was someone in my family that was willing to take me. My dad's mother lived in some shitty trailer about two hours from here. I took her and the little bit of money I could scrape up and got the only apartment I could afford in your school district. I wasn't too excited about the move but getting closer to you was what mattered."

"Me? Why did you come here?"

"Because you killed my father. And you ruined my life. The only thing I could do was come ruin yours. You made it way too simple. I could see right away what your downfall would be. You can't help but help. Even when it gets you in trouble. Even when it takes more than you have to give. All I needed to do to get you to fall for my shit was convince you that you could save me." She chuckles and reaches her hand into her pocket. I don't even consider she might be pulling out something dangerous until I see the knife.

"Daisy, what the hell are you doing? I don't know who your father was."

"Yes, you do. You seduced him. Ruined his marriage and then killed him."

It's alarming how many troubling scenarios I need to run through in my mind to try to figure out what she's talking about. I had done some shady shit to get by. There were lots of married men who'd crossed my path. But they were the villains, not me.

"Who?" I demand, my eyes fixed on the shiny blade of the knife.

"Tucker Rutherford. He was your lawyer when you were trying to get custody of Jules. I was just a baby. He was married but none of that stopped you. You wanted him and you played all your games until you got him."

"You're Tucker's daughter?" If they share any features, I've suppressed his memory too deeply to see it. "I didn't kill your father. He died by suicide. And our relationship was not—"

"You have no idea. See, one night when my mother was about as high as someone can get without dying, she told me. My father was the love of her life and one day she'd found a letter he'd written. A love letter. It was to you. My mother was devastated. She confronted him and he jumped off that hotel balcony just to hide what you'd done to his life. He was gone and it was all because of you."

"I don't know what you think happened between your father and I but—"

"That's what happened. She told me. And we moved to California with my grandparents. For a little while I guess she was okay, but after my grandmother died of cancer my mother just snapped. Started taking drugs. Falling apart. But my grandfather held it together for me. That was until his memory started to go. It was my fifteenth birthday, a month after my mother told me what had really happened to my father, that she overdosed and died on our kitchen floor."

"I am so sorry that happened. But your father was not in love with me. He had a bunch of girls my age at the time that he was sleeping with. I spoke to many of them after he died. This was not about him being in love with anyone. I was your age. I didn't know what I was doing. I thought he loved me, but he didn't." The words are spilling out of me like marbles from a jar, rolling in all the wrong directions. I look down again at the knife clutched in her hand. Knuckles white. Face determined.

"You knew about me. He had a child. You knew he was married. You are such a liar. I read his note to you. My mother had it in her paperwork after she died. That's how I knew how to find you. He wrote you a love note. A damn proposal to start a life together once he could break it to my mother. You did this."

My hands are up on my head as I try to piece together the madness. "You got close to me? Accused my son of assaulting you and then made me look insane by going to the police. Rick never threatened you or made you turn on me?"

"You got it." She smiles hysterically. "The most fun was making you think it was your husband pulling the strings. That part I didn't really plan ahead but once I thought about it, it just felt right. He deserves the hell he's going to get."

"What does he have to do with this?"

"God, you don't know about him, do you?"

"Know what?" I'm gasping out words, trying to make sense of the past and present crashing together.

"You'll see. That car that was following you, Rick really did set that up. I think he knew more about your every move than you think. He's arrogant enough to believe he can hide anything he wants. Prison would be good for him. You should try to keep him there."

She's lost her mind. She has no idea what the truth really is. I try to get the words out to bring her back to reality.

"I promise you that if you let me explain, you'll see that I did not do anything to your father. You said it yourself, he jumped. I had nothing to do with his death."

"You know better than that. Your life has had enough dominos pushed over to realize that the first one, the catalyst, is really the problem. You were the first domino to fall in my parents' life."

"The knife?" I ask, not even able to form a full sentence.

"I'm going to kill you." She says this with the casual tone of someone talking about heading out for an errand. "People will believe you lured me here. Your husband's assault sent you into another psychotic break. Your obsession with me still front and center. We came out here and you attacked me. This knife is from your kitchen. That's pretty clever, huh? I put those notes in your son's bag and grabbed this while I was there."

"You were in my house?" It seems suddenly important as I think of how close to Bryson she'd been all this time. How, if she does kill me, he'll never know the truth. "The notes, how did you know I used to write things like that?"

"My mother had your journal. She was ironically pretty obsessed with you after finding that letter my dad had written to you. She stole things from your apartment when you were out. Had a whole box of your stuff. Your diary was creepy as hell. You needed some serious help. But it made writing those notes more authentic. I have to know, did you wonder for a minute if you actually wrote them? Did you think you were really crazy?"

My eyes stay mostly fixed on the knife. Daisy and I are about the same size but the knife adds an element I can't compete with easily. "I questioned my sanity. I suffered. If you wanted to make me pay, you have. I'll never be able to teach again. I've ruined my marriage. My son, he'll never be the same. You've ruined me."

"It's not enough. When I dream, I see my father and mother together. She's healthy. He's happy. I'll never have that. I'm living in that nasty apartment with my miserable grandmother watching my life disintegrate in front of me. Once people know that you lured me into the woods and nearly killed me, my life will change. I can sell the story to someone. That would be great. I'll be rich."

"People won't believe—"

"They will. You know they will. I'll be very convincing."

"Jules knows. She knows I wasn't really crazy or obsessed with you."

"Great, let her be your insane sister who tries to tell the world her own weird version of the story. Maybe they'll decide she's too crazy to end up as a guardian of Bryson. He'll really be alone then."

"Rick will figure out—"

"Rick will rot in prison. I'll make sure of that too."

"How? He won't sit in there quietly. He'll fight."

"Trust me, he'll stay in prison." She leans in closer to me and winks. I can't figure out what she's thinking. Rick won't sit in prison. He's too smart for that. Too dogged and powerful. Her wink unsettles me, but I try to hold onto the bits of the truth I know for sure. Rick will fight and she's underestimating him.

I can try to outrun her. That's my only shot. If I'm out of her reach, the knife doesn't matter. She's young and fast; if I cut back across the track toward my car, she'll catch me. My best option is the woods. Losing her in there now that it's dark.

"You need to stop this," I demand, using my best teacher voice, hoping to rattle her. "Look at what you've done." I point because I know it's nearly impossible for her not to turn and look. It's human nature. When she does, I bolt in the direction of the woods and let the tiny branches slap against my face freely. The vines try to grab my ankles but I fight through. I run for my life.

It doesn't matter though. Daisy is fueled by something impossibly fierce. Something I have let dominate my life many times before. She hates me. I am the reason she's alone in this world. There would be nowhere I could hide where her hate couldn't find me.

She's on my back pulling me down to the dirt as I scream for my life. The knife is in the air, the silver blade catching the light of the nearly set sun. I wish this was the first time I'd been chased with the intent of being killed. It's not. But I hope with every beat of my heart, that these woods will not be where I die. I've survived so much. I need to fight.

FORTY-ONE

ELIZABETH

Then

The soles of my bare feet are numb, and the uneven pavement beneath them is as volatile as a minefield. I run blindly, not knowing where I'm headed but fully aware that I need to get as far away as possible. My heart pounding in my chest is a frantic beat that seems to match the rhythm of my thudding footsteps.

Whizzing by me in the dark city streets, I see the familiar sights of urban life. The tall buildings and streetlights loom overhead like giants, casting shadows across my path. I catch glimpses of storefronts and restaurants, their neon signs flashing in the darkness. I could run inside and beg for help, but there is no guarantee in the disheveled state I'm in anyone would give me refuge. The city is full of this kind of chaos and I'd be playing the sympathy lottery if I ducked into a store and told them I was being chased by a grown man. Some might usher me into the back and hide me away. But others would shoo me outside, unwilling to get involved in my situation. I can't take that risk. I'd lose the little advantage of distance between me and him.

I told myself I wouldn't do this again. I have custody of Jules now. That was the goal. My life was together and I'd never let it fall apart again. But it's in pieces. Job gone. Housing gone. The man I thought I'd love forever, gone. And even worse, the image I had of him has died too. I always knew better than to trust someone that deeply and now I'm right back where I started. Running for my life, for a little bit of money to buy just enough to keep Jules and I fed.

The man who's chasing me is getting closer with every passing moment, his heavy breathing and angry shouts filling my ears. "Give me back my wallet!" His voice is laced with accusation and I can hear the desperation, the kind of despair that makes people do irrational things. I'm hoping this burst of unexpected exercise gives him a heart attack. That's about the only thing that could save me now.

He's very concerned about the fact that I've swiped his wallet from his nightstand but not with the fact that he was the one who'd brought me to his room in the first place. Now he's probably thinking of his job being at risk. Of his wife finding out. There is irony in his anger, but I don't think he'd listen long enough for me to explain it. With a skid and a quick turn of my body, I dart down an alleyway, hoping to lose him in the maze of streets. I don't let my mind wander to what he'll do if his meaty hands get ahold of me. It's not worth imagining. If I was smart, I'd ditch his wallet. Do away with the evidence. But I'd taken all this risk for the cash I desperately need. I'm not willing to lose it now. As I crouch behind a dumpster, the smell of garbage and decay assaults my senses.

The air is thick with the stench of rotting food and other junk, making me want to retch. Will he kill me? Will he just leave me out here to rot with the other unwanted things?

Every movie, all the books I've read, they have these heroes. And though I am frequently in distress, I am no damsel. There is no knight on horseback about to fight for my life. I tried that and failed. All the men I know are either obviously people to fear or just good at hiding the fact that they're dangerous. I prefer the first kind. The obvious ones. Fewer surprises. Fewer letdowns.

I try to catch my breath and hold it all at once. I don't want to take in more of these putrid smells than I have to or give away my hiding spot by making too much noise.

The sound of approaching footsteps stops my heart. Squeezing my eyes closed I pretend to be somewhere else. The pain in my feet and the smell in the air make that difficult, but I try to conjure up some peaceful place to transport myself to. Leaving my body is the only kind of escape I've ever found.

The clapping of the man's footsteps grows louder, and I can feel my body tensing up, preparing for a fight. It's laughable. I'll be no match, and I've been foolish enough to run myself into a corner, limiting my exits. It was dumb, but fear has that effect.

The image of a beach fills my mind. I've never had one of those magic family days out on the shore. There were never any sand toys or boogie boards. No chairs lugged out from the car or even sandy towels to dry off with. The only time I'd been to the beach was when I'd scratched together the money to stay on the bus long enough to make it there. I'd walked the shore as the waves came in and sat to stare out at the horizon. I'm there now. The salt in the air. The waves at my feet. I am free of this alley and this man.

I just have to be small and quiet. And maybe I'll survive.

When his hand clamps down on my shoulder and yanks me up to my feet I know I won't be able to break free again. I have no power. Some day, I'll be in a fight I can win, because I won't be alone anymore. Some day.

FORTY-TWO

ELIZABETH

Now

When it seems imminent that my life is over, the knife against my skin, I first see the beach. The place I used to go in my mind when my life hung in the balance. Then I see Jules. Her little eyes staring at me with relief when she saw I'd brought food. I see Bryson, the boy who didn't hurt Daisy. The one I knew was good and righteous. I see myself. The little girl with bruised legs and an empty stomach. The warrior who always found a way to survive. I hear her calling my name. Begging me to keep fighting.

The knife plunges downward as a flash of a white shirt emerges from the brush around us and Daisy is knocked off me with force. She rolls, screeches and then lies still, crumpled in on herself.

"Mom," Bryson gasps breathlessly as he gets back to his feet. "Are you hurt?"

"No," I answer, not even sure if that's true. I scurry to my feet and clutch Bryson, in this weird paradox of wanting to protect him but knowing he's the more capable one at the moment.

"How did you find me?" I wonder if he's real. If any of this is. Maybe I'm dead and he's just here to bring me some peace. One last look at the boy I love.

"We all share locations on our phones," he reminds me. "Jules fell asleep downstairs and I thought you were just here walking the track, trying to clear your head. I was going to surprise you. I jogged over. Thought we could walk and talk a little. Then I saw your phone went in the woods and it freaked me out. I heard you scream."

Daisy stirs with a moan.

"We need to run," I beg him, pulling at his sleeve, but he doesn't move.

"Daisy?" he asks, inching toward her. She groans and rolls over, the knife plunged into her abdomen, blood spreading through the fibers of her shirt.

"No," I cry, falling next to her. "Call the police. Tell them we need an ambulance. We need to get the bleeding to stop."

"She tried to kill you," Bryson says, shock clouding his mind and making his words sound far-off and small.

"We need to save her life," I shout, gesturing for his shirt so I can stop the bleeding. "Give that to me so I can put pressure on this. Call for help."

Yanking at his shirt, he tosses it to me. "I'm calling the police. Is she going to be okay? Why would she want to hurt you? You're still going to save her?"

His sweet mind thinks it is some kind of righteous morality that has me trying to keep Daisy alive. Some duty to a student. It is the truth she holds that I cannot allow to die with her. If Bryson and I are out here in the woods with this dead girl, I will never be able to convince anyone of the truth. Even if I could make the connection between me and Tucker all those years ago, who would believe sweet Daisy was out for vengeance? I can't let her die. Because if she does, our lives are really over.

FORTY-THREE

ELIZABETH

"She's in surgery now," the nurse reports as Detective Cole approaches. "We'll update when we know more." He taps the nurses' station desk as a thank you and turns his attention back toward me.

"What the hell happened?" He's fuming. I've made his night worse with yet another messy situation. "You know what, don't answer that. I need to read you your rights and take you to the station."

"She didn't do anything," Bryson shouts, standing between us. "I am telling you, when I got there, Daisy was on top of my mom about to stab her. I shoved her away as hard as I could and she went flying. She rolled over on the knife. It was an accident."

"Kid, I'm not ready to talk to you on this. Another detective will be by shortly. It's your mom that needs to explain why she was out in the woods at night with a student she was supposed to have no contact with."

"I can't explain it." I bury my face in my hands. "It's a very long story."

"Did you ask her to meet you out there?" Cole questions, obviously feeling like it's pretty straightforward. "I see a text message on her phone that was picked up at the scene. Looks like it was from a burner phone. Was that you?"

"Yes."

"So you ignored the fact that you were not supposed to see her and told her to meet you at the track? I'm supposed to believe she was the aggressor?"

"I thought she was in danger."

"Of course you did." He shakes his head, annoyed by how my apparent mental illness is ruining his night. "You were the danger. I'm going to get to the bottom of this. That knife, you brought it from your kitchen?"

"It's from my kitchen, but I didn't bring it." The truth does not feel as though it will set me free right now.

"Elizabeth Meadows, you're under arrest for—"

"Wait," Jules calls as she practically pushes her way through the too slow automatic doors. "Please stop."

"Ma'am, I understand this has been a difficult time for your family but I've got a girl with a serious stab wound in surgery right now. No clue if she's going to make it. We're going to the station."

"Elizabeth," Jules says breathlessly as she ignores Cole. "Bryson called me and told me what happened. Did Daisy incriminate herself? Did she say why she wanted to hurt you?"

"It doesn't matter." I put my arms behind my back for the handcuffs, but she tugs me away.

"Excuse me," Cole barks.

"What did Daisy say?" Jules is demanding an answer as though it would matter. It's her words against mine and at this point Daisy has far more credibility than I do.

"She thinks I ruined her life. That both her parents are dead because of me. This was revenge. She's Tucker's daughter. Do you remember Tucker? Daisy planned it quite brilliantly."

"Tucker's daughter?" Her eyes are worried and shocked. I wasn't sure if she even remembered Tucker, but clearly she does. That whole thing felt like a lifetime ago. Jules so little and painfully unaware of how bad things had gotten. Now the expression on her face makes me wonder if she remembers more about that than she lets on. "Daisy said all that to you?"

"Yes. But it doesn't matter. She'll never admit it, even if she does recover. It's over. And maybe I deserve this for all the shit I've done. I've hurt plenty of people too and—"

"Give me my coat." Jules can't even seem to hear what I'm saying as she strips the jean jacket roughly off my body.

"What the hell is going on?" Cole demands impatiently. "She's under arrest."

Jules pulls back the seam of her coat and reveals a small device with a wire on the end. Pulling it out, she sighs with relief. "If this thing recorded correctly then you'll know that Elizabeth is telling the truth."

"Recorded?" Cole asks, balling his hand into a fist. He's tired of us. I can't even blame him at this point. "Why was she recording a conversation with Daisy?"

"She wasn't. I was. I knew she was going to meet Daisy and I had my reasons for doing it."

"What were the reasons?" Cole is not taking anyone's word for anything right now as Jules grabs a small device from her bag and plugs in the recording piece.

"I had no idea Daisy was playing games and orchestrating all this shit. I thought she had relevant information that she wasn't willing to talk to the police about. Information that could protect my sister in the future. I understood that Daisy didn't feel safe enough to go on record, but I needed to document it all just in case. In case someone wanted to call Elizabeth crazy again or try to take Bryson. If we had Daisy on a recording saying that Rick extorted her into changing her story, it could protect Elizabeth."

She clicks a few more buttons and then holds the device up. Cole leans in and the voices come alive. My voice. Daisy's. Our argument. Her explanation. The talk of the knife. The notes. The family. The plan. All of it.

"Son of a bitch." Cole grabs his cell phone and puts it to his ear. "I need a sergeant to my location as soon as possible. We've got some real serious bullshit to sift through. And get Laurence down here too. He'll be glad to find out he was right."

"Officer Laurence?" I ask, remembering his kind face and gentle instructions as I was carted off to Bayview. "What was he right about?"

"He believed you. Didn't think you were crazy. His radar was going off, but I told him this one was cut and dry. A whacky teacher who went off the deep end. Guess there was more to the story."

"My husband," I choke out the words and look somberly at my son. "He didn't attack me. I set him up. Daisy played us against each other and I fell for it. I thought he was dangerous and I needed to get him away from Bryson."

"Mom, you..." Bryson's world is crashing in around him. The kid was just trying to screw around and be a teenager. Throw a party while his parents were away. He's the one who's supposed to be messing up and needing forgiveness. But all of us are the ones in trouble.

I know I can't make it right with words, but I ache for his pain. I plead with Cole. "I'm sorry. And I'll face whatever consequences I need to for that. For any of this. I just want my husband out and home with my son. They need each other."

"They need you too," Jules cut in. "You did what you thought was best."

"I'm starting to realize maybe I'm not crazy, but I'm not where I need to be either. The only reason Daisy was able to hurt me and my family is because I let my past corrupt my judgment. I should have reported any concerns I had about her and her situation. I should have listened to Rick and his logic. I gave her money like that was some kind of ethical solution. You can't paint someone as crazy unless they hand you the brush. I've got to sort that out." I turn back to Cole, whose head is clearly still spinning. "Can you please do what you can to get Rick out and home with Bryson? You can hear on that recording that he was not in any way involved in any of this."

Cole nods and goes to make another phone call. I pull out my phone and give Bryson a long look. He's floored. Confused. Scared.

"Even after you have the whole story it'll still hurt." I kiss his cheek. "Stay with Aunt Jules until Dad gets home. Everything will turn out okay. I promise."

"Where are you going?" He doesn't ask me to stay and I understand why. He's just begun to realize that Daisy might be the villain in all of this, but that maybe I'm the villain in other people's stories.

"I'm going to call Maggie." I correct myself. We need to be more formal now. "Dr. Harlow. I think it's best for all of us if I do that now. I've got to get my head right."

"I've got him," Jules says, squeezing Bryson's shoulder. It's funny, she looks so capable these days. She's the one saving the day this time. I know she'll say the right things to my son tonight. I know that she's the reason I'm not in handcuffs right now. For the first time, I feel like maybe I can be weak, because she knows how to be strong.

I step out to the front of the hospital and dial Dr. Harlow. I don't wonder what she'll think of this wild tail or my role in it. I'm not concerned with the fact that she'll find out I played her. Lied to her. Manipulated her. I should be worried about that. Embarrassed by it. But I know she'll welcome me into her office again. She'll understand even if she doesn't agree. Because Dr.

Harlow sees something in me I've never been able to see in myself. A whole person. Complete. Fully formed. I am finally starting to see myself the same way. I'll go back, not because she'll begrudgingly take me, but because she'll be proud I chose to. I've been waiting so long for someone to show up for me. And she's reminding me, I can show up for myself.

FORTY-FOUR

ELIZABETH

"You didn't kill her father." Dr. Harlow puts her pen firmly down on her notebook and leans in close to me. "You aren't responsible for his death in any way. You were a child. He was a grown man. He chose to take his life. His wife was a grown woman. She chose not to seek help for her addiction. You weren't the one who told her about the affair or tried to ruin her marriage."

"I just feel like I should have never gotten involved with him. If I hadn't none of this would have happened." She shakes her head in disagreement.

"Daisy is going to get help. She's fully recovered. There is hope for her too. I understand how violently this has shaken your life. It's touched every aspect of your family. But you are strong enough to endure this."

"Maybe individually, but as a family I'm not sure there is enough for us to come back to. It isn't just what happened with Daisy. I don't know that the reasons I married Rick are even right. Tucker was toxic and wrong. I was so damaged when Rick came into my life. We tried to build something on a bad foundation. Things were already happening between us before Daisy came along."

"Something can start out as broken and morph into something beautiful. Your roots don't decide your leaves. I think you've made incredible progress in the last three months. You should be proud. I'm proud of you."

"I hurt Rick so badly. He'll never look at me the same."

"Daisy convinced you he was dangerous. You were trying to protect people."

"I'm the dangerous one." A shiver rolls up my spine and I rub my sweaty hands over my pants. "I've had to take a hard look at myself these last few months. It's just me. No house to run. No classroom full of students to teach. When I'm not pouring myself into something else, I'm only left with me."

"Which has been a very healthy part of this journey. The quiet is where the most important things come to light. You're meditating. Doing yoga. Walking every day. The mindfulness you're allowing yourself right now is really going to serve you well."

"I want to go home." The words slip out like a secret. "I want to be busy again. I want to be needed and part of something. How do I do that?"

"I guess you ask," Dr. Harlow replies with a shrug. "You won't know until you try."

"The idea of him saying no is terrifying. Right now I'm in this limbo. But if Rick rejects me, I don't know what I'll do."

"Yes, you do. You'll talk to me. You'll keep doing the work."

"What do I even say to him? I don't know where to start."

"Try the beginning. That's always a good place."

I have to live with the fact that Tucker never saw his daughter hit any of her milestones, yet I still have the chance to watch Bryson enjoy his life. Tucker and his wife would never have the chance to grow old together. So I can't possibly expect that Rick and I should be able to.

I've tried to free myself from nearly all the secrets. Maggie has become my confidante. My sounding board. A place where my words can flow freely and my memories are not judged.

There is only one thing I've never been able to utter. Not even in the safe confines of Maggie's office. Even Jules couldn't pry this secret from my terrified grip. I take a little comfort in knowing there is not a living soul who could call me out for the awful thing I'd done and the terrible reason I'd done it. The only person who knew was dead.

FORTY-FIVE

ELIZABETH

Then

Tucker lies on my bed, his muscular arms behind his head. It was my favorite way to see him. I think he knew that. I felt the more comfortable he looked at my place the more he was mine. The less he was hers.

It's amazing what your mind can do when you're in love. It can squeeze out reality like a dish towel being wrung dry. You can make it all wash down the drain like it doesn't exist. When Tucker was with me, I felt whole. Seen. When he left, I was deflated and detached. It's why I worked harder every day to try to get more of him.

"Write me a love letter," I plead with the pouty look he loves. The face he begged me to make sometimes while we were in the throes of passion. He went white when I begged him for something.

"A love letter?" He looks down at the stationery and pen I'd tossed onto the bed. "Why?"

"I need something to hold onto while you're gone. If you can't stay with me, at least pretend you want to."

The look of frustration quiets me. "I do want to. Please don't say things like that. You know I love you, and if I could change things I would. I'd never leave this bed if I didn't have to."

I smile to try to soothe him. "Then write that to me. Tell me you love me. That I'm your whole world. Pretend we have a future. Give me something to read when I can't be with you."

"You're crazy." He sits up and positions himself to be able to scratch something down.

"Please really do it. Write what you feel. What you'd say to me if nothing else mattered. I need to hear it." I pout again, but this time lick my lips seductively. It does the trick. He waves me off and begins writing in earnest.

"Can you make some coffee? I'm going to have a late night catching up on paperwork. Plus, you can't be hovering over me while I profess my love."

We'd already been saying we loved each other for more than a month, but I never tired of hearing him say it.

I made the coffee strong. I wasn't sure how long it took to write a love letter but he was sneaking up behind me in the kitchen ten minutes later, kissing his way down my neck.

"That was easy to write. You're easy to love."

Our time was running short. He'd gotten out of work early and come over for an hour. That's all he could manage today. Jules was at dance class until five, so he and I would walk out together. Tucker would have to head home to keep doing some paperwork, taking a piece of my heart with him. I wondered if I'd eventually run out of pieces to give.

But with the few minutes we had left, we sipped our coffee and I read his letter again and again. His words were sustenance. I could feast on them for the rest of my life. Tucker loved me. Our circumstances were complicated but I knew he would be with me if he could.

Reluctantly he peeled himself off the kitchen stool. "I'm going to get dressed. Want to head out together in a few?"

"Sure." He'd gotten very good at hanging his clothes up just right so they wouldn't wrinkle while he was here. I never pawed at him or made it a point to try to get my perfume or lipstick on him to give him away at home. We were smart. Careful. Deliberate. I'd always tried to respect the predicament Tucker was in. Lately though I spent my time daydreaming of what it would be like if things changed. If suddenly we could start our life.

Without enough thought of the consequences, I did something impulsive. I took the letter he'd written and tucked it into a side pocket of his work bag. One I knew he rarely used. Maybe he'd find it. Maybe it would languish there, unseen, forever. Or maybe his wife would find it. What would that mean for their marriage? What would it mean for us?

I busied myself with the dishes as he came back into the kitchen. A sparkle of excitement dancing in his eyes. "One of my meetings on Thursday has been canceled. Can we meet at the hotel?"

I nod and smile my agreement. "I've actually got to make a snack for Jules. I forgot. You go on without me. I'll see you Thursday."

My cheeks flushed with nervous energy as I thought about the letter and what I'd done. It felt too late to do anything about it now. I couldn't admit to him what I'd just done. I'd look like one of those clingy, crazy little girls who can't understand the nuance of a complicated relationship. He'd be angry. Lose trust in me.

"Love you," he calls over his shoulder as he heads out the door.

I don't say it back. The words clog in my throat like a hundred-car pileup. Guilt can have that effect.

The next time I saw him, I'd take the note back. Quickly

and quietly, I'd undo what I'd just done. I'd hide it away and pretend this had never happened.

Next time I saw him, I'd fix this.

I didn't know there wouldn't be a next time...

FORTY-SIX

RICK

My lasagna isn't half bad. The edges are a little burned and the sauce a bit watery, but it's edible. Even Bryson congratulates me on a meal that didn't end with the smoke alarm going off.

I've grown. I didn't think I had to. I felt pretty fully formed. But suddenly when life changed abruptly, I realized how much of myself was underdeveloped.

I put the leftovers in the fridge and wave to Bryson as he heads out the door. His girlfriend has a car. An older woman. Only by seven months, but the joke still makes me laugh. Chelsea is a nice girl who's helped Bryson bounce back through this turmoil.

It doesn't take much at that age. Kids are resilient. Counseling. Transparency. Honesty. They were all important, but I'm not sure anything has made as much of an impact as a date with Chelsea has.

The house is quiet and I flip on the radio to address that as quickly as possible. I can see why Elizabeth was struggling with our lives changing back then. A silent house is triggering.

"It doesn't smell like smoke," Elizabeth cheers, knocking on the screen door but also letting herself in at the same time. It's her house too, but she hasn't lived here in months, so the rules about when to knock are fuzzy.

"That's because I didn't burn dinner tonight. Call the Michelin star people, I'm going to be in the running soon. Do you want a plate? It's mostly like lasagna and a little like soup."

Elizabeth laughs and my chest flutters at the sound I'd nearly forgotten. We haven't laughed together in a while. "No, I've already eaten. I was just coming to drop off Bryson's prescription. This is when he normally starts his allergy medicine for the seasonal stuff and I forgot to tell you."

She shakes the bottle at me and then puts it down on the table. Picking up our dinner plates, she walks them over to the sink.

"I'll get those," I protest, but she carries on.

"I used to get so annoyed when you two would get up from the table and you'd leave your plates for me to clear." She pauses over the sink. "You two were ungrateful slobs. I never thought I would miss it so much."

It's my turn to laugh now and I can see it has the same effect on her. We started out as not communicating at all after I'd gotten home from jail. Then slowly, through Jules, I got every detail of the story.

Last month, we started texting. Just important things about Bryson. About life. Logistics. Now, this was the third time in the last couple of weeks she'd stopped by the house.

"Do you have some time to talk?" She's filling the sink with soapy water as she asks this question. I can tell she's desperate to look distracted in case I say no.

"Is it about Bryson?'

"Not directly."

"About us?" I hold my breath. I have no clue if I want to hear yes or no as an answer.

"I don't know. I think it's about us."

I walk up behind her and turn off the sink. "Want to go for a walk?"

"Sure." She smiles with relief and we head out to the quiet, treelined streets of the neighborhood we fell in love with years ago.

"I've been doing a lot of therapy," she begins, but I already know this. It was court-ordered. Part of the deal she got to tie up the loose ends of the charges against her. I did everything I could to minimize the legal ramifications. I was angry, but she's still Bryson's mother.

"I've had to take a hard look at who I am, and I haven't liked everything I see. I think when you had this vision about my past you saw me only as a victim. In some instances that was true. But other times, even though my motivation was just survival, I did some awful stuff."

"I know about your relationship with Daisy's father while he was married and what that did to her family. Obviously, her seeking revenge was wrong. You didn't deserve—"

"I did deserve it. I knew he was married."

"You were eighteen. He was a grown, married man. No one should blame you for his wife finding out and him ending his life. It's horrible but not on you."

"I made sure his wife found out." She looks away and her cheeks blaze red.

"I thought he wrote you a letter?"

"I put it in his bag so she would find it. Maybe it's not all that different from what I did to you. Our marriage had problems, and at the time I wrongly believed you were dangerous but setting you up like that to go to jail was awful. Putting that letter in his bag was evil. I'm trying to come to terms with the things I've set in motion and the consequences."

I chew on this. Everything has been hard to swallow lately. We've been caught in this mammoth natural disaster and I can't seem to figure out how to get us out.

"I'm sorry I never asked you more about this." I kick at some loose gravel on the sidewalk. "It was wrong of me to just bury my head in the sand and try to pretend you didn't need to talk about it."

"You did ask," she attempts, but I shake my head.

"There is a way to ask when you really want to know something and I never did that. I never gave you space to tell me any of it. I loved you. You were magnificent. And I was afraid to find out you weren't."

"I'm not. I wasn't then. And I'm not now."

"I know." The words probably hurt her, but they're true. "I'm not sure we're really shooting for perfection anymore."

"That ship has sailed." She turns toward me with a look of anguish. "I want to tell you everything. All of it. You deserve to find out if the woman you married is worth still being in love with."

"I want to listen." I brush her fallen bangs out of her eyes and leave my hand to graze her cheek for an extra moment.

"Do you think it's too late for us?" Her fear is palpable.

I open my mouth to answer just as a car comes squealing to a stop next to us. Two men jump out.

"Rick Meadows, you are under arrest for the sexual assault of Daisy May Stevens." Cole is out of the car and slamming me against the hood before I can take another breath.

"What? I didn't—"

He reads me my rights and tosses me in the back of the car before I can offer another word. I watch through the window as he pulls Elizabeth to the side and begins explaining something. She looks at me, confused and then aghast. A moment later she rushes away, her hair bouncing as she charges back toward our house.

We were almost there. Almost back to each other.

FORTY-SEVEN
ELIZABETH

"It's not possible." I bring my hand up to my forehead and try to make the spinning feeling stop. "Daisy has had some serious mental health issues. She can't possibly be a credible witness at this point."

"She went to a clinic the morning after the assault." Cole folds his arms over his chest. "There was an exam. Swabs taken. It's a match for your husband. Seminal fluid. This is not some parlor trick she's pulling to keep screwing with your family."

"Of course it's a trick. We were in the city celebrating our anniversary. Rick wasn't home that night. Why would she just bring it up now?"

"She didn't. We've had her statement on this since the first night she was taken into custody, but it's been incredibly laborious putting all the pieces together. We finally have."

"How can you be sure?"

"The evidence is solid. She used a false name at the clinic. We've been wading through her statement for weeks. Trying to flesh it out. Prove it through. Rick didn't tell you we served a warrant at your house three weeks ago?" He looks perplexed by my lack of knowledge.

"No."

"We found recording equipment. He'd had cameras up in every angle of your house. Judging by the time stamps it was like that for years."

"Cameras?" I stutter the word out.

"Every room. Your bedroom. Your bathroom. He was like big brother, watching every move you made. He'd wiped the old footage, or at least he thought he had. He also had an app that allowed him to mirror your phone and read every text and email you've ever sent. The man had you followed multiple times. We've already talked to the private investigator he hired."

"The red car." I think of every time I wondered how Rick knew so much. I thought he was clever. Like he was reading my mind. But he was watching every move I made. That's how he gained so much control.

He nods. "With our forensic tech team we were able to recover plenty of the recordings from his cameras that he thought he'd deleted. There is footage from the night of the party. Rick came home. It was twelve thirty. I'm assuming he checked the cameras while you two were away and saw the party. Maybe even saw Bryson put Daisy to bed. He left your hotel, probably while you were asleep, drove the forty-five minutes back here and we know now what happened. He let himself in quietly, went upstairs..."

"No." I shake my head vehemently. "Rick wouldn't do that. And Daisy had the opportunity to tell me what happened when we were in the woods and she had a knife. She never said Rick raped her. Plus if she had proof against Rick, why lie and say it was Bryson?"

"We can't comment too much on Daisy's statement on the matter. There is still an open investigation into her own wrong-doing. But from what we can surmise, she didn't feel your loyalty to Rick would be strong the way it is to Bryson. She wanted to make the most impact on your life. That's why she said it was Bryson."

"Rick wouldn't do that."

"We know he did." Cole keeps his voice stern. "There is footage. Rick is the one who assaulted Daisy. He's being charged with it. I'm sorry I couldn't give you a heads-up before now. A man like Rick can weasel his way out of anything. We had to make sure we had the case locked down."

"Rick protects women. Rick fights these cases in court."

The rigid way he replied felt rehearsed as though he'd been dreading telling me this part. "He has a proclivity for young women. You yourself weren't much older than Daisy when you two got together. We've heard rumblings that there might be other young women, clients of his, that were victims. A lot is going to come out. You need to brace yourself."

I physically brace against the porch railing but it does no good.

"How long has this been going on? The young clients?"

"You might want to sit down while I tell you what we found. It's going to be a lot to take in and maybe hard for you to hear."

"More than what you already told me?" I doubt that's even possible.

"Yes."

He gestures to the rocking chair and I make my way there slowly; the subtle rock as I try to sit down has me nearly landing on the ground.

"We spent an enormous amount of time trying to understand Daisy's situation, her statement and how you fit into it. We weren't chalking this up to some hysterical girl out for vengeance. She's facing serious charges and it's been a lot to unravel. That meant digging deeper into her father's situation."

"Tucker."

"Yes. While investigating, we discovered that Tucker

Rutherford did in fact have relationships with multiple underage and young clients. He exploited his position of power and was a predator. At the time of his death none of this was made public, but it had been known privately due to some complaints and an investigation launched by his law firm."

"They knew what he was doing?"

"They were looking into it. They'd hired an outside party to try to check the validity of the complaints against Tucker and compile evidence. That outside party was Rick."

"What?"

"Rick was not only aware of Tucker's crimes; he also had a full manifesto on you. He was meant to be putting a case together against Tucker. That included understanding who the victims were. He knew what was happening to you and was on the verge of turning it over to Tucker's employers so they could take action. Then, Tucker took his own life. It all got buried. But apparently, Rick wasn't finished with the situation. We believe he intentionally interjected himself into your life by orchestrating what looked like a chance meeting. He knew who you were, exactly what you'd been through and he stepped into your life with intention."

"Intention?"

"I think he picked up where Tucker left off. But he did a better job of convincing you to do what he wanted. He'd been following Tucker, had you under surveillance, was likely obsessed. He knew you had nothing, that you would be hurt and heartbroken. Rick wanted to play hero in some sick game. He kept the surveillance up all these years so he could always stay in control."

"We've been married for sixteen years." I cut my hand through the air and reject his points. It can't be. There is no way.

"I know. I'm sorry you have to hear these details from me but I thought it was important you have all the information. It's going to get ugly. Rick is smart, he'll try to fight this every step of the way. Daisy and her troubles have left him with lots of ammunition to do so. I need you to understand who he is and what he's capable of so you can be strong enough to not fall for his bullshit when he starts begging for your support. He doesn't deserve it."

"What do you want from me?" I'm sobbing and clutching the rocking chair arms so tightly the wood might splinter under my grip.

"I need you to keep it together while we tear him apart. Can you do that?"

"Yes." I nod and blink away my tears. I don't want my vision even a little bit blurry as the truth comes into focus for the first time. This is why Rick was so able to step into the hole in my life; he knew the shape of it perfectly. The cameras and the following me around, that's how he kept me under his thumb. I could never figure out how he knew what I was thinking, like he was always in my head. I'd wrongly assumed it was because he was brilliant and I was so simple to figure out. "I never want him to see the light of day again. Can you make that happen?"

Cole smiles with relief. "I don't know if I can, but I'm damn sure you can."

EPILOGUE
JULES

Bryson beams with pride as we fill the back of his SUV with everything he needs for the dorm. He's two years older than most of the other freshmen, but it took a little longer to get ready for this day. Those other kids didn't have the court trials. The sentencing. The newspaper interviews. They didn't know what it was like to find out their father was a monster. Their mother his victim.

It had taken years to unravel it all. To untie the messy knots and lay our lives out flat again. Elizabeth is at my side as he hops into the driver's seat and heads off in the direction of his new life.

"You have an empty nest." I nudge Elizabeth playfully with my elbow.

"We have an empty nest, roomie. I know we've been saying for a while you're going to move into your own place once Bryson is off to college, but we should just admit that's never going to happen. We're stuck with each other. For better or worse."

I smile at my sweet older sister. "It's better. It has to be better than it's been." We both laugh at the absurdity of the last few years.

Elizabeth sighs and rests her head on my shoulder as she speaks. "I don't want to find out another damn secret for the rest of my life. Just keep me in the dark if you have any more."

I owe my life to Elizabeth. Everything I have she fought to give me. Now I have to give her back what I can. I have to give her what she's asking for and keep the remainder of my secrets from demolishing the life she's trying to rebuild.

So she'll never know. No one will. It wouldn't change anything anyway. What's done is done. Rick is in jail. Daisy is in a mental institution. Bryson at college. Elizabeth is healthy. She's dedicated herself to healing up all the old wounds and she's done it beautifully. This last burden to carry will be mine, and I'll heave it along with me until I take it to my grave.

Then

The message on the answering machine was weird. Angry. Tucker had always been so nice to both of us. He's the reason Elizabeth and I get to live together. He brings us meals. Makes my sister smile. She loves him, so I love him. But the message he leaves on the answering machine tonight is scary.

There's a letter, I guess. Something about his wife. I didn't even know he had a wife. He's furious. Wants to meet. Has to. Now. At their hotel. I know where it is. I've hung out in the lobby and done my homework while they meet about stuff upstairs. I know their room number because I was supposed to call if there was an emergency. Now, I know that's why Elizabeth isn't home. Why I'm alone and it's getting dark. They are meeting and I want to know why he's mad. If she's okay.

I slide into my sneakers and walk the seven blocks to the hotel. This is something Elizabeth will yell at me about later but I don't care. I'm tired of not knowing anything. Of Elizabeth treating me like I'm a baby. I know things. I want to find her and tell her that. I want to find him and tell him not to leave mean messages on our answering machine.

I pound on the door loudly when I reach the room and plant my feet. They'll try to send me away. Back downstairs, but I won't go.

The door swings open and Tucker stands there with a knife in his hand and a wild look in his eyes. Pulling me inside, his voice booms.

"What the hell are you doing here? Where is your sister? She ruined my life. I am going to kill her."

The words send my heart down to my socks. He's not regular angry like a person gets, he's lost it. I want to run. I want to go and find Elizabeth and tell her not to come here. He grabs the collar of my shirt and pulls me out toward the open door that leads to the balcony. I smell the alcohol on his breath. Tucker is not steady on his feet. He's wobbling as he tosses me outside.

"Call her. Tell her to get here. I am going to kill her. She ruined everything."

"I can't call her," I sputter out, getting back to my feet. "Just let me go."

"I did everything for you two. I did everything for all of them, and your sister pulls this shit? A letter in my bag? I have a baby at home, you know. I have a life she just blew up."

"Let me go." The knife is still in his hands as he leans against the railing and bangs his other hand to his head. I've seen my dad like this once before. He's still in jail because of it.

"I'm going to kill her. Kill you. Then I'm going to run. I'm going to get the hell out of here and start over." He leans further over and laughs manically, the wobble in his legs getting worse as he seems to slip into more madness. "I'm going to kill her," he yells out into the world as he laughs again and drops the knife to the ground. He's losing his mind. Looking out into the world as though the answer to his problems is there on the horizon. The next time he leans to laugh loudly and proclaim some other insane intention, I muster every ounce of my strength and shove his unstable body over the low railing.

He's gone from the balcony.

He's gone from our life.

He's gone.

A LETTER FROM DANIELLE

Dear readers,

I want to say a huge thank you for choosing to read *The Teacher*. If you did enjoy it, and want to keep up to date with all my latest releases, just sign up at the following link. Your email address will never be shared and you can unsubscribe at any time.

www.bookouture.com/danielle-stewart

I hope you loved *The Teacher* and if you did I would be very grateful if you could write a review. I'd love to hear what you think, and it makes such a difference helping new readers to discover one of my books for the first time.

I love hearing from my readers – you can get in touch through social media or my website.

Thanks,

Danielle Stewart

https://authordaniellestewart.com

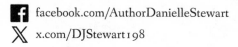

facebook.com/AuthorDanielleStewart
x.com/DJStewart198

9 781837 903160